As Boundless as the Sea

Book Three of the *Coming Back to Cornwall* series

Katharine E. Smith

HEDDON PUBLISHING

First edition published in 2018 by Heddon Publishing.

ISBN 978-1-9995963-6-1

Cover design by Catherine Clarke

www.heddonpublishing.com
www.facebook.com/heddonpublishing
@PublishHeddon

Katharine E. Smith is a writer, editor and publisher.

An avid reader of contemporary writers such as Kate Atkinson, David Nicholls and Anne Tyler, Katharine's aim is to write books she would like to read herself. She has four novels to her name, and one non-fiction guide, written with fellow indie authors in mind.

Katharine runs Heddon Publishing from her home in Shropshire, which she shares with her husband and their two children.

For my brothers, who I don't see often enough.

As Boundless as the Sea

BACK AGAIN

It's hot in the club and the bassline of the music shudders through the floorboards as I sway almost imperceptibly in time with the beat, enjoying the feeling of hands on my hips, warm breath on my not-quite sunburned shoulders.

I lean back. His kiss slides along, from the straps of my sundress, up my neck, stopping just shy of my earlobe, where he whispers my name.

Just as he's moving his hands around my waist, the alarm begins to sound and I turn in a panic, to see beautiful, golden Sam.

"I'm so glad you're here," I say to him.

"I've missed you so much," he whispers into my ear but, just as in all good stories, I wake up to realise it's only a dream.

Sadly for me, I am no longer eighteen and my beautiful, golden Sam is long since lost to me.

But, as I start to come round, blinking sore eyes and cursing my alarm clock, I also take in the light – that special, unmistakable light, just beginning to help the day take shape – and the sounds from outside.

The seagulls calling from the roof.

The street sweeper, making its rounds, although the town is relatively quiet at the moment, tucked as it is somewhere in between the craziness of New Year and the more understated joy of the Easter holidays.

Garden birds and their songs add a sweetness to the

morning; the early risers, unfailingly cheerful and seeming to sing for the sheer joy of another day dawning.

And just there, if I listen carefully – try to strain my hearing past this immediate cacophony – the constant, comforting – exciting – sound of the sea.

Sam may be gone but here I still am, in my beloved Cornwall, and I've survived my second winter here; one entirely without Sam, intact. This is the county that calls to me when I am away from it; rugged and wild, exciting and exotic. The place which makes me feel alive.

Julie, my best friend, my companion that first summer so long ago, is still here, too; tucked away in the room next to mine. These past two years have been eventful for us both. Now we are determined to build on these changes and move bravely forward into our new grown-up lives.

Besides which, the hard bit has been done, surely. It has to get easier from now on in.

1

We've worked hard this winter, the sea and I. There have been three remarkable storms which have really pushed the waters to their limits, coming as they did in fairly quick succession, taking control. Each a pushy commander, insisting that the waves come far out of their comfort zone and trespass into houses, shops, cafes and galleries. The first few exploratory forces just peeping in, some rebuffed by sandbags, retreating quickly, relieved their part of the operation is done. The next coming further, nosing their way in while behind them more and more lie in wait, ready for action. The storm growing louder and more insistent until finally the sea is enraged and will happily trespass anywhere, ravaging anything in its path. All reluctance soaked away. Now the storms are gone, the sky is clear, and the sea is soothed and soothing once more.

High up the town in the Sail Loft Hotel, I was beavering away, happy to be so engaged in my work that I had very little time to think of anything else. Christmas and New Year were the main focus of my attention while the weather was on the turn then January brought an art exhibition and in February the hotel became a writers' retreat, hosting a number of courses and semi-well-known poets and novelists, along with a host of adoring, aspiring writers. These were events which Stefan and I had designed, with Bea's blessing; a way of picking up business in the notoriously quieter grey months of the year.

Stefan's and April's baby daughter came early, in mid-January as opposed to her due date of early March, and needed much medical attention, as did April. Stefan has been understandably absent or else absent-minded. I feel like I've been at work non-stop for months and it is only now that I have been able to take a breath.

Baby Annabel is at home, and April is recovered enough for Stefan to be in work overnight and over the weekend. Last night, as I walked down the hill, I realised that it was almost... very, very nearly... light. I already had the Friday feeling – which I'd all but forgotten about, it had been so long – and something about the light breeze held a promise of spring.

The other challenge about the winter was that in early December, Bea was in hospital and then laid up at home. She and Bob had not long been in Cornwall when she developed a problem with her back (in fact, she's told me in private, it had been bothering her for ages but she hadn't wanted to 'make a fuss'). As it turned out, she needed an operation and this in turn needed a couple of months' recovery time. It turned everything upside down.

David and Martin postponed their Christmas wedding, until next winter, as David couldn't bear the thought of getting married without his big sister by his side. "We've lost all our deposits," Martin told me in a quiet moment, but I don't think he minded too much. They are already living together and have decided on reflection to make their wedding a lower-key affair, which I think Martin is secretly pleased about.

"I can't do it without Bea," David bemoaned while

Martin was in the bathroom, "do you think Martin's cross with me?"

"No, he's not." I said firmly, secretly thinking that if Bea hadn't been intent on not making a fuss, she might have saved us all a lot of trouble, and saved David and Martin a lot of money. "But ask him, not me. I am perfectly sure he understands."

Meanwhile, I had Bob bending my ear, asking if I thought it would be inappropriate if he asked Bea to marry him while she was essentially incapacitated. "Will it look like I'm trying to get to her at a time of weakness?" he'd worried to me. "What if she thinks I'm taking advantage of her? What if I am? She's an independent woman, and I'm pretty sure she's set on not getting married again."

"Just ask her!" I'd laughed. "But don't do it while she's out of it on painkillers and whisky."

Life would be a lot easier if people were open and honest with each other and just said what they meant, to the person who they wanted to hear it. But I know that's easier said than done. I also know I'm not exactly a shining example.

I got through the winter of madness, just as I have now got through another year without Sam. And turning thirty, which happened last summer. When I look at it logically, out of those thirty years, I've spent only about six months with Sam, working out at less than two per cent of my life, if I've done my sums right. Therefore, I have decided, it is ridiculous to be so hung up on him. We've never lived with each other; never even lived in the same town as each other for more than a couple of months. Yes, I still get a pang when I think of him, but I know it's just stupid. I'm becoming convinced that he represents an ideal for me – and it's easy to believe that he is the man for me because he's not here to prove otherwise. Who was it who said love is a type of madness? Probably loads of people. And they are right. I mean, I'm happy for David and Martin; and Bea and Bob – and Luke and Julie, Stefan and April. They're all shining examples of love working. But me and Sam – the more I think about it, the more I think I was deluded. I knew him for ten weeks when I was eighteen and I fell in love. We spent ten years apart only to come back together and be separated again after a matter of weeks. This is not the basis of a strong relationship. This is not two people who know each other inside out and have built a life together. I'm becoming convinced that this type of love may never happen for me, but I'm OK with that. I know what you're thinking: that I protest too much, like somebody with a hangover saying they are never going to drink again, but really, truly, I'm OK with it. I have seriously great friends. The best parents ever. I have a job I love, and plans for the future. Yes, I'm young, as Bea always tells me, and there will be plenty of opportunities to meet 'the one'. It might happen and it might not but, if it doesn't, I've made my peace with that idea.

But enough about love. Let's get back to real life. I am still regularly amazed and delighted that I am where I am at the moment – living in Cornwall, managing a beautiful hotel. Julie and I have been renting David's house since he moved in with Martin; before that, we had been living in his attic. I mean, he knew we were there. We weren't hiding in amongst old trunks and cobwebs, sneaking downstairs for a shower and some food when he went out. We had been staying in the same rooms we'd had when we were eighteen; two tiny bedrooms with a shared, equally tiny, bathroom, a poky kitchen area, and a great view across the town.

This year, though, all is set to change.

David came to see me last night, bringing his customary pizza and a bottle of red wine.

"Hi my lovely," he said, smiling widely and kissing me on the cheek.

"Hello," I'd smiled back, happy to have company on my first Friday night off in some time.

"I've got news!" he'd grinned and I'd known immediately what he was going to say.

"We've been accepted, we've passed all the tests. We're approved. We're approved!" He practically danced into the lounge then turned to me, his eyes alight with excitement.

"Oh my god! David, that is just brilliant. And no surprise at all to me. Of course you've been approved, though, they'd have been mad to turn you down."

Martin and David have been going through the process of applying to be adoptive parents. It hasn't been easy, by any means, and I know they'd worried that delaying the wedding might cause a problem but evidently not.

"Thank you, Alice. I can't believe it. I just can't believe it!"

"So what does it mean? What happens next?"

"Well, I think it's a case of completing all the finalities and then a waiting game. They have to match us with a child. A child!" His eyes filled with tears. "Oh my god, this is so scary. I mean, exciting. I mean, scary."

I laughed. "I bet. I guess this is your equivalent of a positive pregnancy test."

"Ha! I suppose so. But it could happen really quickly – or it could take ages. At least with a pregnancy test you know it's going to be about nine months."

"But it might take less for you..?"

"It could, it could. We just don't know."

"Well, bloody hell. You two are going to be such great parents. You know I already think that."

"I hope so, I really do. But…" his face fell slightly, "… I think we might have to sell this place. I'm sorry, to break it to you like that. But I'd rather just say it to you. So you know. And it's not like we're going to do it right now and boot you out."

"Don't worry," I was quick to cut David off, "I'd always known you'd have to do that at some point and when you two started talking about adopting, I thought this might be the natural next step. It's OK, I promise. I've got to make my own way in the world some time," I laughed, secretly panicking slightly that the time might have come sooner than I'd imagined.

2

After David had gone, I poured myself another glass of wine and took it into the garden. My head was awhirl. I hadn't told him about the plans Julie and I have been making, which I had hoped to concentrate on this year. We want to start our own business. I couldn't easily tell him about it because it's going to mean me leaving the Sail Loft and as he's Bea's brother I have to keep quiet about it all. It's not that I want to keep secrets from either of them but it's a slightly awkward situation with Bea being my boss.

I had really been counting on being able to stay at David's house for the time being. Although Julie will be moving in with Luke later this year, David had told me that he didn't expect me to cover her rent. It was a drunken promise but well meant, and the thought of it has been helping to give me confidence that I might be able to take a chance elsewhere in my life. It's OK for Julie. She has financial backing from Luke which she is not keen on taking advantage of but they're getting married in October and Luke is insisting that his money is hers: "When you and Alice are raking it in, I'll be able to retire."

I, meanwhile, am still trying to work out where I might get some money from. We want to start 'high-end' self-catering (I know, I hate the term 'high end', too) which is essentially not really self-catering at all. Julie and Luke went skiing over the winter, with some of Luke's friends from London, and they had a chef to cook for them in their chalet. Julie says she could do that here; and that together we could provide some extras to help make people's holidays run smoothly, so they can really relax and let somebody else take the strain.

"The only problem is," I said, "I don't know if I want to work for those kind of people. I'm not sure I'm comfortable with people who are too posh to pack their own picnics."

"Hey!" Julie had pushed me, "That's me and Luke you're talking about. We didn't lift a finger when we were skiing."

"Sorry! Well, you know you're a cut above me nowadays." I must admit there is a small part of me that feels like Julie is moving into a different world. I don't really mind; it doesn't matter. Julie will never change that much. But still, she has to think less about money these days, and that can be telling at times.

All that is beside the point, though; I think we have a great idea. There is nothing like that around here. There is an abundance of 'luxury accommodation, furnished to a high standard' and I can feel it within myself; the cynicism towards these people which many locals have. But I know that these same locals probably feel this way about me, and Julie… some people just don't like change, or incomers (or 'emmets' as they call tourists round these parts). And that's not a great way to be but I can sympathise to a certain extent. So, as well as finding the cash, and finding the right place, I also have to find in myself the willingness to make holidays extra special for people whose privilege and possibly sense of entitlement I may have a bit of a problem with.

But I am sure there is a market for it. For people who want the space of self-catering without the catering. And I want to stay here, and be successful. And I really do want to work with Julie. I know we will have our ups and downs but our friendship is definitely strong enough to cope with them.

Now I also have to find somewhere to live. I do know that the staff accommodation at the Sail Loft is an option; which is great short-term but I want a home of my own, plus I don't suppose Bea will be quite so welcoming when I hand in my notice. The very thought of that makes my stomach churn. She has been so good to me, and I really do love the Sail Loft, but if Julie and I can possibly find a way to get our business up and running, we have to do it.

***

I found it really hard to get to sleep, with all those thoughts washing around inside my head. Eventually, I ended up down in the lounge, dragging my duvet along with me and curling up on the settee, watching episodes of *Friends* on Netflix until I fell asleep. At some point I woke up to hear the annoying theme music, and fumbled about for a control, switching the TV off. I tried to get back to sleep on the settee but there was a voice inside me telling me to go up to bed, that I would sleep much better up there. With the duvet round my shoulders like an oversized king's robe, I shuffled through the dark, bouncing off the walls until I found the staircase. I trundled up it slowly, fell onto my bed, and was asleep again within moments.

When I woke in the morning it was already nearly half-ten, and from the sounds outside I could tell that the day had started without me. There were regular footsteps, chattering voices, the sound of cars cautiously edging their way down the narrow streets, the drivers wondering if they become more narrow each year (no, it's just that the cars get bigger). The ever-present shrieking gulls. A delicious feeling came to me. I had the day off. The whole day! Tomorrow, too. When you work 9-5 in an office job you take it for granted that you have a weekend every seven days, without fail. In a hotel, it's different, and with all the pressures of the last few months, I now see weekends as something to be absolutely cherished. And I knew immediately what I would do with this one. I would spend it on the beach.

When we first moved back down here, Julie and I went to the beach a lot. I swore that I always would. However, life has got in the way to some extent and I must confess that sometimes I am so tired, all I want to do is come home after work; making a trip down to the beach before I do that sometimes seems like too much effort. But I must not think like that. I know full well that the rewards are more than worth it. It's like choosing to watch TV over reading a book; it's easier and entirely tempting when you are worn out but you know that a book has the power to transport you and your mood into a different place. Occasionally, TV can do that but generally it's less satisfying.

First, though, I needed a cup of tea in bed. And it was a need, not a want. I wanted to take my time and revel in this unusual feeling of not having to rush up to the hotel, or down from my sleeping quarters there, ready to tend to the needs (or as is often the case, wants) of the guests. I could sit back, sip my tea, rest my neck and my head and my shoulders against the soft pillows; windows open so that the sounds and smells of the town could come and go freely. I tried to take in every detail. David's house has been instrumental in the events of my life; twelve years ago, when I was eighteen, and over the last two years. It's seen love, twice, with the same man. I sometimes wander up to the little porthole-windowed bathroom in the attic and gaze wistfully around, remembering that stormy night when Sam turned up, rain- and grief-soaked. Then I can still cringe when I think of that other night, when Sophie went missing, and I sat at my bedroom window, looking for her. Knowing that Sam was unimaginably angry with me, and that the whole thing was entirely my fault.

All the times I've shared with Julie; from our fresh-faced summer after A-Levels to her own times of turmoil, getting together with Luke, still getting over breaking off her engagement with Gabe. These are the big things but in reality life in David's house has been made up of all the little things: shared meals; watching stupid films and TV programmes; sitting in the garden till late at night. Sharing clothes, towels, secrets, and the ups and downs of life. I am so happy for Julie that she and Luke are getting married, but I am going to miss living with her, so very much.

A slight breeze drifted through the room, breathing onto my face and across the skin of my bare arms. Awakening me, bringing me round from my reverie. It was time to get out there, to face the day, and face life head-on.

3

The slight skip in my step comes naturally as I head down the hill, beach bag under my arm and my sandals slapping the cobbles of the steep street. I pick my way through these oldest parts of town, lined with pretty cottages which used to be inhabited by fishermen and their families, now largely holiday lets with stone plaques exclaiming things like 'cherished getaways' and 'luxury holiday home'. It's almost funny that these houses were once home to some of the poorest people around these parts, whose menfolk risked their lives on the treacherous seas while the women tended to the house, took care of the kids, scrubbed the doorsteps and wore themselves out washing clothes in old dolly tubs. These cottages are still beautifully cared for, but usually by cleaners, with minimalistic interiors and state-of-the-art media systems and coffee machines. As I meander along, following my nose towards the salty sea breeze, I wonder as I often do whether any of these houses' past residents are still around somewhere, somehow... peering out from the shadows with astonishment at what has become of their homes, and the supermarket delivery vans which block the narrow roads every Friday and Saturday afternoon, delivering vast quantities of food and booze, while the newly-arrived holiday-makers prise off the top of a bottle of beer, put feet up on expensive Swedish furniture, and sigh as they start to unwind.

Although full-on summer is still some time away, the town is becoming busy. I smile at the people I pass: families with little kids and panting dogs; young couples too wrapped up in each other to even notice me; older couples walking companionably. I am just desperate to get to the beach. I am wearing my bikini under my dress and hoodie, which may be a bit optimistic. My bag holds my book, a towel, a blanket, a bottle of sparking water, and my phone. I've tucked my keys into the secret place in the garden as I always fear losing them on the beach. Nobody is going to want to nick my rubbishy old phone so I feel fairly safe leaving that while I go for a swim.

The wind from the sea nearly knocks me off my feet as a I round the corner and the beach reveals itself proudly, already teeming with people: family groups securing their domain with a ring-fence of windbreaks; couples and small families more modestly setting themselves up with beach tents; parents digging manically into the sand, finding their inner child while their offspring watch, bemused; surfers, strategically positioned further out from the shore. I slip off my flip-flops and jog down the slipway onto the sand, which feels cold and damp against my toes. The texture changes as I walk along, becoming drier and grainier, speckled with shards of delicate shells and the odd strand of seaweed. I pass the beach bar and wave to Andrew then stop at the shack to get some orange juice and a coffee, picking up a chocolate brownie as an afterthought, then head determinedly along until the groups of people are more irregular, down near the far end of the beach where there are more rocks and fewer people. I find a spot and I drop my bag before dropping myself down next to it. I swivel my orange juice and coffee cups in the sand until I've created nice little holders for both. Then I push my sunglasses up into my hair, squinting at the brightness of the day and the sunshine reflecting on the water. The voices of children down at the shore carry up on the breeze and I feel a slight pang for those afternoons and evenings I used to spend with Sophie. We had a great time down here; in fact, I can see the very rock where we first met, when she spilled her bucket of water on me. This is one area of my life where I am not sure I've done the right thing; I haven't continued to see Sophie because, really, how can I? I am not with her dad any more, and while Kate and I have reached a kind of uneasy understanding, I don't feel comfortable suggesting to her that I take her daughter out. It seems a bit weird. But does Sophie get all that? Does she just think I'm not interested anymore? It's difficult, to say the least.

Still, I am here today for some much needed rest and relaxation. I roll my towel up so I can rest against the rock comfortably, push the glasses back down onto my nose, then pick up my coffee and take a sip, looking out to sea and letting the place and the day, and the having nothing to do, wash gently over me.

After my coffee, I down my orange juice chaser and find a sudden energy rush through me. The sea is eyeing me confidently, challenging me. I pull my dress over my head and carefully fold it over my bag then find a large flat stone to put on top of the pile, to save it being blow away or picked apart by scavenging seagulls. Into the sea I go!

Aside from a very ill-thought-out early morning dip before I started work one Sunday in February, this is my first foray into the cold, salty waters this year. It's still far too early for them to have warmed at all, so I'm not expecting to be in for long, but I need to do this. I plunge in, gasping and holding back an actual shriek as the shallows smoothly claim my ankles and I feel goose pimples jump, outraged, across my whole body. I have to do it, now, I tell myself, or this will never happen. I forge on, until the water is deep enough to push my whole body under. The waves close over my head for just a moment and as I resurface my skin is stinging, my eyes too, but I find myself laughing, jubilant and alive. I swim a short, sharp breaststroke away from shore, then back towards the beach. The sun is strong above now but this is not summer, not yet. Keeping my shoulders under the water, I keep my arms and legs moving and turn to watch the surfers, who would not let a little chilliness put them off their pursuit. Many of them are here year-round, and probably prefer the winter in many ways, with the lack of small children and other swimmers muddying the water.

Already, I am shivering. Staying in any longer would be stupid. For a moment, though, I push myself onto my back, let that icy-cold water fill my ears, and I float, looking up to the slightly insipid blue of the spring sky, and the high-above gulls, whirling and wheeling slowly. All I can hear is the voice of the sea. All I can see is the sky. No ringing telephones; no guests wanting to be checked in or complaining about a leaky tap; no bedrooms to be cleaned, or tables to be set; no happy couples showing me what I've been missing.

Then I am back on my feet, striding out of the sea as strongly as I went in, my whole body on high alert. The wind off the water makes me shiver as it hits my bare skin but it also helps propel me back to my place by the rocks. I pull my towel tightly around me, and slip off my bikini top then somehow manage to shrug myself into my dress and hoodie without revealing any more of myself than I'd like to. I wriggle out of my bikini bottoms and into the leggings I'd brought along, then wrap my blanket around myself and push my sunglasses back onto my nose. With my towel curled up like a pillow once more, I sit back and rest my head, both exhilarated and relaxed at the same time.

The sun is so bright, bouncing off the water, even with my glasses on, that I close my eyes. Now I can concentrate on the sounds of the beach. The voices of children playing; a dad shouting to his son to run 'away from the kite... away!' and breaking into laughter; the gulls; the sea; the occasional car or van passing by on the road above the cliffs. It's hypnotising, I feel my eyelids droop every now and then but catch myself before I drop off. Then, "Alice!"

My eyes flick open and there she is, running towards me. She's grown, I see immediately.

"Sophie!" I jump to my feet and I hug her. It's what I want to do. I've missed her. "How are you?"

"I'm great!" she says, "Well, you know, I don't mean I'm great, I..."

I laugh. "I know what you mean."

I notice another girl trailing slightly shyly behind Sophie. I smile at her and Sophie turns round.

"Oh yeah, this is Amber... did you two never meet?"

"No! But I'm pleased to meet you, Amber, I remember when Sophie first met you. It's good to see you two are still hanging out."

"We've been rock pooling," Amber says, proffering a bucket towards me.

"Let's see," I say. "Did you know, the first time I met Sophie, she decided to chuck a bucket of water, complete with starfish, over my head?"

Both girls giggle.

"Did you?" Amber asks Sophie.

"Noo… well, kind of. But not on purpose. Anyway, I was much younger then."

And she's right. It was only two years ago; not even that, but in that time, how much she's changed! She was a little girl then; now, she is nearly a teenager.

"So what have you got in here today?" I am glad that even if Sophie's growing up, she's still interested in wildlife, as much as she ever was. Just like Sam.

"Actually, not much. Just a couple of CPs."

"CPs?"

"Oh, yeah, common prawns," Sophie says airily. "We're going to try and draw them, for biology, aren't we, Amber?"

"Yeah," Sophie's friend agrees and I wonder if she's as keen on this idea as Sophie.

"Can't keep them too long, in the bucket," Sophie continues, "so we need to get home then bring them back." She looks like she's starting to doubt this idea.

"Well, why don't we take some photos of them? Then you can let them go again and you don't need to worry about lugging them all the way home and back."

"I hadn't thought of that," said Sophie, "but I haven't got a phone. Dad says I'm not allowed."

I hide a small smile. That sounds like Sam. "What about you, Amber? Have you got one?"

"No, Mum and Dad say I'm too young."

"OK…" I bet Sam approves of Amber's parents. He always used to go on about kids having phones and how it was the end of childhood for them, and the start of obsessive behaviour. "Well I've got my phone here. What

27

if I take some pictures and email them to you?"

"Haven't got an email address either," Sophie says.

I look to Amber and she shakes her head.

"OK. I know, I can email them to your mum, Sophie, if she doesn't mind."

"She won't mind; she does let me use her email address for things. She thinks it's stupid Dad won't let me have one, or a phone. She's working on him for next Christmas."

Good luck, Kate, I think, handing my phone to Sophie. She and Amber poke about in the bucket and take out a couple of the rocks so that we can see the CPs, although they are so measly and almost translucent, it's not easy. I help the girls angle the bucket in the sunlight and zoom in with the phone's camera, so that they can get the best pictures possible. Even so, they are pretty blurry.

"Are they going to be OK?" I ask Sophie.

"They're great! Thank you, Alice!" She hugs me tightly and I'm surprised by a couple of tears which spring to my eyes. I'm glad I'm still wearing my sunglasses.

"OK, I'm going to email them to Kate right now so I don't forget. What are you two girls doing for the rest of the day?"

"I don't know, we were going to go home but now we don't have to. Want to go to the harbour, Amber?"

"Sure," Amber shrugs.

"Do you want to come, Alice?"

I smile. "That's really nice of you, Soph, but you and Amber go. Do you know, this is pretty much my first day off all year, I think I'm going to stay here and read. You don't want me cramping your style, anyway."

"That's true!" Sophie giggles. "Don't forget to send those pictures to Mum. Or you could send them to

Dad…" she says, almost slyly.

"Why, is he back?" My heart begins pounding.

"No, but he could send them on to Mum. And I'm sure he'd be happy to hear from you."

"Well, it probably makes better sense for me to send them straight to your mum," I say, trying to not to display my disappointment.

"OK," Sophie says, turning to go.

"Sophie?"

"Yeah?"

"It's really great to see you." I want to say that I miss her, but I am not sure that's the right thing to do.

"You too, Alice." She throws herself at me and hugs me again. "I miss you."

I just squeeze her tightly, and smile at Amber. "It was really good to meet you, Amber."

After the girls are out of sight, I allow a few self-pitying tears to squeeze from my eyes and roll out from under my sunglasses, down my face. It feels like a lifetime away, when I was part of Sophie's world. I used to bring her down here on Monday evenings, when Kate was running her Pilates class. It wasn't long since Sam had left for his course in North Wales and Sophie was struggling with it all. It hasn't escaped my attention that Sam will be back this summer, for a year. Julie's told me that he's got his year's work in Cornwall, before he goes back to Bangor for the concluding year of his course. This had been our plan, initially; this year ahead, we'd have spent together. But it hasn't worked out like that.

I'm still clutching my phone, I realise, and for a second I have this urge to call him, just to say hello. But what would be the point? Instead, I open my email, find Kate's address and start composing my message.

Just as I'm attaching the photos, the phone starts to vibrate and Bea's name appears on my screen. I swipe to answer it.

"Hello?"

"Hello, Alice." I can tell immediately that there is something behind Bea's tone of voice. She sounds happy and excited and secretive, all at once. "Where are you?"

"I'm at the beach." I really, really hope she isn't going to call me into the hotel.

"Ah, lovely. I hope you're having a relaxing day off."

"Yes, thank you," I answer hesitatingly, wondering where this is going.

"And are you doing anything tonight?"

"Erm…" I'd been hoping for a quiet night in, actually. Boring, I know, but much needed.

"Can you come out? I need to see you. I need to celebrate. I'M GETTING MARRIED!" Bea's voice is so loud, I am sure half the beach can hear her.

"What?!" I exclaim; even though I had known Bob was going to propose, this still comes as a surprise. Bea, who had sworn she would never get married again. "To Bob?"

"No, to Barack Obama," Bea laughs. "Of course to Bob!"

"Oh Bea, that is amazing. That is great news. I'm so happy for you."

"Do you want to know when?"

"When you're getting married?"

"In a month!"

"What?!" I exclaim again, truly surprised this time. "What's the rush? You're not pregnant, are you?"

"Ha! No, I just thought, why wait? Why bloody wait? I

just need to tell David; I do feel a bit bad seeing as he delayed his wedding for me and now I'm going to beat him to it. But if I get mine out of the way I can get back to helping him with his."

Get mine out of the way. That is very Bea. I am smiling widely. "Well this is fantastic, Bea, of course I'll come and celebrate."

"Thank you, Alice! Can you ask Julie, too?"

"Yes, definitely. I'll be up at the Sail Loft about eight, is that OK?"

"Perfect."

4

As Julie and I head up the steps to the hotel, bearing champagne and flowers, the sound of happy chatter and music drifts from the open window of the bar. When I get to the top of the steps I turn around for a quick, practised glance across town. This has become a habit and in the nearly-two years since I've been back here, I've seen the town in all sorts of guises: postcard-perfect blue-skied summer; trees turning golden in the burgeoning autumn; gasping for breath in the midst of a storm; moonlit nights; grey, rainy days, and, for about five days during this last winter, the whole place iced with snow, creating a quality of light I have never before seen here. It's possible I have never seen anything so magical. Now, it is almost dark; or, as I prefer to think of it, still a little bit light. Give it a few weeks and the sun will still be shining at this time.

"Alice! Julie!" Bea has somehow sensed our presence and has flung open the front door. I turn to be swept into her laughing embrace, along with Julie.

"Congratulations, Bea!" we chorus together.

Bea laughs even more. "You two always were like twins."

Julie and I look at each other. "Sisters from a different mother," Julie says, her eyes shining against her dark, flawless skin.

"Yep, I don't think that many people have made the observation that we look like twins," I laugh.

"You don't have to look the same," Bea says. "It's obvious that you two were made from the same mould. Now come on in, there's champagne – although I see you brought your own – and are these for me? Thank you so much, ladies. I can't begin to tell you how happy I am."

Julie hands the flowers over obediently and we follow Bea into her hotel. It's nice to be a guest here for once. The bar is full of a mixture of Bea's friends, and guests. I realise that everybody is female.

"Have we got a shortage of men?" I ask.

"No! But this is kind of my hen do," Bea says. "I'm not going to have a chance to have another one, we've already booked the register office, for a month today. Now I need to sort out the guest list, the dinner afterwards, all that stuff. So tonight, let's make merry!"

And that is exactly what we do. It's a really funny mixture of people and Julie and I are definitely the youngest here, by quite a stretch. Bea must be in her mid to late forties; I've never asked but I know David is quite a bit younger than her and he's thirty-nine. Bea's friends that have managed to make it at short notice are mostly from school, along with a few other local business people, and then there are the three Sail Loft guests; Dawn and Treena - a lesbian couple in their fifties - and Miranda, whose husband is apparently happily installed upstairs with a few beers, a bag of nuts, and football on the TV.

Bea is more than generous in supplying us all with booze and Julie takes over the music, linking her Spotify account up to the speaker system in the bar. I see Stefan wander past a couple of times, and he grins and pretends to avert his eyes.

It's not easy to stop myself nipping into the office to check everything is OK but I'm under strict instructions from Bea; tonight I am her guest and work is not on the menu.

Jonathan has knocked up a few trays of food for us all, and champagne and gin are flowing freely; sometimes into the same glasses. Bea is in a simple blue dress and her face is glowing. When she and Julie get into the minutiae of wedding planning, I listen for a while but I have nothing to add so I take myself off to the window, cradling my glass in my hands and gazing across the town. To the far end, I can just see the silhouette of the headland where, somewhere amongst the tangle of thorny trees and bushes, sits the little tumbledown shepherd's hut where Sam and I sheltered from a storm. This was the place I was leaving when I managed to literally fall at his feet, a couple of summers ago; with a swollen ankle and bruised sense of pride, I accepted his offer of help to get me back to town.

I blink rapidly and take a deep breath. Self-pity is not welcome. I run through in my head all the things I have to be happy about, and grateful for: my family; my friends; my job; living in Cornwall – something I never thought I'd be able to do; my health.

Anyway, tonight is Bea's night. I turn back to the room and see her, laughing with Julie and Treena. Bea had a rough time of things with her first husband and she's worked endlessly hard to make the Sail Loft what it is – and she has always been a generous and encouraging person to work for. How can I be anything but happy to celebrate her good fortune with her tonight?

I move to the bar and sit on one of the high stools. Julie smiles and puts an arm around my waist. "If I was a lesbian," she says to Treena, "Alice would be my first choice."

"Julie!" I laugh, checking Treena's face for signs of offence. This is why you shouldn't mix socially with guests. Well, not this situation specifically but you know what I mean.

Luckily, Treena just laughs. "Careful, Alice. I wasn't always women-only, you know. It was meeting Dawn that made my mind up."

"Ha, I think Julie would have fallen for me by now; we've known each other nearly twenty years."

"Could be a slow-burning thing," Bea says, with a twinkle in her eye. "I tell you what, Julie, if you don't think that being a person of colour in Cornwall marks you out enough, perhaps you should try being a lesbian, too. That should do the trick."

I'd forgotten that Julie had once felt that she stood out down here, where in truth there are very few non-white people. However, people are generally not bothered. There may be the odd comment or funny look but that can happen anywhere. I don't think she gives it a second thought anymore.

"It's worth considering," she says, "you know I like to have an impact on a place. What do you think, Alice?"

"OK, I think this conversation's gone far enough, thanks," I smile at Treena, who grins back. "Let's talk about Luke, shall we? Your fiancé, my friend, in case you've forgotten."

"He's not as pretty as you," Julie says, and cackles.

A little later in the evening, there's a knock on the door. I go to answer it, hoping it's not somebody looking for a room. The amount of noise emanating from the bar area will not give somebody a great first impression of the Sail Loft. Bea doesn't seem to care, though.

"Would you jusht get that?" she slurs at me. "Thanksh, Alich, I think I might trip over if I don't shtay right where I am."

Her bar stool wobbles threateningly. I put out a hand to steady her. "No problem."

It's hard to see through the glass as it's dark outside, and the light on the steps is not overly bright, but it looks like just one person. I open the door to find a policeman on the steps.

"I've had a complaint about the noise," he says. "Are you the owner?"

"No, I'm the manager." I don't think I should mention the owner is the reason for all the noise. I look closely at him; he's not one of the usual officers we get round here. Maybe he's new and looking to make a name for himself.

"I have it on good authority that the owner's on the premises. A Bea… Danson?"

"Yes, but she's a bit busy now."

"I don't think she'll be too busy to see me," he says. Did he just wink at me? A light goes on in my head. Oh god, somebody's ordered a stripper. I don't know if Bea's going to like this.

I soon find out.

"Who ish it, Alish?" Bea comes wandering into the hallway, glass in hand. "Oh, hello, Offisher," Her impish grin tells me she's onto him straight away. "Are you here for me?"

"Yes," he says. "Is there somewhere we can go?"

"I guess we'd better go in here," Bea says, leading the way into the bar. I follow on, into a room full of whoops and wolf-whistles.

Julie finds a suitable tune – I wonder if it's her who's arranged this whole thing – and very soon Bea finds herself admiring the undeniably fit body of a very handsome young man, who strips down to his boxers then handcuffs her and makes her lick squirty cream off his chest.

"Would anybody else like a go?" Bea calls. "Alice? You could do with a bit of…"

I can't listen. "No, thank you!" I say, and retreat out of the room before Bea can finish that sentence. I won't remind her of this in the morning. I have a feeling her sore head will be punishment enough.

I hide in the kitchen, pressing my ear to the serving hatch – no longer used, but an original feature of this old merchant's house.

"Whatcha doing?" A voice whispers close to my ear, making me jump.

"Jonathan!" I say, clutching my hand to my chest as I turn to see the Sail Loft's chef laughing at me.

"Shhh!" I say. "I'm hiding from the stripper."

"Really?" He raises his eyebrows.

"Yes, really, Bea was trying to set him on me."

"What, and you're not interested?" Jonathan is standing close to me and I can smell cigarette smoke on his hair and clothes. I thought he'd gone home, banished from this household of women.

"No I am not, thank you very much. I can't think of many things worse."

"You don't like the idea of some fit bloke stripping for you?"

"No!" Those eyebrows raise again. "Not like that, anyway," I qualify, "Not in a room full of shrieking women. It's so… embarrassing."

"Not to mention demeaning to the man," Jonathan

says drily.

"Well, yes," I say, "exactly. What are you doing?"

Jonathan's hands are at his top button, slowly undoing it. "I'm going to dance for you," he says with a straight face, his eyes staring into mine.

"You're an idiot!" I laugh, slapping his arm. "Now shut up or I'll have to go back in."

"I've got a better idea," he says, and leads me quietly through the kitchen door into the dark of the Sail Loft gardens. We sneak over to the veranda that the bar and dining room lead onto, and he climbs over, lending me a hand to help me do the same.

He shushes me as we creep to the window of the bar. Jonathan stands close behind me and I groan as I see it's Julie who is now getting the stripper treatment. She is throwing back her head with laughter as he straddles her, handing over the squirty cream.

"Typical!" I say, "I wouldn't be surprised if it was her who organised it. She wouldn't have told me, she knows I hate this kind of thing."

"All I can think about is how unhygienic all this is," Jonathan whispers to me, "sharing germs. Not to mention what happens when that cream goes off, in all that heat."

"Is that your idea of talking dirty?" I ask quietly.

"Ha," he says, "didn't you know chefs love talking about food poisoning? Salmonella totally turns us on. *Sal-mo-nell-a.*" He whispers this last word right into my ear, making me shiver. "Ooh, you liked that, did you? There's more where that came from. *"Di-arrh-oea ... missed use-by dates ... food handled by somebody who hasn't washed their hands..."*

"You are an idiot," I say, turning to grin at him. His face is close to mine, the light from the bar window falling across it. I can see what Lydia sees in him, not to mention the countless other people who comment on 'my' gorgeous chef. His brown eyes are dancing with laughter and his freckled face is almost school-boyish. How did he get his teeth so white and straight?

"What?" he asks.

"Huh? Oh, nothing," I realise I sound flustered. "I was just wondering if you wore braces when you were at school."

"Oh," he smiles at me, "as a matter of fact, I did. You do ask the most interesting questions, Alice."

"Thanks." I turn back to the window and feel Jonathan's hands on my shoulders. It feels very intimate, out here in the dark. Maybe Bea's unfinished observation was correct and I am in need of some physical contact. Inside, the stripper appears to be putting his clothes back on.

"I hope he puts them straight in the wash," Jonathan says.

I see Julie going to walk the man out, putting some cash in his hand as she does so. "I knew it!" I say.

At the sound of their voices at the front door just round the corner, we disappear back across the veranda, sticking to the shadows, and Jonathan once again helps me over the wall.

"I didn't know you were such a gentleman," I say.

"There's a lot you don't know about me," he grins.

As we head back to the kitchen, I look across at the sparkling moonlit sea, adorned with the twinkling lights of fishing boats and the brighter, star-like lights of a huge tanker which is taking a rest far off the coast. Jonathan opens the kitchen door and ushers me inside.

"And now," he says, "I must disappear before this

coven of witches realises there's another gorgeous man in the house. I'll see you in the morning."

He bows to me, grabs his bag, and vanishes into the night. I smile, thinking about how difficult we'd found it in the early days, working together, then I head back into the bar, feigning disappointment at the absence of the stripper.

"Where were you?" asks Julie.

"Oh, I just had to sort out a couple of things in the kitchen."

"I hope you don't mean Jonathan?" she says. "I heard you two out there."

"Dammit, Julie, can there be no secrets between us?"

"No, my friend, none at all."

"Well, you didn't tell me you'd booked a stripper."

"OK, you're right – strippers are the exception to the rule." She smiles as she pours two glasses of prosecco.

"Champagne all gone?" I ask.

"I think Bea realised we'd have drunk the lot – and by now everybody's too pissed to notice the difference."

"Cheers," she says. "Here's to a year of weddings – and one where I know you're going to find love yourself."

"We'll see," I say, clinking my glass against hers.

"What are we drinking to, girls?" Bea appears at my elbow.

"To love," I say, feeling awash with it for my friends. "A many splendoured thing."

5

There's something about weddings; something about the moment the bride walks into the room, which always makes me catch my breath. I'm sure I'm not alone in this but I am going to have to strengthen my reserves this year; this is the first of four and as Bea walks almost shyly into the ceremony room, I find myself choked up, tears spilling from my eyes.

The music – something by Beethoven but I'm not sure what – started up at exactly the moment Bea and David walked through the grand oak doorway. I can see David's finding it hard to keep it together himself. I look to Bob, standing big and bold at the front of the room, a wide smile painted across his handsome face. That is enough to choke me up again. Oh god, I'm a nightmare! Julie also appears to be silently crying. She smiles through her tears and squeezes my hand.

When Bea reaches Bob, David shakes his hand and steps to the side while Bea takes Bob's arm. The smile he gives her will be forever etched in my mind. That, I think, really is what love looks like.

I manage to quell my tears and I listen and watch closely.

David is a mess; he's not stopped crying since he walked Bea in – before that, even – when we were up at the Sail Loft getting ready, he was snivelling. I went outside with him, at his request, and he lit up a cigarette.

"For my nerves," he looked at me. "Don't tell Martin."

"You're not even married and you're already keeping secrets," I teased. "Don't worry, I won't say anything, as long as it doesn't become a habit."

"Smoking, or secret-keeping?"

"Both."

I look around the wood-panelled room. Bea and Bob have only invited about twenty people to the ceremony. Bob's mum and sister are here, sitting in the front row of seats. Then there are Julie and me, David and Martin, Bob's friend Jack, who he's known since his days in the US Army, Bea's best friend Jane and her husband Peter (David says they're named after some 1970s school books, but I've told him I'm far too young to know what he's talking about) and a handful of people I recognise vaguely from around town.

I take a photo while Bob and Bea are saying their vows, looking into each other's eyes, the celebrant's smiling face just slightly out of focus behind them.

The happy couple exit to the Beautiful South's *Prettiest Eyes*. We follow behind them, humbled and happy in the wake of their love.

Outside, there is confetti thrown by some of Bea's friends, who have turned up to surprise her. Next come the inevitable photos and then it is off to Cross-Section for a celebratory meal before the evening reception. We are greeted by Christian's lovely staff, all dressed in their customary black, offering glasses of champagne or rhubarb & ginger pressé and presenting trays of olives, stuffed mini peppers, artichokes, tiny rolls of pickled herring, smoked salmon on blinis; all beautifully presented.

I sit between Julie and David at dinner; a wonderful aubergine risotto for me and some kind of crazy seafood concoction for the non-veggie guests, adorned with baby squid and some tiny purple flowers, which I have to admit looks stunning.

I steel myself for the speeches; nevertheless, they predictably have me in tears. Bea speaks first:

"Unaccustomed as I am to public speaking;" a gale of laughter at this, "I wanted to stand up to show it is not just the groom who should speak. If this marriage is to be one of equals then that should begin now. But I will keep it brief, I promise. I'd like to start by thanking all of you for being here today to celebrate this most special of days with my husband and me." A brief pause while we all applaud. "I'd like to offer special thanks to my wonderful brother, David, who as you all know delayed his own wedding when I was in hospital and now I've gone and stolen his thunder. But not really, David – and Martin – this wedding seemed like it had to happen now, and I know you understand that, but I can't wait for your big day and I hope that you will be just as happy as Bob and I are. I know exactly how lucky I am to have you, David." At this, Bea's face crumples and David blows her a kiss while Bob puts his hand on hers. She straightens up. "Lastly, I have to thank this wonderful man right here by my side. As all of you know, we met online. He could have been anyone; I was hoping maybe Brad Pitt, but I knew, from the first messages we exchanged, that he was somebody I'd like an awful lot. As it's turned out, he's the love of my life. I've never been happier and I feel so lucky to be spending the rest of my life with you, Bob."

Bob stands and kisses her, taking her by surprise. "To Bob," she says laughingly, then turns to David, "and to my wonderful little brother. My life would be less without you."

David is in floods of tears, and Martin's arm around his shoulders. Julie is sniffling away on my other side. In fact, I don't think there is a dry eye in the house.

The next to speak is Bob. "Well, friends and family, I did have a speech written but I don't think I need it after listening to my beautiful wife. I'd also like to start by offering my thanks to my brother-in-law, David, and to Martin, too. You've both been so generous in letting us get on with this, when you delayed your own wedding for us. I can't help but feel a bit bad about this but your day is going to outshine ours, I know it. This is not a typical wedding; it's small, it's intimate; it's last minute. But it feels one hundred per cent right. And I can only echo what Bea says; from the moment I read her first message to me, I knew she was somebody special. Then I saw her beautiful face on screen, though it did freeze up so she looked a bit like this." He scrunches up his face and crosses his eyes and we all laugh, grateful for the break from the emotional stuff. He turns to Bea, "But I knew, sweetheart, from the start, that you were somebody special. I just never knew how much – and I could never have imagined all this." He gestures around the room to us all, outside to the estuary, then across to town. "I'd been to London before, and around Windsor and the usual places, but I'd never even heard of this quaint little place called Cornwall. Bea used to talk about it and I couldn't really imagine what it was like but I knew Bea wanted to come back and I'd follow her anywhere. Now I'm here, I can see what she loves about the place – and the people – and I want to thank you all for making me so welcome. But most of all I want to thank Bea. My beautiful, strong wife who I love with all my heart."

Oh god, here come the tears again. And next it's David. I've got no hope.

He can barely get his words out to start with. Martin ends up standing with him, his hand on his back, the perfect support.

"As you all know, or most of you at least, Bea and I lost our parents some years ago, when I was in my early twenties and Bea not that much older, though she seemed so much more grown up than me at the time. It's not that Bea has taken the place of our mum for me; it's not like that, but she's always – and I mean *always* – been there for me, and there have been times I have really needed her. When she went off to the States to meet this strange man, I really wasn't sure about it. She has worked her ars- sorry, endlessly hard, to make the Sail Loft what it is and I didn't want her to lose that, or for this unknown character to be taking advantage of her. But I should have known – and I did, really – that my big sister is no idiot and there is no way she'd have left this place for anybody she wasn't sure about. When she got out there, and Skyped me, and I saw her next to this great big disgustingly ugly American brute, I could see immediately what she did. And I could see her eyes shining with happiness. That was enough for me. Now I am so happy they are back here – and as for delaying our wedding, well there's no way that I could have got married with my sister in hospital and I thank Martin for understanding that. This is a truly beautiful and special day, as befitting my beautiful, special sister and her husband. I ask you all to raise your glasses to Bea and Bob."

"To Bea and Bob," we echo through yet more tears. I

take a big sip of my champagne; I need to replace some fluids.

Soon after the speeches, the DJ sets up his kit and more guests begin to arrive. Christian has cleared some floor space for dancing and patio heaters have been added to the outside space, making it inviting even on this cool spring day. I look out at the decking, strung with hundreds of tiny lights and adorned with ribbons and flowers. I can see a mist forming across the waters, just as the natural light of day is dimming. It only adds to the occasion, providing a magical quality to the outside space, and a cosiness here inside. I sit with Julie and Martin while David, along with Bea and Bob, is busy greeting guests. Soon enough, Luke arrives. Julie stands to greet him, with a full-on kiss.

"Steady on!" he laughs. "Had one too many?"

"No, I just cannot wait to marry you," Julie snakes her arms around Luke's waist and he pushes her long dark hair away from her face.

"I can't, either."

I look away, taking a sip of my drink and thinking of Gabe, the man Julie had been engaged to before we came down here, only two years ago. All of that seems a world away; a different lifetime. I always liked him, and I hope he's got himself straightened out a bit now. It broke his heart when they split up and I wondered for a long time if Julie had done the right thing but now, seeing her with Luke, I know without a shadow of a doubt that she has.

Martin reaches across the table and takes my hand, giving me a little smile. He knows, he sees. I'm happy, so happy, for all of my friends, but deep inside there is that tiny sadness, which unfurls every now and then, at times of weakness. I'm only thirty and there is plenty of time for me to meet somebody, if I want to. But I can't help wishing that I didn't have to. That I still had Sam.

As the evening becomes night, the mist thickens, wrapping itself around the building, pressing itself against the windows. The outside lights have faded into the murkiness; it feels like those of us inside are adrift on the sea. We could be anywhere.

I have been sitting with Jonathan and Lydia, who has come back from uni for the weekend. She seems different, somehow, and I can't quite place it. Maybe just a little more self-assured. Jonathan is very attentive to her as well; something I could never have imagined even a year ago. I wasn't keen on this work relationship when it started; Lydia was our morning waitress and also studying hard for her A-Levels. I was well aware of the effect a good-looking chef could have on her life, and her state of mind – particularly as Jonathan was a bit unreliable when it came to his love life – but she stuck with her studies and continued to be her lovely self so that many of the hotel guests would comment on how lucky we were to have her. And to give Jonathan his due, he has behaved impeccably, since those first teething troubles, and now, if anything, the tables have turned. Maybe Lydia holds more of the cards in their relationship these days. Still, he seems proud when she talks about her new course, and her new friends.

"Do you two need a drink?" I ask, having been nursing an empty glass for some time.

"I'm fine thanks, Alice," Lydia says.

"Can I have another pint, please?" Jonathan asks. "I'll

get these, though." He pushes a twenty-pound note into my hand. Another way he has changed in this last year or so. I used to think he was only out for what he could get – largely because he was. Lydia's influence on him has been very good. But perhaps he is just growing up, as well.

I laugh at myself for these thoughts, as I go to get the drinks. Who am I to think that about Jonathan? He's only a few years younger than me. I wonder if I could be any more patronising.

The bar area is busy. I stand patiently behind three rows of people. The Cross-Section isn't really designed for this kind of event; in its normal guise it's a restaurant, so the bar itself is actually very small. I am in no hurry, though. The air in the room feels laden with love, and romance, echoing the promises which Bea and Bob have made to each other today. It's wonderful, and beautiful, but not having somebody to share these feelings with has made me feel ever so slightly detached from the situation. I think I will take my drink outside, despite the mist. I just need to find my jacket as it's going to be cold out there.

"Here, get in while you can." I'm disturbed from my thoughts by a friendly face, allowing me access to the bar. I smile gratefully. The face is a new one to me, belonging to an older-looking man who is somehow holding five drinks at the same time as keeping this space open.

"Thanks very much," I gratefully take up his offer, noting his tanned skin, closely-cut greying hair and cool blue eyes.

"No problem." With another smile, he is gone.

I soon have my two drinks; a pint of bitter for Jonathan, and a vodka & orange for me. I deposit Jonathan's pint and his change on the table in front of him. "I'm just going for some fresh air," I say.

"You sure?" Lydia asks. "It's gonna be cold out there."

"Yeah, I kind of like it," I grin. I manage to find my jacket on the overladen coat stand. I shrug it on then open one of the wide sliding doors out onto the decking.

"Don't let that mist in, love," a loud-voiced man calls from a nearby table.

I smile, and slip into the darkness, closing the door so that the music and voices are nearly obscured and replaced instead with the whispering of the mist.

"Who goes there?" A voice reaches me, before the shape of a person becomes apparent.

"Erm…" I don't recognise the voice, though I realise I can smell cigar smoke. The shape becomes more human and I realise it's the man from the bar.

"Hello again," he says.

"Hi."

"Out for some fresh air, too?" He grins, holding his cigar up. "I shouldn't really, but it's a special occasion. And it was getting a bit much in there, I wanted to be out of the room for the first dance."

"Oh, yeah… I'd forgotten all about that."

"I hate them!" he says. "My wife and I – ex-wife, I should say – danced to bloody *Lady in Red*. Her choice, I hasten to add. And she was wearing white."

I laugh. "Chris de Burgh probably won't be my choice, if I ever get married."

Urgh. Where did that 'ever' come from? I must sound desperate.

"There's no rush, is there? You don't look old enough to be married. Take it from me, live life a bit first. I was only mid-twenties when I got married, my wife a bit younger. Two kids by the time I was thirty. Great kids;

nearly grown up now of course, and I'd never regret them, but I think I was too young. We both were. Divorced before we were forty."

"I'm sorry," I say.

"Don't be!" he laughs. "We're OK. We rub along as best we can, and we're better off apart."

I'm not sure what to say so I take a sip from my glass, inadvertently shivering as I do so. I've found my way over to the rails at the side of the decking and here, amid the swirling mist, the fairy lights are once more visible, doing their best to pierce the darkness. I can hear the sea below, rushing and whooshing, spitting against the rocks. It is almost dizzying, knowing it is down there, but not being able to see it. I have a sudden thought that I am out here with a strange man. What if he was to attack me? Push me over the banister? The music is so loud inside the restaurant nobody would hear me.

"Here," he says, slipping his jacket off and putting it around my shoulders. I'm touched by the gesture, although I do wonder if it's a bit too smooth. Still, he smells good, and as he smiles at me little lines appear, as though his face is well-used to smiling.

"Thank you," I say. "Now you're going to be cold, though. And I'm already wearing my own jacket; this definitely feels a bit greedy."

"Oh no, I'll be fine. Don't you know, real men don't get cold?"

"Of course! Sorry, I'd forgotten, you're not like us fragile little ladies."

His laugh is strong and sudden. "You're Bea's manager, aren't you?"

"Yes, I'm... have we met before?"

"No, not as such. I've seen you about town, though.

I'm Paul." He offers his hand.

"Alice," I say, surprised by the warmth of his skin. "Sorry, my hand's cold."

"Ha! I'm not bothered by such trifles. I'm a man, remember?" He shivers now, and I laugh.

"Maybe it's too cold out here. I might have to go back in. First dance or not."

"Mind if I join you?"

"Not at all."

Back in the warmth, Paul and I find some seats and he gets a bottle of champagne from the bar. "Sorry, I'm not being flash, I promise. And I don't always drink champagne. It's just I've got a long day tomorrow and I know I can have a glass or two more of this without feeling too bad. If I start to mix the drinks now I'm going to have a raging hangover. This is one of the downsides of getting old."

How old are you? I want to ask but it seems a bit rude. I'm guessing maybe mid- to late-forties, a similar age to Bea.

Julie walks by, catching my eye but not stopping. I can see the look on her face and I know exactly what message she's trying to convey. I must admit, I am quite happy to be sitting here with Paul. As he refills my glass, I take the chance take a better look at him. I'm no expert on clothes, by any means, but I can see that Paul's are good quality and fit him very nicely, from his shirt to his suit trousers. I've handed him back his jacket, which is now slung on the back of his chair. I'm going to sound very cheesy here but he appears to have looked after himself very well; there is no belly hanging over the top of his trousers and his greying hair is cut well around his tanned face and neck. I sneak a glance at his hands. His nails are cut neat and short.

"What do you do, Paul?" I ask him.

"I… I'm a… a businessman," he says. "Which I realise sounds very vague. I own a couple of businesses."

"Oh, right. Doing what?"

"Logistics, and catering. Not the most exciting things in the world. But I like what I do."

"Well, that's all that matters, isn't it? I love my job," I say. "And I used to find my old one very dull. I worked for a stationery company up in the Midlands, where I'm from. It was OK, but I am so much happier now."

"I can see that," he smiles at me. "And you're right. If you can enjoy your work, not much else matters. Well, I don't mean nothing else matters." He stops and looks at me.

I hold his gaze for a moment, feeling a strange combination of flustered and confident at the same time.

"Have you got a boyfriend?" he asks me.

"No."

"Girlfriend?"

"No!" I laugh.

"Well, that's good news. Maybe I can take you out for a drink sometime?"

"I… that would be great," I say. I have a strange jelly-like feeling in my legs, and my stomach is doing cartwheels. I want to catch Julie's eye but she's busy whispering into Luke's ear and judging by the smile which is spreading itself his face, they won't want to be disturbed.

"Here," Paul slides a card across the table to me. "I never like doing this, either. Ordering champagne… handing out business cards… I'm not trying to be a slimeball, I promise."

"Ha!" I say, pulling out my wallet and fishing about for one of my crumpled cards. "You can have one of mine. Even though you know where I work."

"Alice Griffiths," he says, turning my card over. "And have you got a mobile number, Alice?"

"Yes," I say, "have you got a pen? I'll write my number on the card."

Even Paul's pen seems expensive, and stylish. It's weighty and writes so smoothly. I don't want to give it back; I feel like I could write all day long with a pen like this.

"Thank you." When I hand my card back to him, he tucks it into his own business card holder. "I will be in touch, I promise. But I guess we're both going to have to do some mingling soon, or people will talk – you must have been in town long enough to know just how much people like to talk around here! What if we finish these drinks and go our separate ways? For now." That direct look again.

"OK," I say, knowing he is right but feeling disappointed.

"I'd love to spend all night with you... that sounds wrong, sorry... I would love to spend the evening sitting and talking with you," Paul grins, "but I hope there'll be time for that."

We clink our glasses together, then Paul insists on topping up my glass with what is left in the bottle before we part ways.

"I'll be in touch, soon," he says, his face close to mine. A further shiver goes through me but it's not the cold this time.

"I'll look forward to it." I take my glass and head over

to my friends, kicking myself all the way for the 'I'll look forward to it'.

The rest of the night is a whirl of happiness and festivities. Paul seems to have got under my skin, in a good way. Even if he doesn't call, it has been a nice little ego boost, and I feel full of energy and confidence. Every now and then we catch the other's eye and smile. And when Bob and Bea take to the dance floor for their first dance – INXS's *Never Tear Us Apart* - we grin at each other. It's like we have some kind of unspoken secret. I like it.

The bride and groom are whisked away before their guests, in a fancy car, to an undisclosed location. Bob had apparently insisted on booking their honeymoon, and has not told anybody where it is going to be. I hug Bea before she leaves. "I'm so happy for you."

"I'm so happy, too!" She twirls me round, bringing me back to stand face-to-face with her. "It just goes to show, Alice, you don't know what life's got in store for you. And you're so young! You've got so much to look forward to!"

"I hope so," I say, quickly adding, "In fact, I am sure of it. Now, go and have a very, very well deserved break with your handsome husband."

"Are my ears burning?" Bob says, appearing at my shoulder.

"Let me see… no, I don't think so," I pretend to examine his ears then stand on my tiptoes to kiss his cheek. "Have a great honeymoon."

"I intend to!" Bob grins at me.

After they have gone, we make our way out into the night to find one of the taxis which have been arranged to take the guests back to town. As Julie follows Luke onto the back seat, I feel a hand on the small of my back and turn.

"It's been really nice to meet you, Alice," Paul gives me a kiss on the cheek.

"You too," I say. He holds the door, shutting it once I have clambered inelegantly in. I smile at him as the car pulls away and in a moment, Paul has disappeared into the mist.

"So what did he want?" Julie asks.

"Oh, he's just a friend of Bea's, a local businessman. We were just talking work."

"Don't give me that!" she laughs. "I can recognise an Alice Griffiths flirtation from a mile off."

"What's this?" Luke turns to us, his eyebrows raised.

"Oh, nothing," I say, not comfortable with Sam's best friend hearing this conversation.

"Alice snagged a silver fox!" Julie laughs.

"Oh yeah? Who is it?"

"Paul… hang on…" I reach for his card. "Paul Winters."

Luke's eyes spring wide open. "Fucking hell, Alice, that's good work."

"What? Why?"

"He's one of the richest men in Cornwall. Well, if you don't count the thousands of second-home owners – and I don't."

"He's..?" I don't know what to say. This is interesting, and exciting. It does cross my mind briefly that Luke doesn't seem too concerned, as I thought he might given he is Sam's best friend. Perhaps this is proof that Sam has got over me and moved on. Which means that surely it is time for me to do the same.

6

While Bea is away, the Sail Loft is fully booked every day – the beginning of another long, busy season.

I have received just two short messages from Bea, saying that they are having "most relaxing time ever". She still won't say where they are and I don't ask. Workwise, it feels like when she first went over to America. Now that she is back in Cornwall, although I've retained the position of manager, I'm always aware of her presence and the place feels less 'mine' (I know it's not, it's Bea's). It's not that Bea is heavy-handed, but I am realising that I really do want to be my own boss.

Julie is equally keen to get our business started and so we've been spending our evenings trawling through property and business residential websites, and looking through papers like *Daltons Weekly*. The sticking point, as always, is our budget.

"This place looks amazing, Alice," Julie pushes the paper towards me, a large red circle around an ad for a former smallholding which has already been converted into holiday lets. "It's got land around it, and it's only just outside town. It's perfect."

I read the particulars. It does sound perfect. Five self-contained units: two two-bed, two six-bed and one larger one, for ten. It's about two miles from the edge of town, and on a bus route. Not that the people who we're looking to make our clients are likely to be the type of people who rely on public transport.

"I know what you're thinking," Julie continues, "it's too expensive. But Luke says he can loan us most of the money. And you said your mum and dad might…"

"I think it's a bit beyond what they're capable of loaning me," I say. "And I know what you're saying about Luke. I know, but it's different for you. He'll be your husband soon. I just don't feel a hundred per cent comfortable with him footing most of the costs."

"But we'll pay him back!" she says earnestly, "it's in the plan. And what's the difference between borrowing from Luke and borrowing from a bank?"

"Hmmm."

Ideally, I would sell my flat back home – and I am trying, but it's proving really hard. And not being nearby makes it even harder. Mum and Dad have been round and given it a 'lick of paint', as Dad says. Julie's brother, who was renting it, left a month ago so it's just an empty flat and actually starting to cost me money.

If I think too hard about things, I start to feel a bit anxious. I'm paying the mortgage on my flat, and I need to find somewhere to live down here, sometime soon. It's going to cost a lot more than what I'm paying to live in David's house. It seems a bit mad to be also looking to borrow a load of money to start a business, which in itself is a huge risk. I know I have to break it down, try to deal with one thing at a time. And I also have to remind myself that I came down here to escape the mundane, predictable life I used to live. It requires some strength of will to overcome that side of me that values stability but I know that the potential rewards are more than worth it.

"Let's go and look," I say, surprising myself, and Julie's face lights up.

"Really?"

"Yes."

"Alice!" Julie hugs me. "I love you! I have such a great feeling about this."

Her enthusiasm is contagious and I hug her back. "I do really want to do this, Julie. I hope we can make it work."

"We will. I know it."

So it is that the following Sunday morning, we are driving up the hill through town, in the little red car, out onto the narrow lane which scoots along parallel to the coast for a while then takes a pronounced left turn, towards a great little village with a pub that's been newly taken over by some friends of Christian's. Shortly before the village, Julie says, "There – that left turn!"

There is a battered old gateway which I would have missed had it not been for Julie. Attached to the gatepost is a carved wooden sign which reads 'Amethi'.

I break sharply and find myself on little more than a track, which we bump along for nearly a mile, finding ourselves seemingly deep into some woods before we reach an opening. If you didn't know this place was here, you'd never find it. I already know it's perfect.

We've deliberately arrived half an hour earlier than we'd arranged to meet the agent so we can have a look round before somebody else arrives and starts telling us we should buy the place. We get out of the car and smile at each other then walk across the cracked old hardstanding.

"We'll need to sort this out," Julie says.

"You sound like we're definitely doing it!"

"Just thinking positive," she grins.

The closest building to us is the biggest; the old

farmhouse, apparently – this will be the ten-bed place. I peer through the windows, into a large, empty space. There are dark Cornish slate tiles on the floor, and I can see patio doors on the other side, leading into what looks like old stable yard. I press myself against the stone, feeling its age, wanting to find guidance there. I turn to see Julie smiling inquiringly at me.

"I know it's nice, Alice, but I'm not sure I want to make love to it."

"You haven't given it a chance," I say, and take her arm, pulling her towards the next part of the building.

From our view from outside, it looks like all the units have been finished in a similar way: the same dark slate tiles; magnolia walls; polished wooden banisters and worktops.

"Why on earth would somebody sell this place when they've gone to so much effort?" I wonder aloud.

"Maybe they've run out of money," Julie suggests.

"That seems a shame."

"For them!"

"I had no idea you were such a mercenary cow," I laugh.

"Yes you did. Anyway," she says seriously, "who knows why they're selling? Maybe they just changed their minds? Or maybe it was a builder just getting these into a saleable state. It could be anything, or anyone. What matters now is what we think of the place."

As she says this, we hear the sound of an engine and another car bumping its way along the narrow track. We start guiltily and walk back towards our car but not before a sleek, shiny black Mercedes has emerged from between the trees. A smiling woman waves at us and pulls her car neatly next to the shabby little red number we've come in.

"Getting an early look around? Very wise!" She continues smiling as she gets out of her car, and I like her immediately. "Sally James," she says, shaking hands with Julie and then me.

"We were just…" I say.

"Oh, it's fine. Sensible, if you're thinking of this kind of outlay!" She pulls the particulars of the place from her bag, and jangles a set of keys. "Shall we?"

She unlocks the door to the first building and we walk in, our footsteps echoing on the tiles. The house smells of fresh paint, and cement, and something indefinable.

"Oh, it's beautiful!" It's almost like Sally's looking at the place for herself.

"Have you not been here before?" I ask.

"No! My husband, John, has had all the dealings with this place, it belongs to a friend of his."

"Really?" I say, intrigued. "Do you know why they're selling?"

"Yes, I do. He's had a change of heart as it's too different to his normal business, and he says he needs to concentrate on that. In honesty, I think he bought this place as a favour to the guy it used to belong to – another old school pal, who used to live here with his family before it all went wrong. Anyway, you don't want to know all that." Sally is reading the reaction on my face. "It was very sad but he's OK now, the original owner, and living upcountry, by the Tamar, running a canoeing business, doing quite well I think."

"So you don't need to feel guilty, Alice!" Julie says laughingly.

Sally smiles. "Why don't you two have a good look around? I'll go and unlock the other buildings, if I can work out which of these 500 keys fits which door! Just give me a shout if you've got any questions."

Julie walks up the stairs, which are a polished redwood with a thick cream runner up their centre and which turn invitingly up towards a high-ceilinged landing which leads to three bedrooms. A further set of stairs goes up to the other two bedrooms, encased in the sizeable attic space. Each room has its own en suite. All the rooms up here have exposed beams and wonderful views. This is a beautiful house, there is no doubt about it. I look at the fixtures and fittings, not really sure what I am looking for, but feeling that I need to see as much as I can of this place.

Julie is in one of the other rooms.

"I love it, Alice!" I hear her muffled voice.

"I do, too!" I say, but I can't shake the feeling that it is a dream too far. Still, we are here now. We go through all the rooms then all the other units. Three of them are joined together, converted from the stable block, hayloft and whatever else was here. The second of the two-bedroom places stands apart a little way, its back turned to the main complex.

There's a barn just over a small grassed area, which has been done up to create a large space with no clear purpose. The floor of the barn is polished concrete and there is a small kitchen as well as a cloakroom and toilet.

"This wasn't on the particulars," I say to Sally. "Is it part of the complex?"

"Wasn't it? I'll kill John! Yes, it is, I think the owner was entertaining the possibility of this being a place for work get-togethers – you know, conferences, team-building events, that kind of thing."

"This … is … perfect," Julie breathes.

"We could rent the whole place out to groups of friends, or families," I say. "God, we could get a wedding licence! It would be perfect for a secluded, intimate wedding."

"It would, wouldn't it?" Sally smiles.

I'm not much of a one for a poker face, and neither is Julie. Sally can clearly see how enthusiastic we are. "Have another look round if you like, ladies, I'm in no hurry. John's got the kids and I'm making the most of it. I know it's not exactly a spa afternoon but I've got to take these opportunities where I can!"

"Thanks, Sally." We take her up on her offer and wander slowly back through each building. I stop outside and take in the sound of the birds; the trees moving in the slight breeze which caresses my face. I close my eyes.

"This is it, isn't it, Alice? I know it!" Julie's voice makes my eyes spring open. My friend is standing in front of me, looking more excited than I have ever seen her. "Alice, you know that we've known, ever since our golden summer, that we're meant to be here. In Cornwall, I mean. And now I think we know what we have to do. I can't imagine working with anybody but you, and I know you love the Sail Loft but it's not yours. It's not ours. Let's make something that's ours."

I laugh and a memory springs into my mind, of this time two years ago, when Julie talked me into quitting my job at World of Stationery and coming back down here. I was reluctant; I was scared, but I knew it was what I wanted to do and her drive and determination were catching. I began to allow myself to feel excited by the idea. I feel exactly the same right now.

7

On the way back to town, I feel my phone vibrate a couple of times but as I'm driving I leave it be. Instead, Julie and I talk non-stop about Amethi; what we loved about it, what we could do with it. I know we had an idea before but there was something about being in the place which has set both of our imaginations alight.

It has to be equal, though; we have to be even. This means I have to foot my part of the bill myself. No matter how much I love Julie – and Luke – I know that if I am in debt to them from the outset, it's going to do something to the balance of the business, and the way we work together. And I am already well aware that Julie and I are not going to always see eye-to-eye.

So this is what I have to do. Alongside managing the Sail Loft, and developing plans with Julie, I have to raise that money. I have to sell my flat, and I have to speak to my parents. And once all this is done – if it can possibly be done – I have to speak to Bea. I really hope she doesn't feel like I am throwing her generosity and loyalty in her face.

Oh yes, and I need to find somewhere else to live. It's probably a good job I'm single; I don't think I have the time or the energy for a relationship at the moment.

It's only when I take my phone from my pocket that I remember feeling it vibrating when I was in the car. I check the missed call number but I don't recognise it. I open the text message.

Hi Alice. This is Paul. We met the other night at Bea and Bob's wedding. Please can you get back in touch at your convenience.

It's an odd message – half friendly, half business-like. Maybe he's out of practice. Having seen that twinkle in his eye, however, and felt the smoothness of his gesture in loaning me his jacket, I somehow doubt it.

I am not sure whether to ring or text but as he didn't leave a voice message – and because it's just easier – I opt for the latter.

Hi Paul. Thanks for your message. Sorry I missed your call, I was out with a friend.

Does that mean you were on a date? His return message is quick to appear.

No! Not a date. I was out with Julie – who was also at the wedding.

Oh, well that's OK, then. Can I call you?

Sure.

My heart suddenly starts beating ten to the dozen. What does that expression mean anyway? I don't have time to Google it, or to get any more nervous, because my phone is ringing.

"Hello?"

"Hi, Alice. It's Paul, in case you hadn't guessed. How are you?"

"I'm fine, thanks. How are you?"

"Oh, good… just taking a break from some work, actually."

"Well, it is Sunday – traditionally the day of rest."

"That's what I'm thinking. So I guess you're not working this weekend?"

"No, Stefan – the night manager – is in all this weekend."

"So you're free now?"

"Erm… Yes."

"Can I take you out?"

Now this is what I call fast moving. I hadn't expected it at all. But really – what else am I going to do this afternoon? OK, OK, I've already made a list of all the pretty major things I have to do with my life. It's Sunday, though; what can I get done on a Sunday?

"OK," I say.

He laughs. "Don't sound too excited."

"Sorry! It's just a bit… unexpected."

"At the risk of sounding totally up myself, I am usually working or travelling, or both, so I have to grasp these opportunities when I can. You seem like a good opportunity."

It's my turn to laugh.

"OK, that was cheesy! Sorry."

"That's fine, I just don't think I've been described that way before."

"Well I could think of other ways to describe you… but maybe I'll save them for later. Pick you up in an hour?"

"OK. Great. I'll meet you at the front of the Sail Loft. It's easier than getting stuck down in town." It also means

I don't have to tell him where I live. Although why do I have the feeling he's one of those people who knows everything anyway?

"Fantastic. See you shortly."

Argh! An hour! "Julieeeee!"

"What is it?" My friend comes rushing from the kitchen, swinging herself round the bottom of the banister.

"I've got a date!"

"You've what?" She grins. "The silver fox?"

I nod.

"When?"

"In an hour!"

"Shit, we need to sort you out! Where are you going?"

"I don't know!" I wail.

"Well, how do you know what to wear?"

"I don't! This is why I need you."

"Right, you go jump in the shower. Don't actually jump, I don't want any injuries before your *first date in two years.*"

"OK, rub it in," I say sourly. "Anyway, it's not two years."

"Well, near enough. Go on, I'll find you something to wear."

"Thank you, Julie."

"No problem. God, I feel like your mum! I'm so proud of you, angel."

"Shut up, you idiot."

I shower quickly and thoroughly, unable to quell my nerves. I step back into my room and Julie has laid out three different lots of clothes on the bed.

"Right," she says, "get yourself dried off and your hair wrapped up and we'll work out what the best option is." I can tell she's loving this. "OK, so you don't know where you're going. Could be posh, could be a greasy spoon."

"He doesn't seem like a greasy spoon kind of man," I observe.

"No, he didn't really look like it. Although… every man is a greasy spoon kind of man, really."

"Agreed. But I don't think he's going to be taking me to a truckers' cafe."

"OK, so what I was thinking was you could wear these…" she holds up some black trousers, "which can be dressed up or down. Wear this top, which is nice and strappy, and cover it up with a cardigan. It's too cold for strappy tops really anyway but if you end up in a lovely restaurant, you can slip the cardigan off and he can admire your shoulders. If, however, you end up walking hand-in-hand on a beach looking at the sunset—" I whack her on the arm "Ow! What? It could happen. As I was saying, if you end up walking on the beach, you can wrap this cardigan around you and it's so soft and beautiful, he's going to want to wrap you around him."

"Julie!"

"Come on, Alice, of course he already wants to do that."

"You don't know that."

"Oh, I do. I saw the way he was looking at you."

I can't deny a little thrill passes through me at this thought. I know nothing about this man and from first impressions he and I are probably very different – but he was pretty gorgeous and also very different to Sam, which I think can only be a good thing.

I get dressed and Julie dries and straightens my hair then offers me some make-up advice.

"I'm not going to wear any."

"You're – really? On a first date?"

"Yeah. Really. Either he likes me, or he doesn't. And actually – more importantly, for me – either I like him, or I don't. Make-up can't change that."

"I love you, Alice," Julie says.

"Ha! I love you, too. And I don't want to look haggard. I love the clothes you've chosen. I just – I don't know. I want to be myself."

"You are always yourself."

Julie follows me downstairs and passes me a pair of her sandals to wear. "You might not want to wear make-up but please don't go out in your smelly Birkenstocks."

I laugh. "OK, I will concede to you on this. Thank you, Julie."

"It's a pleasure." She puts her hand on my shoulders. "Look at you. All grown up."

"Shut up, you idiot."

"Have fun! And I'll have my phone. If you need a quick getaway, let me know."

"I will."

I walk up the road, smiling at the people walking the other way, towards town. I keep my cardigan on but it's just about warm enough not to. As I approach the Sail Loft, I turn to the familiar view of the town and the sea and I am hit by the promise of approaching summer. It swoops into me and I want to laugh out loud. I don't because I don't want people to think I'm mad as a hatter.

I don't have long to wait. I'm just trying to decide whether or not I should sit on the steps of the Sail Loft – a) will a guest see me and harangue me about some kind of work-based issue? and b) will it look far too casual for somebody like Paul? – when I hear the sound of an engine and a smart dark blue convertible pulls up alongside the kerb. Paul is smiling at me from behind his sunglasses. He turns off the motor and steps out of the car.

"Alice! You look lovely," he kisses me on the cheek and opens the passenger door for me. "Shall we?"

"Yes," I say, feeling unaccountably flustered. I steal a quick glance at the hotel as I try my best to climb elegantly into the car. Why did I ever think meeting somebody for a first date outside my place of work was a good idea?

Paul walks round to the other side and slides easily back into the driver's seat.

"Where are we going?" I ask.

"Well, I wasn't sure what you'd fancy. Have you eaten?"

"No, not yet."

"Great. How about we go out of town and just see where we end up? It's a beautiful day, and it's not going to be dark for a while yet."

"Sounds perfect," I say as Paul reaches into the back of the car. I wonder what he's up to and the image if a beautiful bouquet of flowers pops into my head. I laugh when I realise he's passing me a blanket.

"In case it gets cold," he says.

"I'm not an old lady!" I protest.

"No, but I promise you, it can get a bit chilly with the roof down. And I want you to travel in maximum comfort."

I can see lines crinkle out from the corners of Paul's eyes when he smiles, which I think is a good sign. He either smiles a lot or he's got a severe squint.

Just as he pulls away, I see Jonathan rounding the

corner of the road. I smile and wave and he does a double-take then raises his arm in a vague wave.

Soon we are on the road out of town, weaving along between the moors, catching occasional glimpses of the sea. The blanket comes in handy, as it turns out. I tuck it around me and realise with a little relief that it is too noisy to really hold a conversation. It buys me a bit of time to calm down and just get used to being with Paul. I surreptitiously take in the details. The faint smell of his aftershave which reaches my nostrils intermittently; his short, greying stubble which looks like it's only a day or so old; the cleanliness of the car; his leather jacket, his jeans and shirt, which look casual yet still expensive somehow, and like they have never been creased. I check out my own clothes and try to pull out any signs of wrinkles. The polish on my toenails is not chipped, I'm pleased to see, and my fingernails are cut short as usual. I'm glad to have had Julie's help in getting ready and I can't help wishing that I might have put on a little make-up. *No,* I tell myself firmly, *either he likes you as you are, or he doesn't. And anyway, you have to decide if you like him or not.*

We find our way onto the coast road. Paul clearly knows these roads well, and is a confident driver. I look at his hands on the wheel, noting the veins and the fair hairs there. He glances across and smiles. "Would you like to stop at a beach?" he half-shouts so I can hear him. "We can have a walk, and I've just thought of the perfect place for dinner."

"Sounds great," I say as loudly as I can.

Paul takes the next right-hand turn, which finds us on a very narrow lane, lined either side with hedges which are just coming into bloom. After numerous twists and turns, and a close encounter with a 4x4 going the other way, we pull up on a little patch of ground, next to a high brick wall which I guess must enclose somebody's garden.

"It's a bit muddy, sorry," he says, "but once we're on the path down to the beach it should be better."

I look around for a path but I can't see one anywhere. Paul is already out of the car and opening my door for me. He gestures towards a small gap in the trees, and there I can see a pathway of sorts.

"I hope you don't mind a little walk," he says, "but this place is worth it, I promise."

"I don't mind at all." I pick my way across the muddy ground to the path. The trees are tall and well established and the brick wall which I noticed at the top follows the same route as the path. All around, there is birdsong, filling the air.

"I love this time of year," I say to Paul.

"Me too. I always think it's summer that I love best but there's something about spring. It's full of promise. We don't know yet if summer's going to be a let-down. I don't think spring ever is."

"No, that's true, I hadn't thought about it like that. Right now we can tell ourselves we're heading towards a beautiful summer but when it happens it could be just… crap."

I kick myself for my unsophisticated wording but Paul laughs. "I'm glad you could come out this afternoon. I didn't know whether you'd be busy. Or whether you'd want to."

"No, erm, I was out this morning and I hadn't got much planned. Julie, that's my friend… my housemate… will be with her fiancé later so I'd have just been kicking around the house on my own."

"Have you known her long? Your housemate?"

"Oh yeah, we've known each other since we were eleven. We met at secondary school. In fact, it's her fault that I'm in Cornwall at all." I explain to Paul where I'm from, and how Julie got me to quit World of Stationery and come down here. "We'd spent a summer here when we were eighteen, and just fell in love with the place." I don't mention that I fell in love with Sam as well.

"I don't blame you. But I remember when I was eighteen, I was desperate to get away. Now, I wouldn't be anywhere else in the world but I spent a good few years away, and I'm glad I did. I needed to see the world."

"And you still travel a lot?"

"I do. But I also have people to do that for me. Sorry, that sounds terrible. But I've been lucky enough to hire some great people, who are more up for all that. I don't think it helped my marriage that I was away so much, and I feel like I missed out a lot on the kids growing up. So now I suppose I prefer to travel for fun, and I like to take my kids with me when I can."

"How old are they?" I am picking my way carefully down the stony path but my foot slides on some loose stones. Paul grabs my arm for a moment.

"Steady on there! They're nineteen and twenty-one. Both at uni. I know, I don't look old enough, do I?" He laughs. I like his laugh. His sunglasses are pushed up onto his head now we're in the shade of the wooded path, and I can see those eyes and those laughter lines more clearly.

"You don't," I agree and, just as I say it, I see the path ahead open up, to reveal sand and sea. I want to take a photo, this is such a beautiful sight. "Wow!"

"I know, I really do look good for my age, don't I?"

"No, I…" I look at Paul to see he is grinning at me.

"I know, you meant the beach, not my good looks."

Well, actually, I'd say both, I think, but I'm not letting that thought out of my head. When we get to the sand, I ask Paul if he minds hanging on for a minute. I want to take off my sandals, and roll my trousers up.

"That's not a bad idea," he says, and he takes off his socks and shoes. I hadn't clocked the shoes until now but they look expensive, to my inexpert eye. He puts his socks carefully together and places them in his left shoe then he places the shoes on a rock which is jutting out of the top of the beach.

"What if somebody nicks them?" I ask.

"They won't," he says. "Nobody ever comes here."

"Really? Do you come here often?" Oh god, did I really just say that?

"Maybe." He smiles, "Leave your sandals there too, come on!" He starts jogging away so I drop my sandals next to his shoes and I follow him onto the cool sand. The beach is not huge but there is enough space to run and I feel swept up in the moment, just Paul and me on this beautiful expanse of sand. It's like having a private beach. I run down to the shallows and feel the ice-cold water pinch my feet. But I stand there and let it, goose pimples running all the way up and over my skin. Paul comes to join me and we stand close to each other, not touching, looking out to sea. Just for a moment. Then I turn and look back.

"Look at that place!" I say, clocking the huge modern-looking house tucked into the woods behind the beach. That garden wall must mark the boundaries of its grounds. "Somebody's lucked out there. I bet they've kept that path as closed in as possible so nobody knows this place is here."

"Yep," Paul says, "you need to be in the know, or

you'd just pass straight by."

An idea crosses my mind, and I smile. "Shall we leave them a message?" I ask. I jog across the sand before Paul has a chance to answer, and before I've considered whether this is really a good idea. I root around at the bottom of the path and find a big strong stick. Paul walks up to join me.

"What have you got in mind?"

"You'll see."

I run back onto the sand, to the other side of the beach, and I start carving out letters in the sand. Paul stands at a little distance, watching with interest. Gradually, the words appear in large, bold letters across the beach.

ALICE WOZ ERE

Paul, grinning, has managed to find his own stick. He adds some more letters under mine.

(AND PAUL TOO)

He adds a large emoji with a sticking out tongue.

"I wonder if they're watching us right now," I say, "but maybe that was them we passed on our way here. I bet they'll be delighted when they come back and see we've ruined their perfect view."

"It's just a shame it'll get washed away."

"We'll have to come back and do it again."

"We will," he agrees. "Listen, I did bring a drink down here, if you fancy one. Then maybe we can head off for something to eat." He produces two small bottles of prosecco from inside his leather jacket then he takes his jacket off and lays it on the sand. "You can sit on my coat if you want to."

"No, I'm fine," I say, "I don't mind a bit of sand." I marvel at how easy I feel with him already, and realise that I really don't care what he thinks of my clothes, if I'm covered in sand or my nail polish is all chipped away. He's got a very nice, easy-going air about him.

"Me neither." We both sit ourselves on the beach, and he opens both bottles, handing one to me.

"Don't think I'm the type to drink and drive," he says, "I promise I'm not. I won't finish this anyway, I just wanted to have a sip. But I want you to enjoy yours. I'm sorry I don't have any glasses."

"Glasses would be all wrong on the beach, anyway. This is perfect."

We clink our bottles together and take a sip, looking out to sea. A sailing boat glides into view and we watch its progress, not speaking for a while, but it's not an uncomfortable silence.

"Are you cold?" Paul asks, and I realise I am a little. He slips his jacket around my shoulders. I don't think now is the time to tell him I don't really wear leather. And I think of Bea's beautiful office chair anyway, a guilty pleasure of mine.

"Thank you," I say instead.

"My pleasure."

The walk back up the path is slightly more challenging with a glass-and-a-half worth's of prosecco inside me. Paul gallantly let me finish his as well. "I'm not trying to get you drunk though, I promise."

At the top, I catch my breath. "I wish we could take a photo of our beach art!"

"Ha, yeah, I'm sure it looks great from up here. Now,

are you hungry?"

"Yes, I definitely am."

"Great. I know a pub which does an amazing steak."

"Ah, yes, I'm kind of vegetarian," I say.

"Oh, oh no, and I made you wear my jacket!"

"It's OK, you didn't make me. And I hate to say it but I kind of like it."

"Well, look, let's see what else this pub does, shall we? I'm sure there'll be some good veggie options, and if not we can go somewhere else."

"I'll be happy with a bowl of chips," I say.

"Me too. Well, we could just move along till we find a chippy..?"

"I'm happy with that."

We get back into his car then it's back up that winding road, without passing any cars this time, then off we fly. I have already tucked the blanket around myself and the prosecco has added to my warmth. I sit back and enjoy the ride as Paul expertly manages the twists and turns then pulls fairly suddenly into a layby where there's a fish and chip van.

"I know this place," he says reassuringly. "Is it just chips you're after? You're sure?" I nod, and Paul jumps out of the car and goes to the van, returning with two paper-wrapped parcels, and two polystyrene cups. "Can you hang on to these? We're only a few minutes away from a little place I know."

"You know a lot of little places, don't you?"

"I do, but as we've already established, I am very old, so I've had lots of time to learn about them all. And I did used to bring the kids to lots of them at weekends, so I've got quite a collection stored up."

Our cargo keeps me warm as we head off once more,

arriving just moments later at another layby, which leads into a little car park. There are benches and a wonderful view of the sea. The only other people here are a couple in a campervan, who have set up a barbecue, and whose dog is running excitedly around, sniffing the air. We smile and say hello then go to the furthest-away bench, sitting companionably side-by-side as we unwrap our chips and take the lids off the steaming cups of coffee.

"Not exactly a posh date," Paul says, "I hope you don't mind."

"Far from it," I say, aware that in actual fact I have just latched onto the fact he's called this a date.

"It's a refreshing change, in honesty," Paul says. "Without sounding like too much of a twat – I hope – I spend loads of time in upmarket restaurants and hotels, for work, and I find it all a bit stifling sometimes. This afternoon has been a very welcome break from all of that."

"I'm glad." I look at him as he turns to me and we smile at each other. I am the first to break my gaze and I look back at my chips but I'm pretty sure there was something in that look and it's made me feel a bit light-headed.

As we sit on our bench, I hear birds calling but I can't see them, hidden somewhere in the long grass. It's a familiar call. I can't place it and I know that Sam would in a flash but I don't want to think about Sam now. The daylight starts to dim and by the time we head back to the car, it's close to dark. I can't wait for the nights to stretch out even further. It's coming, I can feel it.

On the way home, we have the roof up and it creates a different atmosphere. With the heaters on too, the car is cosy and intimate. I tell Paul a little about my family and he tells me about his. It's strange to think that his kids are closer in age to me than he is. All too soon, we are back at the Sail Loft and I realise that I don't want the evening to end. I don't know how to end it.

"Can I drop you back at your place instead? Save you walking home in the dark," Paul says.

"That would be great, thank you." I give him directions and we are there in about three minutes. Paul gets out of the car and comes round to my side, opening my door for me. I am scrabbling for my keys in my handbag and as I fish them out triumphantly, I look up and Paul puts his hand on my waist.

"It's been a great day, Alice. Thank you."

"Thank you," I say, "it has been really lovely."

We look at each other for a moment then he leans forward and kisses me, just briefly, on the lips. "Can we do it again?"

The kiss? I wonder, finding I am thinking, *Yes, please.* But I know he means going out. "I'd like that."

"Great. I'll call you."

He steps back and I put my key in the door. Should I ask him in? I kind of want to. But no, not now. Not yet.

"See you, Alice."

"See you, Paul."

I step into the hallway and close the door with my back, then reach for the light switch. Paul's car engine starts up and I smile to myself as he pulls away into the night.

8

So how was the big date?

Julie's text pings in while I'm lying in the bath, pretending to myself that I'm not waiting for Paul to text me. I make myself wait a whole three seconds after hearing the ping of the message arriving in my phone and then assume the expression of somebody who's not disappointed that it's their best friend sending a message. Actually, I can't help grinning.

It was good thanks. I send this back, knowing full well that it will not be enough for Julie.

Good?

Yep.

Like, he's with you now kind of good?

Nope.

Did you kiss?

This isn't the *Guardian* Blind Date column, Julie.

Griffiths, I know full well what you're doing. And

I also know it means you kissed him. Alice and Paul sitting in a tree...

Damn. She knows me too well.

Just a very polite kiss at the end of the evening.

Polite? Sounds boring.

It wasn't.

Ha! Good. You can tell me all tomorrow night.

I sink back into the bubbles, smiling and thinking of the kiss. It was not full-on, but it was more than a perfunctory kiss on the cheek, and it was very definitely on the lips. Maybe this is what it's like to be a grown-up, I think. I know I'm nearly thirty-one, and I have a very responsible job, but somehow I feel that my true self is still young. Not a kid exactly but definitely not a grown-up. Then again, maybe nobody ever really feels like a grown-up. Perhaps it's what is perceived by those younger than us. I often see myself as on a level with Lydia but realistically, she probably thinks I'm really old. She's not twenty yet and I am over thirty. I wonder how Paul sees me. An equal? I don't feel it somehow. Not in a putting-myself-down kind of way, but he's seen so much, done so much. Been married. Had two kids, who are about the same age as Lydia. Travelled the world. Developed a very successful business, from what I can see. I have done none of those things.

But side-by-side on the beach – mucking about writing those stupid messages – eating chips out of paper at that picnic table – all these things felt easy and comfortable and I would very much like to see him again. I hope he wasn't just being polite when he said he felt the same.

There are bubbles prickling and popping and fizzing in my ears and my hair, which I need to wash and dry before bed. It's back to work in the morning and I am already up too late to have a full night's sleep but there is so much going on in my mind.

It's not just Paul, it's Amethi. What a beautiful place, and with so much potential. I really do want to get this business going with Julie. It's time to get serious.

I tip my head back to soak my hair then lather in a good amount of almond & apricot shampoo (Julie's), before rinsing away all the bubbles with the shower attachment. Wandering into my bedroom, it hits me again that I also need to start looking for a new place to live. How am I going to get all this done? I just have to take a deep breath, take things one step at a time. I towel-dry my hair and put on my pyjamas then head down to the kitchen to make a hot milk, which I hope might help me sleep. The curtains are open but the dark outside is not unnerving. Opening the door into the garden, I take my milk with me and sit on the bench. This is the place where I sat when Julie was urging me to text Sam, when we had only been back in Cornwall for a month or so. It's also the place where Sam and I sat the night before he went away to uni, when we thought we had it all sorted out. I miss him still and my heart aches sometimes when I think of the kind, beautiful man I always thought I was meant to be with, but circumstances dictated otherwise and it's not like I'm the first person who has had to get over a broken heart.

I sip my milk, surrounded by the night. Footsteps echo

along the street, reminding me that in a matter of weeks the annual exodus to the town will begin, with holiday-makers grabbing their week or fortnight in this place. Their presence is unwelcome to some locals, who see only that these people jam up the streets and turn this beautiful place into something akin to an amusement park. On foot or in their cars, the incomers take up so much space, create so much noise and strain on already stretched resources. But I was one of these people myself and I know exactly what it's like. There is a finite amount of time to be here, and this place can seem like a different world to that back home, with office blocks and busy roads and the drudgery of day-to-day life. I may live here now but I know that to some people I will always be an incomer. I have a small concern as to how this business of mine and Julie's will be received by the local community, as it will be bringing more visitors, taking away more buildings which could have been bought by locals. It's important that we are sensitive to this and that anything we do can contribute positively to the local area.

Bea is a key member of the local business networking community and it would be so good to be able to consult her about our ideas, but to do that will be giving away my intention to leave the Sail Loft Hotel and I don't think I am quite ready to tell her yet. Not until we have some firmer plans. Not until I have some more money.

I take a deep breath, leaning my head back to look up into the sky. There's a satellite passing overhead, picking its way between the stars. I count to ten, and try to clear my mind of all the thoughts which are pressing against the sides, clamouring for attention and space. I need to go back to Pilates, or maybe yoga. I should ask Kate about it.

Taking the last sip of my milk, I head in and lock the door behind me, leaving my mug in the sink. Upstairs, I brush my teeth and only as I am about to switch off the light in the en suite do I remember my mobile, left on the stand by the bath.

Paul Winters (1)

My heart jumps for joy.

I'm sitting outside with a whisky, looking at the stars, and thinking what a great time I had with you today. I wanted to say thank you and wish you goodnight. P.

Taking my phone to my bed, I slide under my covers before I compose my reply.

I had a great time, too. Thank you for taking me out. See you soon x

I add the kiss on the spur of the moment and resolutely put my phone on the bedside table. I am not going to wait to see if he replies. It's after midnight, I need some sleep. *Ping.*

It was definitely my pleasure. I'll work out my diary tomorrow and then maybe we can make another date. Sweet dreams x

Ha! He sent a kiss back. I wriggle down under the covers, smiling to myself, and fall asleep still holding my phone.

9

It's a rainy Monday morning and I splash to work through the numerous puddles which have gathered in the dips of the pavement. The road is lined on either side with runnels of happily flowing water, which is making its way back to the sea, where the whole process can begin again. A quick glance from underneath my umbrella towards the sky shows me a solid block of grey, which looks like it has no intention of shifting. This, though, is a place where it might look like this at breakfast time but by lunch the whole vista may have changed, the clouds blown away across the water or inland, making way for the dreamy blue skies and seas which draw so many people here.

I skip up the steps to the Sail Loft and fold down my umbrella, giving it a good shake over the bush at the side of the steps and noting as I do so some fat buds nestling in between the leaves. I am not sure what type of plant this is but its flowers are large, reddish-orange blooms, which appear in the spring and keep on going until autumn. There is a postcard some of the shops in town sell, which features the Sail Loft and this beautiful foliage, against a backdrop of sapphire-blue sky. In an interesting contrast, some shops also have postcards with pictures of Princess Di on them.

"Morning, Alice!" Stefan greets me as I step through the door. I can hear the sound of voices, and cutlery on crockery. It's early for anyone to be having breakfast. I look at Stefan quizzically.

"It's the Bernardsons. They've got a hot date with a… a erm… I can't remember, some rare bird that might be down at Land's End today. They asked for an early breakfast and Jon obliged."

"Who served?" Our current waitress, Angie, can only get in for 7.30am, after she's dropped her kids at breakfast club at their school.

"Jon did it," Stefan smiled.

It doesn't seem that long since I had some trouble with Jonathan – he wanted the glory of being the chef without any of the inconvenience it entailed. He called in sick when he actually just had a hangover, and to make matters worse it all tied in with him getting together with Lydia. More correctly – at first, anyway – messing Lydia about. She was a love-struck A-Level student and he was a handsome, charming chef. I have to hand it to him, though; since then he's really turned it around and I love working with him now. I'll find it very hard saying bye to him, and to Stefan, should Julie and I ever get our business off the ground.

I wander into the dining room to say hello to the Bernardsons, both of whom are dressed from head to toe in muted greens and browns, with thick cream walking socks pulled up over the hems of their trousers.

"Can I offer you a packed lunch to take with you today?" I ask.

"Oh thank you but your chef's already seen to that. Such a pleasant young man. We're having a wonderful stay."

"Well, that is wonderful to hear. I hope you get to see the… erm…"

"Eastern olivaceous warbler," Mr Bernardson supplies.

"Oh yes, of course… I hope you get to see it today."

"Would you like to hear what it sounds like?" Mrs Bernardson asks, brandishing her mobile phone.

"Yes, sure, that would be great."

"This app is great, it also recognises birds by their song, if you're not sure. We don't often need it for that though, do we, George?"

"Ha! Not likely."

I listen reverentially to the sound of the Eastern olivaceous warbler then make my excuses and head into the kitchen.

"Nice work with the Bernardsons!" I say to Jonathan, who is busy prepping for the rest of the guests.

"Oh yeah, thanks. Did they make you listen to the Eastern Olive Branch Line Wobbler?"

"Yes," I smile.

"Think you could recognise one now if you heard it?"

"I think I'd need a second listen, to be honest."

"We should play it outside their bedroom window tonight!"

"That is an excellent idea… if I wasn't the manager here and you weren't the chef. Now, get their lunches through to them and let them get on their way. If you're lucky you'll get to hear all about it tonight at dinner."

As Jonathan goes through to the dining room, I head to the office for my handover with Stefan. I say hi to Angie, who is just coming through the door.

"You're soaking!" I say to her. "Sorry, you probably already realise that."

"Yeah, the kids were messing about and then I couldn't find the umbrella, or my proper coat."

"You poor thing. Look, grab the key to room ten as it's

empty, go and dry yourself off and warm up a bit. Get a cup of tea, too. The Bernardsons have already had breakfast so that's one less table for you to worry about, and there's no sign of anybody else yet."

"Thank you, Alice."

"No worries, just make sure you leave the door open so Rita knows she needs to put clean towels in and give the room a once-over. I'll try to remember to tell her, too."

In the office, Stefan is sitting at the smaller desk. This is something he started back when Bea was away, and it was just me and him – and occasionally Lydia, when she needed peace and quiet to study – using the room. Now it's a bit odd because if Bea is there, I feel I have to cede to her as the owner of the hotel, even though she says I don't need to. I think that she misses the hands-on work, if I'm honest. She built this place up and it really was just her back then, with support staff like me and Julie in the summer. She is great, and gracious, and generous, but I don't feel quite the same running the place as I did when she was in the States. Now she's away on honeymoon, it feels a bit like old times.

"Anything I need to know, Stef?" I ask.

"Nothing major – a new booking yesterday, for a week in June. Oh, and my mum wants to stay here when it's the wedding. She wants a week, too. And my auntie, a week. Then some cousins, just for the weekend. Can we do it, do you think?" he asks anxiously.

"Let's see, the wedding's July." I open the booking system on the computer, and the large book, which is really more for show than being any actual use. It's just annoying having to enter details in both, but Bea insists on it. And actually, if the IT system goes down then it is good having another point of reference.

"I know, I know, why didn't I do this before?" Stefan chides himself. "I have checked and there's some rooms free but maybe not enough. I actually… I actually didn't know if they would come. They are not happy that I am getting married here and not in Sweden."

"Oh I'm sorry, Stef, I had no idea."

"Well, they say it's because I already live here, why could April not let us have the wedding at home? They don't get it, though. This is home. And the children… travelling with them will be hard. We want to just relax and enjoy the day, you know?"

"Yes, I think I do. Let's see… how many people are there?"

"Now, I think just fourteen."

"Fourteen!" I exclaim, without meaning to. I'd thought he'd meant maybe five or six people. The Sail Loft only has twelve rooms, and eight of these are already booked for the dates Stefan needs. We've blocked the place out for wedding guests, for the three days over the wedding weekend. This will mean squeezing fourteen people into eight beds. I'm not even sure if the insurance will cover it, if it is indeed a possibility. "Leave it with me. I'll speak to Bea when she's back, we'll see what we can do."

Stefan and April are planning a fairly modest wedding – although with fourteen members of Stef's family, it's suddenly become quite a bit bigger. That must be sixty-odd guests now. And the wedding reception is being held here. Thinking about it, all the other guests at that time are members of April's family. Maybe we will be able to work something out. It really depends just how flexible these people are happy to be. As Stefan's getting married, I will be managing the hotel, and also attending the wedding. It's going to be an interesting combination of roles but Jonathan has possibly the harder job, as he's going to have to cook for everybody. Lydia is going to help out, and Stef and April have hired some extra staff to do drinks and serving. It's a matter of cost as much as anything and they are trying to do so much of it themselves, I want to make sure they get to enjoy their day.

"Thanks, Alice."

"It's no problem, it's going to be a fantastic day. Do you want to go through your menu with Jon again this evening? You'll need to ask your fourteen guests for food preferences too, in the next few days. We need to get everything on order and make sure we've got enough extra chairs, decorations, and all that."

"There's not long, is there?" Stef's face has gone suddenly pale.

"No, just weeks now! But that is a reason to be happy. Come on, Stef, we can do this, it's all going to be fine, I promise."

"I hope so."

"Promise. Now go back to your beautiful fiancée and beautiful children and get some rest!"

Stefan doesn't need to be told twice. He takes his coat from the stand and leaves with a smile. I lean back in Bea's leather chair and think through what I have just promised. There will be a way, I'm sure of it. I just need to make sure it's all in place well before the big day. And I can't ask Bea until she's back from honeymoon. I expressly promised I would only contact her in the case of a dire emergency. This is important, but not on that scale.

I hear my phone vibrate within my bag so I fish it out while I scroll through the next few weeks' bookings.

There are very few vacancies now until September and going by last year, they should fill themselves. I look at my phone.

Paul Winters (2)

I just wanted to wish you a good morning. Still thinking about yesterday. Are you busy Weds pm? x

Then

I don't want you to think I'm a stalker, texting you again already. I'm not. I'm just keen to see you. P

My stomach does a little tumble of excitement. I had not expected this, at all, and I'm really flattered that somebody like Paul is keen to see me. I tell myself not to think like that – after all, Paul is a person just like anybody else. But I suspect he and I mix in very different circles. I love his air of confidence, and he seems so at ease with himself. When it comes down to it, he is just so different to anyone I've been with before. It's making for an exciting change.

I don't think you're a stalker... at least I hope not. Yes, free Weds. I'll be home from a little after six. What are you thinking of?

I can't tell you what I'm thinking of right now, I don't know you well enough. But if you'd like to come out with me for dinner, that will be a step

in the right direction. I can pick you up at 8, if that suits.

Am I reading between the lines correctly? Is this some fairly heavy flirting going on? I'm not sure, and I am not quite ready for replying along the same lines, just yet.

Sounds fantastic, thank you! See you then x

As I press 'send' I think I've basically put him off sending any more texts till Weds. But maybe he'll know from the kiss that I am not being overly cool. Argh, I hate texts. It's so ridiculous, pulling apart these little messages to find hidden meanings, or just the correct meaning. My phone vibrates again. Phew, maybe I'll have a chance to send a slightly more enthusiastic-sounding response. I don't want him to think I'm not interested.

Julie (1)

Hi lovely, hope you're having a good day. I just wanted to let you know Sam is back this week – an unplanned visit but some of his lectures have been cancelled so he's back till Thursday. Just so you know. Jx

My initial reaction is *Damn, it's not Paul,* swiftly followed by a twinge at the thought of Sam being in town. Why does everything have to happen at once?

Thanks for letting me know! I have another date on Weds anyway.

Paul??!

Yes – who else?

I can't help but feel excited. This is exciting! I am being taken out by a real, grown-up, successful and very attractive man. So Sam's back too – so what? I probably won't even see him but even if I do, we won't be able to avoid each other at Julie's and Luke's wedding in October so maybe it's better to just start getting on with it now.

10

On Wednesday, Bea and Bob turn up at the Sail Loft, looking tanned and relaxed, and ridiculously happy.

"Hello!" I kiss them both in turn, "I wasn't expecting to see you till next week. Where have you been? Why are you back so early?"

"Barbados," Bea grins.

"And we're back early because our flight got in last night and Bea wasn't interested in staying in London a few nights. She wanted to get back here."

"Barbados!" I exclaim then laugh at Bob's words. "Bea, you should have made the most of your honeymoon."

"That's what I said," Bob agrees.

"Oh, but I did – we did – and when we got back to Heathrow the only place I wanted to be was in Cornwall. Barbados was just amazing, and I didn't fancy a city break after that."

"OK," I concede, "that makes sense. But you shouldn't be here, at work!"

"We are just here to say hello, aren't we, Bea?" Bob looks at her sternly.

"Yes, of course, I just… have to check something in the office."

"No!" Bob and I say together.

"You're on honeymoon," I finish.

"I know, I know," Bea says apologetically, "but once I get this thing done I promise I won't be back till next week. And I won't even mention the Sail Loft," she says to Bob.

"Whatever you say, sweetheart." Bob rolls his eyes at me. "Good job I knew I'd always take second place to this damn hotel."

"Hey, don't call it a damn hotel," I protest, "you'll hurt its feelings."

"Oh my god, you're as bad as her. Listen, ladies, I'm going to beg a cup of coffee of Jon then sit in the garden till you grace me with your presence, good lady wife."

"Come on, Alice, you can fill me in on what's been going on," Bea loops her arm through mine and turns me towards the office.

"I will not," I say resolutely, "not till Monday, remember!"

"I don't mean at work," she mutters quietly. "Rumour has it you're being taken out by a certain local businessman."

"What?" I feel the blood rush to my face. "Bea, you've been in Barbados for nearly two weeks, how can you possibly know anything about that?"

"Come on, Alice, you've lived here long enough to know that there are no secrets! But I notice you're not denying it." Bea ushers me through the heavy polished wood door and shuts it behind her. She sits in her leather chair, leaving me to sit on the smaller chair, at the smaller desk; it seems uneven, somehow, and I am reminded as ever that I will never really be in control here. "So it's true?"

"It's... we've been out once."

"And are you seeing him again?"

Do I tell her about tonight? I feel annoyed that I seem to be being talked about, and slightly put out at Bea's interrogation. It seems out of character.

"Yes, I am, I'm..."

"Okay, well I don't blame you at all, Alice. He's quite a catch. But I just wanted to let you know a bit about him, seeing as you're obviously not on the gossip grapevine just yet."

And I have no intention of being, I think, but I feel warning bells ringing in my mind.

"OK then, what's there to tell?" I ask defensively.

"Well, you know he's divorced?"

"Yes, and I know he's got two kids. What's the problem?" I am finding myself increasingly irritated.

"Well, when he and his wife were still together, there was talk that he was having an affair."

"OK…" I say slowly. What am I meant to say to this? What am I meant to think? "Do you know if this is actually true?"

"I don't," Bea admits, "but I have known Paul for quite some time, and I know what a charmer he is. I knew him when he was married and he really was quite a flirt."

"Being a flirt doesn't mean he's a cheat," I say.

"No, I know. And I also know it was a long time ago. He and Melanie – his wife – really did marry young. And from what I can tell, they still get on well, and his kids are great. Both at uni now, of course."

I feel really uncomfortable with this conversation. Bea is displaying the gossipy side of her nature which she does not often reveal, and I'm learning personal things about a man I have only met twice; things which really don't concern me.

"OK, well I'll bear all this in mind," I say, forcing a smile onto my face. "Now go and get that husband of yours and don't let me see you here again until next week! Everything is under control, we're getting there with Stefan's wedding – I'll go through all that with you

95

on Monday – and the weather is really picking up so make the most of living here before next week."

"OK!" Bea laughs. "And I'm sorry, if you think I'm sticking my nose into your affairs. It's none of my business, and it's all so long ago. I like Paul," she adds and I wonder why, then, she felt the need to tell me anything. "It's just I know how hard it's been for you to get over Sam so I don't want you getting hurt again."

"I've been on literally one date with the man," I protest.

"And it's none of my business anyway, I know. Enjoy yourself, Alice. You deserve some happiness."

"Thank you, Bea. Now go on, get out of here!"

For the rest of the day, I try to push Bea's words out of my mind. It is none of her business, and who knows what was going on in Paul's life all those years ago? I can't help wondering when this supposed affair took place – how old his kids were at the time, and who it was with. I have images of a seedy fling with his secretary but I really don't want to believe that is the kind of man Paul is. I'm just annoyed that something which has been making me feel happy and excited now seems slightly tainted.

Nevertheless, when my phone pings to let me know I have a message, my heart leaps. And I'm right, it's him.

Hi Alice, really looking forward to tonight. Can I pick you up a bit earlier, maybe 7.30? I want to take us out of town. Px

Seems a good idea, I think, *it will keep us away from the gossips.*

Perfect, I will be ready and waiting x

I feel defiant suddenly, determined to enjoy myself with Paul now that I have been warned off him.

xx

Those two kisses make my stomach churn with excitement and I can't stop smiling. Bea is right, I deserve some happiness, and even if this goes nowhere, I am going to enjoy it for what it is.

When Stefan arrives in the late afternoon, I sit with him in the office and go through the notes for the evening and overnight.

"Ms Bolton, in room 7, has diabetes – just for info. She says she likes people to know as she's on her own. She says it's well controlled but always likes to warn people that if she starts acting a bit strange or you think she's drunk, you might need to get medical help. Get her to check her blood sugars if you can. She says she doesn't drink much so it's more likely to be her blood sugars than being pickled."

"Pickled?" Stefan smiles at me.

"Yes, it's another word for being drunk. It's – well I guess it's to do with pickling your liver and kidneys, or something. I don't know!"

"You look happy, Alice."

"Do I?"

"Yes, you do. Is there something I should know?"

"Well, it seems that the rest of the town already knows so why not you? I've got a date."

"Oh really! With Sam?"

"No, not Sam."

"Oh, it's just I saw him earlier. I thought maybe you

two…"

"You saw Sam? Did you speak to him?"

"Just a quick chat, you know, I was being dragged to the playground by Reuben."

"Oh, right. Was he OK?"

"He seemed fine," Stefan smiles kindly.

"Great. Well, I'd better be off."

"Have a great night, Alice."

"I will… I hope! Thanks, Stef."

I shrug my coat on, although actually I think it may be too warm out there for a coat now. I experience that familiar thrill as I open the front door of the hotel and am greeted by the sparkling sight of the sea at the foot of the town. If I wasn't going out, I'd head down there now. Its pull is magnetic. I make a promise to myself that I will go to the beach after work tomorrow. Maybe Julie will be able to come, too.

"Alice!"

I know who it is before I've turned round and I don't have a chance to compose myself. Hurrying along the street to the side of the Sail Loft is Sam.

"Hi," I say, weakly, and he reaches me as I get to the bottom of the steps.

"Hi," he smiles. "How are you?"

"I'm fine, thanks. Julie said you're back. Are you here all week?" Oh god, I sound so utterly dull. When did our conversation become so perfunctory?

"No, only till tomorrow. I have to get back to Bangor."

"Of course. Is it still going well?"

"Yeah, great, but I've got my year off coming up."

"Oh yeah, that's come round fast!"

"Yeah, kind of."

I wonder if Sam is thinking the same thing as me.

When he got on that course, it seemed like the end of the world. This point in time, when he'd have completed those first two years, seemed a world away. Now it seems like nothing at all. I dare a proper look at him. He is as beautiful as ever. His hair's a little longer on top, which means it's a little bit curly, tumbling over his blue eyes. He's not as tanned as I remember but I suppose we're only just through the winter and I am guessing he's spent a lot of time indoors, studying.

"Do you know where you'll be?"

"No, not yet, but they know I want to be back in Cornwall if I can."

"Sophie will be really pleased if you're back here," I say. "I saw her and Amber a few weeks back, at the beach."

"She said. I think she misses you, Alice."

Don't say that, I think. It touches some part of me that I've tried to bury deep inside. I smile. "It was great to see her. I need to get home now, though, Sam."

"Of course, I bet you're shattered. Mind if I walk with you?"

"Oh, er, no, if course not."

"Is work OK?"

"Yes, it's great, thanks. Bea's been on honeymoon, and Stefan's getting married soon – we're having the reception at the Sail Loft and I want it to be perfect."

"I'm sure it will be."

"Thanks! How's life in Wales?" I am aware that we are walking close together, and I wish I hadn't put my coat on. For one thing, this situation has put me on edge and I can feel my armpits are damp from the nerves. For another thing, if my arms weren't covered I'd be able to feel Sam's skin brush mine. I know it's sad. And I know I am going on a date with another man tonight. But I can't deny it's true.

Before I have too much of a chance to think about this, I feel my phone vibrating inside my bag. We stop while I rummage for it and Sam laughs.

"I see some things never change," he says.

I give him a mock-stern look as I retrieve the phone, registering my dad's mobile number on the screen. "Hi Dad!"

"Alice." Straight away I can tell there's something wrong. "Alice, love, try not to panic, but your mum's in hospital."

My stomach drops like a weight. "She's..?"

"She's in hospital. We think it might have been a heart attack. She's OK. She's OK." It sounds to me like he is trying to convince himself.

Sam's is looking at me with concern all over his face.

"Are you with her, Dad? Can I speak to her?"

"Not... not right now, Alice."

"I'm coming up," I say. "Right now, I'm just on my way home then I'm coming."

"OK, love."

The fact that Dad doesn't try to dissuade me only makes me panic more. "See you in a bit, Dad, I'll ring when I'm on my way. I love you."

"I love you, too."

"What's going on, Alice? Is it your mum?" Sam's face is full of concern.

"Yes," I sob, "she's had a … they think it's a heart attack. I have to go. I have to see her."

"OK, no problem, let me help you." I'm grateful for Sam taking control. I can't think straight. "What can I do? You go home and get your bag packed, I'll get up to the Sail Loft and tell Stefan what's going on, then I'll be right with you. OK? OK, Alice?"

Sam lifts my chin so I'm looking at him. He's trying to pull me through my shock.

"Yes, yes, OK. Thank you, Sam."

"Is there anything I can tell Stefan? Anyone you need to speak to, anything to cancel?"

Cancel. *Oh god, Paul,* I think.

"No, no, I don't think so," I say.

"OK, then get moving – the sooner you get packed up, the sooner you can be there."

As Sam heads back up the hill, I hurry towards home, fumbling with my phone. I will have to cancel Paul and I'd rather get this done before Sam's back with me.

Hi Paul, I am really sorry but have to postpone tonight. My mum's in hospital. I have to go and see her. Ax

In just a moment, the phone vibrates.

Oh god, I'm really sorry to hear that. Is your mum nearby?

No, I reply, feeling teary and sorry for myself, **Back home, in the Midlands. I have to get packed and go, I'm sorry x**

Of course, don't worry. Get sorted. I'll speak to you soon. Take care. I hope things are ok xx

I put my phone back in my bag and get to my house, unlocking the front door and letting it swing open. I dash through the sunlight which is streaming through the stairwell window, two steps at a time, and swing round the banister, up to my room where I throw things into my bag.

"Alice!" I hear Sam's voice from downstairs. It's so familiar, and so welcome.

"Up here!" I say and I hear his footsteps bounding in my direction.

"Right, I've decided," he says, "I'm going to drive you."

"You're..? You can't."

"I can, and I will. It's a long journey, you can't drive while you're worrying about your mum. The only thing is, my car's in the garage for a service, so can we use yours?"

I am overwhelmed by his kindness, and despite my need to see my mum I also find I want to fall into his arms. But I can't. I need to get to my parents as soon as I can.

"Are you sure?" I ask. "What about Sophie, won't she be expecting to see you?"

"She's at Amber's tonight," he smiles. "And anyway, I'd say she owes you one after all that messing about."

I can't acknowledge what he's referring to at the moment – the times that Sophie engineered her dad's attention when he and I were meant to be together. "But what about you going back to uni? And picking your own car up?"

"I'll sort it," he says calmly, "now stop finding reasons not to do this and let's get going!"

"Thank you, Sam, thank you so much."

"It's my pleasure. I promise."

I look at him properly, seeing both the eighteen-year-old boy I met so many years ago and the man he has turned into. He has lost none of his kindness over the years.

"What?" he asks.

"Nothing," I half-smile at him. He knows.

"Well if it's nothing, let's go!"

He's down the stairs before me, heading for the hooks where Julie and I keep our keys.

"Alice," he says, "where are the car keys?"

"On the hook," I say, panic prickling over me at his question.

"They're not – look."

Shit. He's right. Which means … Julie. I scurry into the kitchen and there, sure enough, is a note from my friend.

They want me in Truro so I've had to take the car – I hope that's OK, I know you're off out tonight anyway xxx

"Shit," I say.

Sam reads the note over my shoulder. "She could have called you," he says, annoyed.

"Yes, but she thought I wouldn't need the car this evening. I was meant to be…" My sentence drifts away but it seems Sam isn't thinking about what I was meant to be doing.

"Trains!" he is saying, digging out his phone. "There must be a train. I know it's not ideal but let's see what the options are."

At this moment, the doorbell goes. We look at each other.

"I don't want to answer it," I say.

"I'll go. You check Trainline to see what we can do –

103

we can always get a taxi to Penzance if that's more direct."

I start tapping in the details, half-listening to Sam striding across to the front door. Then the door opens and... oh shit, is that Paul?

"Alice!" calls Sam, and I hear a note of civility in his voice; a politeness which was not there moments ago and which immediately creates a distance between us. "I think your journey problems are solved."

I walk into the hall, my face flushed, and see Paul and Sam both looking at me.

"I've come to give you a lift, Alice," Paul says. "I thought you might not want to drive when you're worrying about your mum."

The front door is still open and I can see Paul's sleek, shiny car pulled up outside. I can also feel Sam's eyes on me. But what can I do? I need to see my mum – that has to be more important than anything right now.

"Thank you," I say, "we were just trying to work it out weren't we, Sam?" I look at him but his eyes seem to have glazed over slightly.

"Yeah, but it looks like you've got a knight in shining armour."

"I ... yes, erm Sam, this is Paul."

"Nice to meet you," Sam shakes Paul's hand. "You'd better get on your way. I'll let Julie know what's going on if you like, Alice."

"That would be great, thanks Sam."

Paul, seeming to sense there is something not being said, goes back out and gets into the car. I pick up my bag and follow Sam out of the house.

"Sam," I say, and he turns. "Thank you so much. You were going to drop everything to help me."

"Just a shame it was such a fuck-up, eh? Lucky Paul's here to help."

"Yes, he's … well, I just need to get to Mum as quickly as I can."

"You do," Sam's features soften slightly. "Of course you do. I hope she's OK, Alice."

"Me too." I kiss Sam on the cheek and try to make him look me in the eyes. "I really mean it, Sam, thank you so much."

"Any time, you know I'll always help you."

I can feel the tears coming and I can't afford for that to happen right now. "I'll let you know when I get up there."

"You do that. Drive safely, mate," Sam calls to Paul and then he is off up the street while Paul pushes open the passenger-side door for me. I climb in, easing onto the scrupulously clean seat, while Paul starts the engine. As we move off, I glance back and see Sam moving one way while I go the other.

11

There's something about hospitals which brings out a kind of awe in me; a sense of almost other-worldliness. From the entranceway where people stand talking into mobile phones, others just feet away chain-smoking cigarettes – some drawn so strongly by this addiction that they're willing to stand in full hospital gown, drips following on like sullen teenagers.

Once you step inside, it's busy, it's hectic, and there's a sense of urgency, as if all those emotions which occur in this place every single day have been sucked here and remain, tumbling around each other while the staff try to maintain a sense of orderliness amidst the chaos. Toddlers scamper about as their harassed-looking parents try to keep them occupied, pulling books and toys from their bags or proffering bags of crisps bought from the vending machines.

On the corridors, though, as you approach the wards, this mayhem dies away and it is here that the hospital really takes on the form it is striving for. Hand gel dispensers at each door. Neat signs, pointing patients, visitors and staff in the right direction. Uniform wooden doors, with names or numbers, and small opaque windows which throw no light either way. Tidy nurses, healthcare assistants and doctors stride purposefully and efficiently, completely focused. A buzzer allows communication with the sealed-off wards, the disembodied answering voice empowered to allow or deny entry.

As I rub my hands vigorously with the gel, I am buzzed through. To my left are rooms, wide wooden-framed windows with curtains drawn; to my right, the nurses' station.

"I'm here to see my mum," I tell them, "Jane Griffiths."

"Of course," the nurse says. She looks young to me, but is sure in herself as she checks through the papers. "Sorry, I'm only just on shift so I haven't had a chance to get to know who's where yet. Ah yes, she's in room three – just there."

The door is adjacent to where I am standing. "Thank you," I smile and knock on the door then push it open to see my mum sitting up in bed, wires attaching her to a machine. My dad is on a chair drawn right up to the bed. If anything, he looks worse than she does.

"Alice!" they both say and I am relieved to see Mum smiling. I hug her, then Dad.

"I am so happy to see you," I say, finding my eyes filling with tears.

"It's OK," Mum says, even now the comforter. "I'm fine. Just had a bit of a scare, that's all."

"It was a bit more than that, Jane," Dad says sternly. "But don't worry, Alice, Mum's going to be fine."

"I know, well I think I do. It was quite a relief when I got your message."

In the car on the way up, my phone had lost signal for a while and when it returned I had a voicemail from Dad, telling me Mum was OK and on the ward and that the doctors weren't too concerned.

"How do you feel?" I ask Mum. "And you, Dad? How

are you?"

"We're both OK," Dad says. "Relieved, like you, love. But we're in the right place now and Mum's resting. The nurses are wonderful."

As if summoned by this testament to her greatness, the nurse who I saw earlier pushes open the door. "Just come to do your obs," she smiles. "Do you need another chair in here? I'll get you one in a moment."

"That's OK, I'll get one, if you point me in the right direction," Dad flashes her a smile, ever the charmer.

"Right you are, Mr Griffiths, there should be one right next to my desk out there. I guess one of the doctors took it from in here earlier. Typical, not returning it!"

Dad disappears momentarily and when he's back, Mum already has a blood pressure sleeve on her upper arm, and what looks like a crocodile clip on the end of her right index finger.

"Good… this all looks good," the nurse tells us. "I'll be back again in an hour but just press that buzzer if you need me in the meantime – or, in fact, just open the door as I should be right outside again when I've done my rounds."

"Thanks so much, you're an angel," Dad says.

"*You're an angel*," Mum mimics when the door has closed and they grin at each other. I can't believe that just hours ago I thought she might be dying and now she's back to her usual feisty self – well, almost.

"How are you feeling, Mum?"

"You asked that already!" she laughs. "I'm OK, I promise. Just tired. But at least I know what's going on with me now. I think I've had a few clues over the last few months but I didn't know that's what they were."

"You must be exhausted," I say.

"She is, she'll need to get some sleep soon," Dad says. "But we wanted to wait for you first, so you can see your mum's OK, and because Mum was desperate to see you." I realise that now he's close to tears.

Mum puts her hand on his. "I will, if you don't mind, try and get some sleep now. You two should go home and have a glass of wine. I will be fine, I promise," she cuts short Dad's protestation. "But come back as soon as visiting hours start tomorrow, will you? And can you bring my book, off the bedside table? And maybe the paper, so I can do the puzzles…"

"We'll sort this out in the morning," I say. "You can let us know whatever you want. Keep your phone on, and send me a message if you think of anything. Night night, Mum. I love you."

"I love you, too. Thank you for coming, Alice. I didn't mean to worry you."

"No, of course you didn't! I know that. I'm just glad you're OK." I hug and kiss Mum then step outside as Dad says his goodbyes.

As we walk out of the hospital into the night, I feel an immense relief flood through me, and also exhaustion. It's close to midnight.

"Where's your car?" asks Dad.

"Oh, I er, Julie was out in it. I got a lift."

"All this way?" Dad asks. "That was kind."

"Yes, it was."

"It wasn't Sam, was it?" Dad took a real shine to Sam and has never let me forget it. If Mum was with us she'd be elbowing him in the ribs and giving him her Look but without her he has free rein to be as unsubtle as he likes.

"No, Dad, not Sam, although I did see him earlier. He's back from uni this week. But he didn't have his car,

109

either."

"Well, I'm just glad you got here tonight, for your sake and your mum's."

"Me too, Dad."

I follow him to the car and get in. We drive quietly back to my childhood home, the radio on at a low volume but not interrupting our thoughts. I am running back through the events of the last few hours in my mind, and I am sure Dad is doing the same. He must have been terrified when he got that telephone call, and I can't imagine how he felt as he drove to the hospital. Mum had collapsed in the kitchen at work, apparently.

Oblivious, I had been able only to think about my date with Paul. It seems like another lifetime now. I draw my phone out to text him, and see I have a number of messages. I scroll through them,

Sam Branvall (1)

These words still have the ability to make my insides flip over.

I hope your mum's OK and you are too. Let me know when you have news.

Julie (3)

Thinking of you. Love you.

Give my love to your mum and dad.

Love you, love you, love you xxxxx

Paul Winters (1)

Just stopped for coffee and fuel. Hope you and your folks are all OK. I enjoyed our journey – not the date I'd hoped for but lovely to spend time with you nevertheless xx

Bea Danson (1)

Alice, just heard about your mum, I hope she's OK. Let me know if I can do anything to help xxx

David Danson (1)

Alice, is your mum ok? Are you? Love you loads. You know where I am when you need me. Love David (and Martin) xxxx

Somehow I hadn't quite been expecting this onslaught of messages. I decide to reply to them when I'm in bed. I am sure nobody's expecting to hear from me right away. I think of Sam; his face when he realised that there was somebody else more able to help me. I allow myself to acknowledge how gutted he looked, when Paul turned up. In honesty, I would have accepted a lift from almost anybody, to be able to get to Mum as quickly as possible, and while I am incredibly grateful to Paul, would I have preferred it if it had been Sam?

***

When I step into Mum and Dad's house, I am greeted by the ever-familiar smell of home. Each house has its own unique scent; a combination of washing powder, perfumes, aftershaves, shower gels, cooking… but also something less tangible. Something attributable only to this particular family, person or couple. I never really knew this until that golden summer, returning home from Cornwall, full of myself and my mind full of Sam. I hadn't wanted to come home; I had wanted to stay in Cornwall, no matter how unrealistic that was, but when I walked through this same doorway, into the place which had been my home ever since I was born, I was surprised. I felt a strong sense of belonging and, more than that, I felt safe.

Now, I experience something very similar but mingled with a strong sense of relief and a need to release the emotions of the last few hours. Dad turns to me, his face older than I've ever noticed it before, and I hug him. We hold on to each other in the bright ceiling-sunk lights of the hallway for some time, neither of us speaking but nevertheless acknowledging the fear we both felt today.

"Come on," he says after a while, "I need to let people know your mum's OK, and I expect you've got text messages and emails you need to answer. Let's get the kettle on; the heating, too."

He's right; I realise I am shivering. It has been an exhausting day and my body is now protesting. Dad trots upstairs and I hear the whoosh of the flame as the boiler springs into life. I realise that we are both turning on lights as we go, as if warding off the darkness. In the kitchen, I switch on the kettle then I sit at the table and pull my phone from my pocket. Who to answer first? I go for the easy choice – Julie. After all, I reason, she is part of our family. She has the most personal interest in what's happened to mum.

She's OK! I slide my finger across the screen, watching the swoosh of the stripe as my finger swipes across the correct letters and my phone detects the words which I need to form. **I'm home now, with Dad, and they're keeping Mum in for a day or two, but nobody seems too worried about her. She might have an operation in a few weeks, but she's OK. I'll ring you tomorrow xxx**

Thank God. Sleep well, Alice. Love you so much xxx

Julie's reply is close to instant. I smile.

Thank you, Julie. I love you, too. Sleep well. xxx

Next – Bea. Well, she will need to know what's going on for work.

Mum's OK, thank you Bea. She's in hospital, I've just got home with Dad. I'll ring you tomorrow xx

David next – OK, OK, I admit it, I'm delaying having to choose between Sam and Paul, as if the order in which I text them bears any significance.

Thank you, David (and Martin). Mum is OK, she's resting, and I'm back at their place now. Thanks for thinking of me. Xxx

As I am sending this, a message pings in from Bea:

No problem, Alice. I've got everything covered. X

Thank you, Bea, I am so sorry for ruining your honeymoon xx

Don't be ridiculous! We've had our honeymoon and you know I can't stay away from the Sail Loft, anyway. You've given me a reason to be there without Bob being mad at me. Take as much time as you need with your parents. And get some sleep! X

Now for the hard part ... I am just being silly, I know. In fact, I am being ridiculous, but not in the way Bea thinks. Dad comes into the kitchen and busies himself making two cups of hot chocolate. I decide to just get on with it. Sam first, my reasoning being that he has met Mum – and she loved him.

Thank you, Sam, and thank you so much for being there for me. Mum is OK, she's in hospital and I'm back at home with Dad now. Ax

I wasn't really sure how to sign off, but it's OK to put a kiss, isn't it? After all, we still care about each other.

And finally, Paul – then I determine to put my phone away and concentrate on Dad.

Hi Paul, just to let you know that I am now at home with Dad and Mum is doing OK. Thank you so much for driving me up here, I'd

**probably still be on the train if it wasn't for you!
Ax**

An identical sign-off. I don't wait to see if either Sam or Paul texts back; I switch off my phone and put it away. Dad sits opposite me, tipping his own phone from one hand to the other; at once agitated and contemplative.

"Have you contacted everyone you needed to?" I ask.

"Yes, I think so. Well, I set the ball in motion. Your mum's got a lot of friends, you know."

"I know," I smile. "I'm sure there'll be the trickle-down effect. Are you OK, Dad?"

He smiles thinly. "I am now. I wasn't earlier. I don't think I've ever been so scared."

"I can imagine."

"It's time for some changes, Alice. I kept thinking that, while I waited to hear if your mum was OK. She works too hard but it's going to take some convincing to get her to agree. She doesn't want to retire for another couple of years but you hear about it all the time: people working their guts out then retiring and not lasting long enough to enjoy it. We'd be OK financially if she stopped working now."

"Do you think she would? I wish she would," I admit. "Especially now. As long as you two don't end up driving each other mad!" I laugh and he laughs, too.

"We'd keep busy, keep out of each other's hair. We'd have to, or your mum would end up divorcing me!"

"Well let's see what we can do," I say, "but we'll give her a day or two to get over the shock of all this, eh?"

"Yes, I think that would be wise."

Dad and I sit and sip our drinks, each taken with our own thoughts. After a while, I collect both of our mugs and put them in the sink. "They'll wait till tomorrow," I say. "Now you need some sleep and so do I."

Dad looks up and nods. He looks exhausted. We head upstairs and hug on the landing before going our separate ways. Neither of us switches off the lights.

In the morning I am confused for a moment, but it doesn't take long for everything to flood back to my mind. In honesty I've woken many times during the night, my restless mind playing tricks on me and refusing to let me sleep. Now, with the sunlight pouring in through the thin curtains of my room, I lie for a few moments, letting my eyes adjust to the light and my mind to the reality of the new world I am living in. One where I've seen my mum's mortality and it is no longer an abstract concept. Even though I have seen friends lose their parents – most recently, Luke – I gave found it impossible to imagine that Mum or Dad will ever actually die. They are a firm fixture of my life, they're going nowhere. Yesterday, I faced up to the fact that actually, Mum might have died, and I wouldn't even have had a chance to say goodbye to her. I sob now at the thought, and I wonder if Dad is awake, suffering similar torments. However, a clattering from the kitchen below alerts me to the fact he is already up. Moments later, I hear his footsteps on the stairs and a knock on the door.

"Come in," I say, sitting up.

The door opens and Dad appears with a tray, bearing a plate of toast, a small pot of tea, a cup and a jug of milk. "Breakfast is served!"

"Wow! Thank you, Dad. Have you had any sleep at all?"

"Not really," he admits, "so I thought I'd make myself

useful."

"You've certainly done that," I smile. "This is great. I feel like I'm in a hotel."

"Well, you deserve to be waited on for a change."

Dad puts the tray on my bedside table. "I'll leave you to it. Then maybe we can get to the hospital."

I look at the clock – it's 8.34. I never sleep this late. "Of course! I didn't realise that was the time. I'll get dressed."

I move to get out of bed but Dad puts a gentle hand on my shoulder. "No rush, sweetheart. Have your breakfast – your Mum'll kill me if you don't – then have a shower and we can go. OK?"

"OK," I agree.

Dad leaves the room, closing the door softly behind him. It feels nice being in my old room – even though it's changed. There's a double bed these days, and new curtains, and a complete absence of the hundreds of photos which used to adorn the walls. But somehow it still feels the same. I sneak out of bed and get my phone from my jeans pocket, switching it on. It takes a few moments to come to life then the messages ping in. I feel my heart lurch, wondering who has replied.

5 New Messages

Five? That seems excessive. I go into my inbox and see two from Julie, then there are two from Sam and one from Paul.

It turns out three were sent last night so I go through them in order.

Julie: **Don't forget to give my love to Phil, and Jane tomorrow when you see her. Tell them to** come and have a break in Cornwall when they can xx

Sam: **I will always help you if you need me, I hope you know that. I'm glad your mum's OK.**

Paul: **My pleasure xx**

These were last night's – this morning's are as follows:

Julie: **Morning, my lovely. The sun is shining in Cornwall and I hope it is back home. Just wanted you to know I'm thinking of you all. Keep me posted and let me know if there is anything you need me to do here xxx**

Sam: **Good morning, I just wanted to check everything is still OK. And also to say I'm glad you were able to get up to your parents'. I would have helped if I could but luckily somebody else was able to. I'm off back to Wales today. Take care x**

Urgh. There's something about that message from Sam that I don't like. It seems so… formal, and it makes me feel uncomfortable. I miss him still, if I am honest, and I can't bear the thought that we might end up being 'civil' to each other. We used to have so much fun. Still, what must he have thought when Paul turned up with his flash car? I can be nothing but grateful to Paul, though – Mum came above everything else yesterday and I am sure that Sam must understand that.

I don't reply any of the messages for now. Instead, I eat

my toast and drink my tea, then I step into a hot shower in Mum and Dad's newly refurbished bathroom. The water is hot and powerful. I shampoo my hair and soap my body then allow myself a few minutes' pummelling, remembering my journey up here last night.

Paul was great; he allowed me to be quiet but also kept me from sinking too far by asking questions, about Mum and Dad, and life before Cornwall. I described my job at World of Stationery, and my manager, Jason. How he'd wanted me to come back and work for him but how I had decided to stay in Cornwall.

"Well, I'm glad you did," Paul had smiled over at me. "And do you like your work now?"

"I do," I say, "I love it."

"There's an unspoken 'but' at the end of that sentence, isn't there?"

"There's… yes," I thought that there was no point in denying it but was also aware that Paul is a friend of Bea's (though he might feel slightly less friendly if he knew what she'd told me about him). "I love the hotel, I love working with all the guests, and we've got a great team. Bea is a great boss. It's just…"

"It's getting too small for you?" he suggested.

"Yes," I said thoughtfully, "that's a good way of putting it. And it's not that I'm not grateful to Bea – I am and I always will be. But it's *her* place, and I'll never feel quite the same way about it that she does. I'll always be working for her. Not that she isn't great to work for."

Paul had laughed. "You don't need to keep justifying what you're saying. I know where you're coming from. You've been at the Sail Loft, what … two years? And you were the boss for part of that time, while Bea was away. Now she's back and you're not quite the boss anymore.

119

There's nothing wrong with wanting to be, you know. There is absolutely no shame in being ambitious."

I surreptitiously looked at him, taking in his easy manner and confidence. Here was somebody who had the drive and belief in himself to start a business, and make a success of it. I began to suspect that I could learn a lot from him, and I began to think that I would like to be more like him.

"I'm not saying it's not hard work," he continued. "It is – and it can take over your life. But if you want to move on up from working for somebody else, you should do it. What would you do, Alice? Your dream job? Run your own hotel? Or something totally different?"

As well as distracting me from worrying about Mum, Paul seemed to be inspiring me with his drive and determination. Life is too short, people say, and I knew this more surely than ever. Before I knew it, I found myself telling him about Julie, and our plans, and how we had found the right place and were just now trying to find the money.

"Is this place in Cornwall?" he asked.

"Yes. Not far from town, actually."

"Well, I'm glad to hear that," he smiled. "So what's it like?"

I described Amethi to him and as I did so I could just feel the place, somehow. I know it sounds weird, but as I pictured the different buildings, and how the whole plot is encircled by trees, tucked away, it almost felt like I was there again.

"But I have to acknowledge there's a good chance somebody else will get it. I still have a long way to go to raise my part of the funds. Julie's fiancé has offered to fund a huge portion of it, as a loan, but I don't know – it's

OK for Julie, she's going to marry him – but it just doesn't sit right, somehow."

"I get that," says Paul. "So how are you going to do it?"

I loved the way he said that – with the conviction that it was going to happen. "Well, I've got a flat up here, near my parents. If I can sell that, I'll have a bit of cash, and a bit more of a chance of borrowing from the bank. Which I know sounds stupid – why not borrow from Luke, when I'm going to have to borrow from somebody?"

"Because he's your friend, and your friend's partner, and your partner's partner – and you need to go into this on an even footing. That's why. You are completely right not to want your business to ruin your friendship, or your friendship to ruin your business."

"I'm sure Julie thinks I'm just being stubborn but it's not that, at all. I have to get somewhere new to live in Cornwall too, though," I admitted.

"You really have got it all going on, haven't you?" Paul sympathised. "But you know what? It's times like this, when you're up against it, that you find out just what you're made of – and when you can really make things happen. I have a feeling you're going to do just that, Alice."

"Thank you, Paul, I really hope so."

"Have faith," he had smiled.

When we'd got to the hospital, I'd thanked him again for the lift. He just squeezed my hand gently and smiled. "Don't mention it," he said. "I wouldn't have done it if I didn't want to."

I felt sure he was telling the truth.

***

When we get to Mum's room, she is free of wires and sitting in bed drinking a cup of tea. Her TV is pulled round and I can hear the sounds of some kind of daytime antique- or house-related programme.

"Bloody hell, love, that was pretty extreme just to get a morning in bed," Dad smiles and kisses her.

She returns the smile. "Can you believe this time yesterday I was just at work as normal? I had no idea what was in store for me."

"I've got to say, you look pretty relaxed about it all." I hug my mum, taking a seat on the opposite side of bed to Dad. "Now, what's this rubbish you're watching?"

"I think it's called *Antiques under the Hammer*."

"Sounds very impractical," I suggest.

"Yes, but I always have liked an element of danger."

"As you proved yesterday," agrees Dad. I'm surprised and dismayed to see Mum's eyes fill with tears.

"Hey," I say quietly, putting my hand on hers and looking at Dad.

"What?" he protests but relents. "Sorry. I don't think I'm very good at these kinds of situations."

"Really?" Mum sniffs but it seems Dad's ineptitude has lightened her mood. "I'm sorry, too, not for getting upset, but for putting you two through all of that yesterday. I thought I was… I thought I was going to die, quite honestly, and I wasn't ready to leave you."

This is enough to send the tears coursing to my eyes. "You can't leave us, Mum. Not now. Not ever."

"Well, I think that might be stretching it," she smiles at me. "But I'll do my best. I am under strict instructions from the doctor to take it easier."

"Does this mean..?" Dad asks.

"Retirement? I don't know. I can't quite believe I'm old

enough to actually retire."

"I've been retired for two years," he says.

"I rest my case. But really, I don't want to give up work completely. Dad and I have been discussing this for a while, though, Alice. I don't know if he mentioned it to you?"

"Kind of…" I wait for her to say more, not wanting to put words in her mouth.

"I suppose it's been more of an abstract concept until now," she says, "but I lay awake for a long time last night thinking through what had happened and how it had happened. Maybe it is time for a change."

"Definitely," Dad says. "I couldn't agree more. We always did think on the same wavelength," he takes her hand and a look passes between them that I cannot miss, and which can only be described as love. I am at once proud to see that they still feel this way about each other after so many years together and embarrassed, as though I am trespassing on a private moment.

"When you get home," Dad continues, "I am going to take care of you. You won't have to lift a finger. I just can't wait for you to come back."

"I think it's going to be a day or two yet, you know," Mum says, "and I'll be back for an operation, they say. It's a stent," she turns to me to explain. "Something to help keep my arteries open and my heart working as it should. The doctor says they're really effective."

"OK," I say slowly, "but what about these changes? What are you thinking?"

"Well, for one thing, I think we need to sell the house. Move somewhere smaller. Maybe even newer. It seems like ever since we've lived there we've been repairing the place, or updating it, or both."

"OK..."

"And, yes Phil, I will think about work. There'll be occupational therapy time as a matter of course after something like this but," she intercepts him, anticipating what he is going to say, "that does not mean I am necessarily going to stay in that role. I just don't want to jump into anything."

"Fine. For now." Dad seems partially satisfied.

"Shall I get us some coffee?" I suggest. "Are you allowed coffee, Mum?"

"Actually, no, not really! And I've just finished an unsatisfying cup of decaf tea, but if that's the worst I have to put up with then I really can't complain. You go and get your dad and yourself a cup, Alice."

I head out of the room and off the ward. There's a proper coffee shop along near the entrance. It feels like weeks since I was heading the opposite way, desperate to see Mum, yet it isn't even twenty-four hours ago. I'm aware again – even more so than yesterday – of the heightened emotions in this place. I am lucky enough to have spent very little time in hospital in my life so far but it strikes me that you could be in severe distress, or deliriously happy and relieved, or horrendously bored. It seems that very little of what goes on in these places is done by halves.

I step into a Ladies' toilet before I go to the coffee shop; looking my mirrored reflection in the eyes, I splash water on my face and embolden myself. This is an important time, I think, and I need to be on the ball. I need to be strong for my parents. A role reversal. I dry my face with a hand towel and walk out to the queue for coffee.

While I am waiting, I feel my phone buzz. It's a local

number; the estate agents, if I'm not much mistaken. Probably giving me another pointless update, as they do every month. "We're sorry, the recent time-wasters/nosey gits [delete as applicable] thought it was a great little space but it just wasn't right for them. They were looking for something a little bigger/a house with a swimming pool [as before]." I'm just glad I don't have to show the supposed prospective buyers round myself. I let the call go to answerphone.

Back outside Mum's room, I can see she is reclining with her eyes shut, a small smile on her lips. Dad looks up at me through the glass of the door and puts his finger to his lips. I creep in as quietly as I can but, true to form, Mum's eyes spring open. "Why don't you two get out of here for now? Go for a walk or something. You've seen me, you know I'm alive and kicking, but I really could do with some sleep and I don't want to have to listen to you slurping your coffee, Phil."

"Ha!" he says. "Great idea, though. What do you say, Alice? Fancy a walk?"

Through the window I can see that the sky is blue, with flimsy fast-moving clouds. A beautiful late spring day. "That sounds great."

We kiss Mum goodbye and head out. I can't help but feel relieved as we exit the hospital. I am in awe of the people who work here. Dad and I walk to the car in silence, clasping our too-hot coffee to ourselves. Once safely installed, seatbelts on, we look at each other.

"Are you OK, love?"

"I'm fine," I say. "How about you?"

"I think so. A walk sounds great, though – your mum always knows the right thing to do, doesn't she?"

"Yes," I agree, "she does. But maybe we won't tell her

that."

Before I know it, Dad is sobbing. I put my hand on his arm but don't try to stop him. He must need this, to let it all go. I just sit quietly and after a time he rubs his eyes, looks at me, and is about to speak.

"Don't say anything," I say. "You needed that. Now let's go and have that walk."

"And a pub lunch?"

"And a pub lunch," I agree.

We head off to the Malverns, which are about forty minutes' drive from here, and park at their feet, clambering eagerly out of the car and scrambling up until, out of breath and panting, we reach the top. To the right and the left, the range of hills stretches away, and out in front of us the rural landscape is spread like a picnic blanket, spring deepening the green of the hedgerows and new leaves. A tiny tractor chugs along through one of the distant brown fields and miniature cars meander along the narrow lanes. Meanwhile, a kestrel hovers at eye-level, its head perfectly still while its wings beat furiously, eyes focused on its prey.

It's windy up here but I feel like I need to feel the force of the weather. As clouds hurry across the sky, chased by their shadows down below, the sun's rays warm me.

"It's good to be alive," I say but with the noise of the wind Dad doesn't hear me and I don't mind. I wasn't really speaking to be heard. Just acknowledging something great.

"Let's walk," I say more loudly. Dad nods in agreement. We head along, following a slope into a more sheltered area, and are able to talk once more.

"So, who did drive you up here?" Dad asks conversationally.

"Oh, just a friend. Paul."

"Paul? I don't think I've heard you mention him before."

"No, well I haven't known him long. I met him at Bea's wedding."

"Oh yeah?" Dad looks at me slyly.

"Yep," I say, wanting to give nothing away but knowing that in the brevity of my answer I'm telling him all he needs to know.

"And will he be giving you a lift back?"

"I hadn't actually thought of that," I say. "I haven't thought that far ahead. But I guess not; I'll probably get the train, I think."

"OK." Dad doesn't press this point any further. "So how's the Sail Loft? Getting busy again, I bet. Maybe me and your mum should come for another visit soon."

"Yes, you should. When Mum's better, that would be great. I meant to say, Julie says you have to come and visit."

"Not long till her wedding now," Dad says. "We'll be there for that anyway."

"Oh, but come before then, won't you? Come when it's hot and sunny and you can make Mum relax on the beach."

"If we can find a quiet spot!" Dad laughs.

"Ah, well, I know a great little secret beach now," I say, thinking of my date with Paul. "It's only a few miles from town but you have to look hard to find it. I can point you in the right direction though, for a small fee."

"Very generous of you."

"I thought so. When I'm back at work I'll see when we've got availability and book you in."

"OK, you do that, love."

"I have been meaning to talk to you about work, though, Dad."

"Oh yeah?"

"Yeah, well, you know me and Julie have…"

"Julie and I."

"No, *me* and Julie. This has nothing to do with you. Anyway, we've found the perfect place…"

I tell him all about Amethi, describing it in enthusiastic detail. But also how much it will all cost.

"It sounds perfect, and very exciting, Alice. Do you know, if your mum and I can sell the house, we might be able to help you more than we'd thought before."

"That's so kind of you, Dad, thank you, but I have a feeling this place is going to be snapped up before too long. I think we're going to have to think again," I say sadly.

"What about your flat?" Dad asks. "Any news on that?"

"No," I say then remember the phone call. "Though that reminds me, the estate agent called earlier."

I pluck my phone from my pocket and dial voicemail. "Probably something and nothing," I say to Dad but listen to what Janet from Hills Estate Agents has to say.

"No way!" I exclaim, cutting off the message and looking at Dad with delight. "No bloody way!"

As I say those words the sun escapes its brief cloud cover and soaks Dad and me with its warmth.

"It's not… it's never?"

"It is!" I say, practically dancing for joy. "Somebody's made an offer on the flat! The full asking price! I can't believe it."

12

After a few days, Mum is back home and it's almost as though nothing has happened, except we all know it has. And Dad and I are not likely to let her forget it.

She gets annoyed when we talk to her about work, though. "Look, you two, I know you're only saying this because you care about me but you have to understand, I've worked bloody hard to get where I am and the thought of giving it up just like that isn't easy. I love my job. I love working."

"Sorry, Mum," I say, thinking how I might feel if I had to give up work all of a sudden.

"It's OK. And I am going to make some changes, I promise, but in my own time. I've got the occupational therapist coming round next week to talk. I'll give it some serious thought before then and see what my options are."

Mum's worked in HR for years, and for the same company for the last twelve years. They make beautiful woollen rugs and wooden furniture, and employ about 250 people. It's Mum's job to manage all the human resources requirements. As a consequence of working for this firm, my parents' home is beautifully furnished, but also my mum has some long-term friends – many younger than her – who I know she loves dearly.

"I think you just don't want to be stuck with me every day," Dad teases.

"Well of course I don't! I'm not mad. But seriously, that would be a big change for both of us, too. We need to give this some thought."

I know this is something Mum and Dad need to decide together. "I'd really better get back to my job, too," I say. "I'll look into train times and head off tomorrow. Now I know that you're home, safe and well, Mum."

"Sounds like a good idea. I did hear you got a lift up," Mum casts a sly glance my way.

"Yes," I say defensively, "I did."

"Must be someone who thinks a lot of you to drive you all this way."

"Well, we'd had plans for that evening and… Oh, you two!" I exclaim, as my parents grin at each other. "You need to grow up!" I can't help grinning myself, though. "Paul's a friend, I haven't known him long."

"Well, that's fine, and he's obviously a good man to look after you like that."

"He seems to be, yes. But it's early days."

"It's good, Alice! Don't be so touchy. You deserve some fun. You're a fine one to lecture me about working too hard!" Mum puts a hand on my arm.

In truth, Paul and I have been texting like mad since I've been up here. It's like an addiction; if I'm not texting him, I'm either trying to make myself wait so I don't look too keen, or listening out for the ping of my phone, waiting for him to get back to me. I've also sent Sam a couple of messages, to let him know things are OK with Mum. I feel bad about the way Paul kind of usurped him, but Sam's not being drawn on this. His replies have been short; perfunctory. I've relied on Paul to lift my spirits instead. Oh, and having the offer on the flat – which all looks to be going ahead. There's no chain on either side so it shouldn't take long. While I still had a mortgage on the place, I'll get enough from the sale to go a little way towards the business. If only I didn't have to worry about getting a place to live, too. I know I really need to sort that out before I commit to Amethi, which I am still a way off being able to do anyway.

I called Julie to talk it through. "I don't know what to do – I just can't get Amethi out of my head."

"Me neither, and look, Luke's still happy to help us both. I know, I totally get why you're not comfortable with that, but if it means the difference between us getting the place and not…"

She's so keen, so up for it, but it's easy for her. Or easier. This is her soon-to-be husband. She's moving in with him soon. They will be sharing everything anyway.

"Look, when I'm back, I'm going to start looking at places to live. I've already been searching and I think I'll be OK in a little one-bed flat. It will have to be up the hill, and it won't be anything like we've had at David's, but if I can get somewhere not too expensive then I'll be in a better position to go for it with you. And I'll go to the bank."

I've got so much to do; it's piling up in my mind again and I know I need to get back to Cornwall to get on with it. I need to find a place to live; David's going to want to put the house on the market soon and I don't think it will take long at all for his place to sell. I need to complete the sale of the flat here. I also have to work out whether I'm ever going to be able to do this with Julie, or else let her down gently but quickly. I also am desperate to do it so I have to find a way. And then I will have to tell Bea. On top of this is Stefan's wedding; the silly season at work; Julie's hen do: Julie's and Luke's wedding. Oh, and making sure Mum and Dad are OK. I don't want to leave them; my heart is tugging at me to stay but I have to go, I have to get on.

Paul is a very welcome distraction from it all and I've promised him we'll go out again when I'm back – once I've made up for my absence from the Sail Loft – and also that I will come to a party he's having at his place next month:

I do it every year. It's mostly a lot of local business people, you'll know some of them. It might be a bit of a yawn but having you there will keep things interesting for me xx

I'm half nervous and half excited about the party. I don't really know if it's the right place for me but I suppose if I'm serious about getting the business going with Julie it won't hurt to make some more connections. Maybe I'll get some inspiration, too.

***

Julie and Luke meet me at the station.

"I've missed you!" Julie cries, flinging her arms around me while Luke looks on, grinning at his fiancée's dramatic ways.

"I've missed you, too," I say, smiling at my friend as I pull back. She is brimming over with excitement; in truth, she has been since she and Luke got engaged. After she asked him to marry her and he said no, she was gobsmacked when he asked her a year to the day later.

Luke takes my bag from me and swings it onto his shoulder. "I'm glad your mum's OK, Alice." He swoops to kiss me.

"Thank you, Luke."

Julie links her arm through mine as we head across to the car park. "I've been trying to call you all morning," she says.

"Ah, yes, I had my phone off." I had given myself the length of the train journey to escape the world; let all my thoughts and feelings about Mum and Dad wash through me, and forget as much as I could about all the things waiting for me back here.

"You bugger!" she laughs, "I've got so much to tell you and it's all happened while you were on the train!"

"Oh yeah?" *Here goes,* I think, and I steel myself.

"Yes, now, the one I think you'll be most interested in is that there's a bit of a complication with Amethi."

"Oh no," I say, thinking that maybe the decision's being taken out of my hands.

"Yes, but not in a bad way – well, maybe not. I don't know. See what you think."

"Just tell her, Julie!" Luke laughs from behind us.

"Well, Sally – you know – from the estate agents?"

"Yes, I know Sally," I say.

"She rang to say that there's some kind of covenant on the place which they've only just become aware of. One of the buildings – one of the two-beds, you know the detached one? Away from the main block? We can't rent it out as a holiday let."

"We can't..? Oh. Well what are we meant to do with it, then?"

"Well, durrrr … you can live there, can't you? I mean, you could. If you'd like to. If we're going for it."

I know full well when my friend is trying to play things down. Shit. This could be the answer to one of my

133

problems. But…

"I know, I know, would you want to be on site with our clients? And would you want to be out of town? But the great thing is, because of it, the seller has reduced the price."

"Really?" I ask.

"Yes, I know, we thought it was odd, too, but it's something to do with it not being wholly commercial premises now."

"Bloody hell." This is a lot to take in.

Julie opens the car door. I drink in the view of the sea, over the car park wall, before resigning myself to the back seat of Luke's car. I've gone from a phone-free, leisurely train journey to full-on one-hundred-miles-per-hour Julie. It takes a bit of building up to.

Nevertheless, no matter how high Julie's enthusiasm right now, I do know she'd never expect me to do this if it wasn't right for me. I can feel my heart pounding and my breath shortened by it all. And we haven't even left the station car park yet.

The next day I'm back at work at the Sail Loft. Julie wants me to go with her to see a lawyer, but there is no way I can ask Bea for time off again when I've just got back.

"You can go without me – or take Luke. Get the ball rolling," I said, sitting at the opposite end of the settee to her, both of us holding large glasses of red wine and a half-eaten pizza congealing in its box on the table. I think we both realised we couldn't eat. Tensions and nerves are just too much right now.

"No, no way am I going without you. If we're going to do this – and I know, it's an *if*, we need to be taking all these steps together. I'm just so bloody impatient!"

"I know," I laughed, "and I am, too, I promise. I know I seem more reticent but that's really only because of the money, although I can't say I'm too keen on telling Bea about it, either."

"She'll be alright, won't she? She's a strong, independent businesswoman, and she'll understand you want to be the same."

"Let's hope so."

Still, there is no point in mentioning anything to Bea right now – not till I have something definite to tell her. And her hug when she greets me at the top of the steps on my return is so warm, I feel a sense of guilt that I'm just turning my back on everything she's done for me. *Don't be stupid*, I hear Julie's voice in my head. *You've done a lot for her, too.*

It's true, I think; I've introduced new elements to the Sail Loft; the Christmas and New Year celebrations; the writers' workshops. And she may not have been able to go to America to meet Bob in person if I hadn't agreed to take on the management of the place. So it hasn't all been one-way but between her and David, who's made sure I've always had a place to live, I can't deny I feel a debt of gratitude to the Dansons.

I push this all to the back of my mind, though, and hug Bea back. "I'm sorry for ruining your honeymoon!"

"Alice, we've already been through this. I was glad to get back here and it was like a little holiday in itself, running this place again. Not that Bob can understand how in the world I'd consider it a holiday. Just because he's retired. I don't know how he fills his time but he does, somehow. I can't bear the thought of not having some kind of structure, though. If I'm not working, I

135

think I may as well curl up and die."

"I know what you mean," I smile.

"I know you do – we've got the same work ethic, you and I. That's why we work so well together."

There goes that twang of guilt again. I steadfastly ignore it, for now. "So how are things here? Anything exciting happen while I've been gone?"

"Not really – we had a couple of last-minute bookings at the weekend so we had a full house. And aside from that, it's been ticking over nicely. Really, I've been helping Stefan sort out wedding stuff."

At this, I feel a little put-out. This was my job. I have been loving helping Stef and April, but it's only a matter of weeks till their big day now; I couldn't expect them to wait for me to come back.

"Oh," Bea continues, "I've also got some dates for your parents to visit. There are a couple of options so let me know what's best for them."

"Thank you, Bea, I think some sunshine and sea air will do Mum lots of good. Dad, too."

"Of course it will, there's nothing like it! Do you know, Barbados was all well and good but give me Cornwall any day. Don't tell Bob, though."

"I won't!" I grin and head through to the kitchen.

"Alice!" Jonathan turns and sees me. "How are you? How's your mum?"

"I'm fine, thanks – Mum, too. It's been a bit of a shock, though."

"I can imagine. Is she back home now?"

"Yes – and she's threatening to be back at work next week. But the OT is coming to see her today so I hope they can talk some sense into her. She's as bad as Bea. Did you know she said it's been a treat running this place while I've been away?"

"Ha, she's mental," Jonathan grins. "I've definitely missed you, too – she's not half as much fun."

"Ahhh, thank you." Here is another thing to feel guilty about. I can't bring Jon with me as Julie is the chef. And while she may need some help at times, I don't see him taking to the role of sous chef – or either of them being able to share a kitchen with the other, come to think of it. "I missed you, too."

"Did you?"

"No."

"I knew it. I'm not sure Lydia's missing me that much anymore, either," he says more glumly.

"Really? Why do you say that?" I was afraid this might happen; surely it must happen a lot when one partner goes off to uni. Especially at Lydia's age. Still, there must also be relationships which last the course of university. Not mine and Sam's, obviously, but we had other complications on top of being apart. Maybe Jonathan and Lydia will be luckier.

The day passes uneventfully and at handover time Stefan comes in, beaming. "Alice, it's so good to see you. And guess who's getting married in just over three weeks' time?"

"You!" I say, "I know, because I've arranged half of it, you idiot!"

"I know, I know, I'm just so excited! And Reuben is going to be my best man. Can you imagine?"

"That is going to be very cute," I say, "is he organising your stag do?"

"Ha. No, Jonathan is seeing to that. Just a few of us – you know Marvin, of course. And my brother, he'll be here by then. And Sam."

"Sam? My..?" I stop myself. He really isn't *my Sam* anymore.

"Yes, I hope you don't mind, I saw him when he was back and I just mentioned it to him, he said he's around, he'll have done his exams by then I think, and he'd like to come. And he's going to come to the reception in the evening, that is if it's OK with you."

"Well of course; and it's not up to me, anyway. Is he… will he have anyone with him?"

"Yes." My stomach drops. "He's bringing Sophie." I'm flooded with relief, and happiness at the thought of seeing my favourite eleven-year-old.

"OK. Well, we need to make sure everything's in place for the main event," I say, pulling out the folder. "Shall we go through it now?"

"Yes, let's do that. And while you were away, Bea sorted out the problem with accommodation, too. My cousins will be at the Hollies next door so we don't worry about overcrowding or insurance or anything like that."

"Well, that's a relief," I say. Stefan pulls his chair over to mine and we run through the guest list, the menu, the order of events and the entertainment. They have opted for a traditional wedding DJ and I really hope that the weather is good because there is precious little space for dancing in the Sail Loft bar but we can spill out onto the veranda if it's dry. It's going to be a beautiful day and I can't wait, but there is much to do and now I have Sam's presence to gnaw away at me. At least I can busy myself in my role as hotel manager/wedding planner, though, if things get really awkward.

I head off home with a spring in my step, intending to give Mum and Dad a ring when I get in. I'm going to hold them to booking a holiday down here, and I also want to know what the OT has had to say to Mum about her return to work. Almost every house, hotel or B&B that I pass has flowers blooming from pots, window troughs and hanging baskets. The breeze, though definitely there, has a warm edge to it, and I breathe it in, hoping to scent some of the flowers as well. I have to remind myself sometimes to appreciate all this but right now, while summer teeters tantalisingly on the tail end of spring, it is no effort at all.

When I get to the top of the street, I see the little red car pulled onto the pavement outside so there is just enough room for another car to squeeze by. It's a good job it's later in the day and not yet high season. As I get closer, I see the engine is running. Julie opens the driver-side door.

"Get in, Alice! I've been waiting ages!"

"Where are we going?" I ask as I reach her.

"Amethi!" she says.

"What?"

"Well, I happened to see Sally today…"

"Oh, you just happened to see her, did you?"

"Yes, she was… in her office when I went in. I thought we should go back, make sure it's as beautiful as we remembered."

"OK," I laugh.

"And you need to take a look at your future… I mean *potential* future… home."

To be honest, I can't think of anything I'd like more. As Julie takes us down through town and back out again, I seize the chance to ring my parents.

"Is everything OK?" I ask Dad.

"Yes, I'll get your mum, she'll tell you how it went

139

today."

"Hi Alice." At the sound of her voice I feel the familiar relief at evidence that Mum really is OK.

"Hi, Mum, how did it go today?"

"Oh, it was fine, thank you. Tim said that I can come back next week but just for half-days at a time, and I'm not allowed to travel anywhere."

"Well, that sounds sensible."

"And I told Tim that I'll do what he says. But... your dad and I were talking some more last night and I think I'm going to give it up at Christmas."

"Really?"

"Yes, really."

"How do you feel about that?"

"I can't pretend it's not strange but I think it's the right thing. I can't do it forever. And I was talking to Pat – you know, she lives down the road. Number eight."

"Oh yes," I say, having no idea who Pat is.

"And she said something similar happened to her but she's a lot older than me, of course."

"Of course."

"And she didn't want to give up work – she was a headteacher – but when she did, she didn't look back. And she's still really busy. She does loads of stuff..."

Mum's voice starts to break up. "Mum? I can't hear you. I'm in the car with Julie, I'll ring you later."

"Pat... work... cake... jam."

Jam? "Mum, I'll call you later," I shout and the phone goes dead. I'm sure she'll work it out. Moments later, we are turning onto that dirt track, which looks drier than the first time we came, and bumping along to Amethi. How is it that this already feels like coming home?

As we emerge from the wooded driveway into the clearing, I think Julie and I share the same reaction. Since we were last here, it has become greener, and the once-well-tended gardens around the buildings have truly come to life. There are roses in bloom, trailing up the walls towards the roof; dahlias and fuschias bursting from the flowerbeds and planters. The lawns and the paddocks, which have been left to grow as they wish, are swathes of long, unkempt grasses, waving in the breeze which has found its way to us from the sea, even in this sheltered spot.

There is no sign of Sally. "Oh no, she's not coming," says Julie mysteriously.

"What, she just gave you the keys?"

"She… yes, she did, actually. I've, well I've kind of made an offer."

"You've *what*?"

"I had to. Well, I didn't have to, but Sally rang today, and she was talking about other people showing an interest, and while you were away, Luke and I put our heads together to work out the new costs, taking into account that you might be living here. Which I have here–" she waves a folder at me "– to go through with you."

"I can't believe this," I say, and I really do not know how I feel. Well, actually, I do. My over-riding feeling is of anger.

"Alice, I know, I'm sorry, I shouldn't have said it without you. I didn't want us to miss out. Nothing's finalised yet, anyway; I just made an offer, and the owner's accepted it. And it's a great offer – look."

I push the folder away. "For fuck's sake, Julie!" I exclaim. I don't think I have ever sworn at her before.

"What was all that about us having to start on the same footing? As equals?" There's something about the way that she and Luke have worked out the costs, while I've been up with Mum and Dad, that rankles with me as well.

"We are… we will… look, I can call Sally now and withdraw the offer."

"I think you should," I call her bluff.

"Really? Don't you want to look through all this first?"

"No, I don't," I say, and I storm away from her before I say something I might regret. The ground is uneven and I twist my ankle in my haste to get away. The sharp reality of pain brings me to tears and I stalk as best I can round the corner, where I sit against the wall of the stable block. The thick stone of the wall is warm on my back but I don't register it immediately, I'm so annoyed. How dare Julie do this? It's typical of her. I think of the way she was at school; she'd plan our weekends – ice skating, cinema, parties – and I'd happily go along with her wishes. Then there was the way that two years ago she'd arranged our jobs down here without my knowledge. Now she's made a huge decision on my behalf and she hasn't had the decency to consult me first.

"Alice," Julie comes round the corner, "are you OK? I'm sorry. Look, I'm going to call Sally."

"No," I say, "Don't. Not yet." Although I'm annoyed at the way she's gone about things, the memory of her arranging for us to come back to Cornwall has shaded my viewpoint slightly differently. I wouldn't be here if it wasn't for her. And I must admit that as I finally acknowledge the warmth of the wall at my back, the sight of the waving grasses and flowers, and the protective wall of trees which stand firmly around the site, my anger starts to dissipate. I begin to realise that this could be ours. Our business and, more than that, my home. What would it be like, living here? What if there were no guests and it was just me out here? I realise I like the idea.

My friend sinks down next to me, sitting close. I look at her and see that she is genuinely upset. "I'm sorry," she says again. "I've done it all wrong. And I know what it must seem like – Luke and I planning something which is actually meant to be yours and mine. But I wanted to help, while you were away; I wanted to make sure that we didn't miss out on something great. And then today it hit home that we really might. It seems obvious to me – but I shouldn't assume that it's the same for you. Oh my god, Alice, I'm a shit business partner. And I'm not even a business partner yet."

"You're not," I say, "not a business partner nor a shit one. You're an amazing friend, even if you do drive me mad. You also make me do things I might not otherwise. You know I'm not a risk-taker."

"No, but that's a good thing. I'm… I'm ridiculous."

She's crying openly now, and so am I. And we both must be ridiculous because we sit there, on that stone floor, crying in each other's arms, for some time.

It's me that breaks away. "Come on," I say. "Give me the keys. I want to see my new house."

"Your…? You're up for it?" Julie draws back and looks at me, examining my face.

"Well, I – subject to quite a few things, yes I am. I am!" I laugh.

"Shit! Shit, shit, shit, shit, shit! This is more exciting than getting engaged. Don't tell Luke," she adds. She fishes the keys from her pocket and we run across to the little house which sits slightly apart from the main block of buildings.

"Here," Julie hands me the key. "Your house, you open it."

I do, and as I unlock the door I am greeted by the smell of a place which has been locked up for months; warmed by the sun and freshly painted, it does not yet smell domestic – but it could. I step forward with trepidation into the hallway, opening the door to my left which reveals a large kitchen, its slate floor covered in a thin film of dust, and a fly buzzing in the sunlight which streams through the window. I go to let the fly out and I see what I would every day if I lived here. There is a small area just outside, made from warm creamy-coloured gravel, and a little bank of grass with an overgrown but colourful planter made from railway sleepers. Behind this is a paddock, and behind that the trees. I close the window and turn to face Julie.

"Shall we..?" I ask, pointing to the next door. We've already been in this building of course, but not with the same perspective as we have now. This could be my home, I think. Through the door off the kitchen is a small utility room, a toilet, and the back door, which leads into the little gravelled garden. I smile at Julie but say nothing, ducking past her and back through the kitchen, into the room on the other side of the hallway. This, too, is slightly dusty but instead of the slate tiles there are exposed floorboards. There is also a small fireplace, and a window at either end of the room. From one window, I can see across to the main block of buildings, while the other shares the same room as the kitchen.

"Come on!" I say, scooting past my friend once more and up the wooden staircase, my footsteps ringing out against the bare walls. My eyes feel tired from crying but my spirits are soaring. At the top of the staircase is a bathroom, with a bath, a shower and a sink. This is not what I am interested in. I turn left towards the main bedroom, above the kitchen. It is big, and has a large picture window to the rear, which displays a matching view to the kitchen window's, only elevated. There is no view of the sea, which I would dearly love, but does that really matter?

"I know what you're thinking," Julie says from the doorway. "Where's the sea?" How does she always know what I'm thinking? "Well, apparently in the winter, when the trees are bare, you can see it – just about. It's one of those sea glimpses," she laughs.

"Oh my god," my heart is beating so fast. It can't be. It's too good to be true, surely? I know there is so much to do from a practical perspective and my head is beginning to hurt from just beginning to contemplate what we would need to do. How would it work, if I live in a place but Julie and I share the business? Would I buy the house and if so, where would I then stand legally? Could I even afford to buy it? Or, would I rent or lease the house from the business? What if Julie and I fell out? Or if the business went drastically wrong? All of these thoughts are beginning to converge in my mind but at the same time it is also sinking in that this place really could be ours. And this little house I am standing in right now, this could be my home.

We go together into the other bedroom – smaller than the main room but cosy and peaceful – then I scoot back to the other bedroom again. I stand in the doorway, trying to picture my things here. It isn't difficult.

"I'll see you outside," Julie says. "I'm going over to the

main block."

"OK," I say, "I'll be right with you." I stay rooted to the spot for a few moments more, listening to Julie's footsteps down the stairs then away outside, until I can hear them no more and it is just me, and this quiet house, and the ever-so-gentle breeze which lets itself in through the open door, bringing with it the freshness of the summer air, and filling my heart with hope.

13

Now that our minds are made up, it feels like things should be going full steam ahead with Amethi but in reality it is a long, slow process. I still have to secure the funds; although the sale of the flat is nearly complete, I am still going to have to borrow against the business. Luke's offer remains but although I have now decided that if it comes to it, I will gratefully accept, I don't want to borrow from him unless I have to. I'm one hundred per cent behind this now and I will do everything I can to make sure that it goes ahead.

The owner of the property is away abroad, Sally tells us, but has accepted our offer in principle, which was exciting in itself. Now, though, is the nail-biting time, when we have to see people like solicitors, to draw up the agreement between Julie and me, which is made more complicated by the fact I will be living in one of the buildings. I still can't believe that; no matter how many times I say that is going to happen, it feels like it's just words, like it's not actually ever going to happen. We've decided it will be best if I lease the building from the business, to start with at least, with the option to buy it in five years' time. Five years! I'll be nearly thirty-six by then. Which, really, is nearly forty. There was a time when I'd assumed I'd be married with kids by that point in my life – and probably married by this point. But that was when I'd imagined myself taking the route which has been followed by so many women over the years, it's been carved deep into the landscape of life in this country. Grow up, get a job, get married, have kids, quit your job. Maybe return to work at a later date. This path has taken a slight divergence over more recent years in that women are no longer expected to rely on their men for the family income – I don't suppose that would even be possible for most people these days – but from what I can see, more often than not it is the woman who sacrifices career for family. And I'm not saying that's wrong, not for one minute. It must be kids before job, surely; but for me, and Julie, with no kids to think of (and for me, no partner to consider), we have decided to jump the barrier and go our own way.

What happens if Julie and Luke have kids? It could very easily happen. I know they want them. We will just have to deal with it if and when that happens. But I know Julie and I know the driving force she is; I've been driven by her so many times, and she'll find a way. I'm aware that it all sounds a bit too rosy, and too good to be true, but that is also what people said about us moving down to Cornwall. We made it work. We will make this work, too. If only we can get through the legal and financial wranglings.

Oh, and finish the renovation job; furnish the houses; get the marketing right. Not to mention me telling Bea I'm leaving the Sail Loft. But still, I can't do that; not yet, not until I know it's a done deal. And so likewise I cannot tell David I have somewhere new to live. I don't like keeping these things from my friends but I really don't want to rock the boat.

Besides that, there is Stefan's wedding to think of. Oh, and soon Sam will be back in town. Paul has been called away on business, off in Germany, so I haven't seen him since I've been up at Mum and Dad's. To be honest, it seems a bit of blessing with everything else which is going on. It also means that I'm enjoying some increasingly flirty text conversations with him, which provide a very welcome distraction and a splash of excitement.

***

The day before the wedding, I am just making sure that the rooms are all furnished beautifully for Stefan's family. I've put vases of fresh flowers in his mum's and aunt's rooms, at the top of the Sail Loft where there are the best views, and left little baskets with Cornish tea, biscuits and fudge on their dressing tables. I open the windows in his mum's room briefly, flooding the space with fresh air. Across the rooftops, the sea sparkles and oscillates splendidly under a deep blue sky. Windows shine and glimmer in the sunshine and the town hums with life. We are entering the heart of holiday season; schools are about to break up so the make-up of visitors is slightly different to how it will be in a few weeks' time. Older people; couples, and families with pre-school children. Making the most of the lower prices before the school year ends and the cost of a holiday triples.

I feel proud of this place and excited that Stefan's mum, who has yet to visit Cornwall, will get to see us at our best. I close the window and smile as I turn to give the room one last once-over. The bed covers are pulled tight and there is not a spot of dust to be seen.

I scurry down the stairs, enjoying the unusual peace of the hotel. From now until Monday, the only guests staying will be Stefan's and April's relatives. Jonathan is out collecting the cake, and Bea is at the florist's. It is just me alone in this beautiful building. I stop on the last flight of stairs, and take it in. Dust flurries in the thick chute of sunshine which slides through the staircase window. The grandfather clock in the hallway ticks on as it always does; steady and reliable. I sit on the thick carpet of the staircase and allow myself a moment to take it all in. To feel this place and all the people who have passed through here in its lifetime. It is sad to think of leaving, but now is not the time for sadness. I allow myself a few moments more then propel myself onwards. I will not stop again until the wedding is over.

Once Jonathan is back, the cake beautifully boxed up and carefully installed in the kitchen larder, I go through the various menus with him, from the breakfasts to the main wedding meal and the evening buffet. We run through lists, check and double-check the guests' names for allergies, or other dietary requirements; make sure we have food choices for each person. I can feel my energy levels rushing higher; adrenaline pumping through me as I build up to making this happen and not just happen but ensuring that it is an unforgettable day for April and Stefan. Jonathan, who is usually as enthusiastic as I am about these things, does not seem to be getting into it. He's with me, he's organised, and I have no doubt he's going to get all this done, but he seems subdued.

"Are you OK?" I ask, putting the paperwork down.

He doesn't really look at me; instead, he stands and goes to the coffee pot, plucking two mugs from the hooks and pouring us both a cup. "Yeah, well sort of… it's Lydia."

I thought it might be. I say nothing, waiting for him to

continue.

"I just… well, I'm finding it difficult, her being away. I mean, I'm happy that she's loving uni, of course I am. But if she's not studying, she's out with her new mates. Or I'm working. It's really difficult having any time for each other. The difference is, I don't think it's bothering her the way it bothers me."

"Ah," I say. "That is difficult. I think it's hard being the person left behind. You have the same life as before, only that one key person isn't in it. They've left a huge hole in their wake." I'm speaking from experience here, knowing exactly how I felt when Sam went away. Jonathan nods glumly, sitting in front of me and clasping his hands around his mug as if to warm them, only it's far from cold in here. "I suppose for Lydia especially, after having such responsibilities with her family, and her job here, not to mention her studies, she's just enjoying spreading her wings, having a bit of freedom."

"I know," Jonathan says. "I get it, I really do. And I don't resent her for it, at all. I remember what it was like being at uni… which may be part of the problem."

"Is she coming back today?" I ask gently.

"Yes, I'm going to meet her this afternoon."

"Maybe you can have a bit of time with her tonight?"

"I can't, it's the stag do."

"Of course." I'd forgotten that Stef's decided to go down the traditional route; a few drinks with his mates the night before the wedding. He wanted to wait for his cousins to be here, too. I'm well aware that this also means Sam is in town. I'll be so busy that I won't have a chance to bump into him, though, which at the moment is a bit of a relief. "Well maybe you'll have the chance to talk tomorrow. I mean, between cooking breakfasts, then

151

going to the wedding, then cooking the wedding dinner, and getting the buffet out. There'll be loads of time."

This at least gets a laugh.

"I'll make sure we have a chat," Jonathan says. "But the last thing I want to do is hold her back. Or become one of those people who's always whingeing at their partner, or about their partner."

"Well, the fact you're thinking like that means you won't become that person," I say. "And I'm sure Lydia will appreciate that."

"Thanks, Alice."

"It's no problem. Now come on, we've got a wedding to put on. And Bea will be back any minute so we'd better look busy."

***

I must have had just three hours' sleep the night before the wedding – all in the early morning. I remember drifting in and out of consciousness, lists running unbidden through my head, the early-rising bird population singing their tiny hearts out. By 5.03am I know I have to be up but, typically, it is only now that I feel I could have a really, really good sleep. If I just close my eyes for a moment…

NO. This won't do. There is a wedding to get up for, and I need to make sure it goes perfectly, or as close to perfectly as possible.

Over the two years Stef and I have worked together, I have really grown to love him. Initially, he was just a fantastic fellow manager and I knew from the outset that I could count on him. It didn't take long to discover his sense of humour, and his complete love for his family.

Having seen him, and April, go through all that stress when Annabel decided to show up early, I feel like they are especially deserving of a celebration today, with their beautiful children. Oh god, I feel like I could cry already and the day hasn't even begun.

Into the shower I go. Fully dressed and hair still wet, quietly, so as not to wake Julie and Luke, I tiptoe down the stairs and check my wedding clothes, which are zipped into a suit carrier and hanging from a doorway. A sneaky peek through the stairwell window on the way down has confirmed what I already knew. It is going to be a beautiful day. I close the front door gently behind me and stride breathlessly up the hill. Today I have to be hotel manager and wedding guest and I'm not sure quite how it's going to work but I'll just have to make sure it does.

The front door of the Sail Loft is wide open. Bea waves at me from behind a huge floral display on a pillar. She puts her finger to her lips. Stefan's mum, aunt, and the other guests are asleep upstairs. We have all this to do and we have to do it quietly. A quick peek into the dining room reveals the rest of the flowers. All cooped together for now on a long trestle table. There are apricot and cream roses, luscious green leaves and tiny, delicate white flowers. Amidst them all are my favourite flower, one which has always reminded me of Cornwall, somehow: the fiery crocosmia, alongside open, creamy amaryllis. The entire room smells amazing and as I wander along to the hallway I realise that the scent is drifting through the whole house. I push open the kitchen door.

"Hi Jon," I whisper. He is frantic already; preparing the breakfast trays for all the rooms. Lydia appears at the open doorway.

"Hello!" I say in a stage whisper, and I go to hug her. "Those trays look amazing."

Each is laid out with a tiny cream cloth, and a gleaming silver tea or coffee pot, alongside a cup and saucer, an equally shiny miniature milk jug and cutlery and a highly polished glass for fruit juice. Behind each tray sits a silver dome, ready to be placed over the scrambled eggs and salmon when it is time. Jonathan looks at them. "Lydia's sorted them all out," he says proudly, beaming at her.

At 8am, the trays go up to the bedrooms. Already, the Sail Loft is transformed. As well as the pillar in the hallway, there are garlands of flowers strung along the banisters, the dado rails and doorways, and the reception desk.

When Stef's mum comes downstairs, she exclaims, "Oh, this is beautiful. Stefan is very lucky to work here. I can see why he has stayed."

I smile. "You must miss him."

"I do, and I miss the children. I miss seeing them grow up. But he is happy, and April is a good girl. I must make sure I come to Cornwall more, that is all."

"Well, you're always welcome at the Sail Loft," I smile, wondering if I have the right to say this when if all goes according to plan I won't be here in a few months' time.

"Thank you, Alice. I have heard a lot about you from my son as well. He loves working with you."

"I love working with him," I say, wondering if I can feel any guiltier.

"Stefan and Alice are both wonderful," says Bea, appearing at my shoulder. "They've changed my life, which sounds a bit dramatic, but until they came along it was just me here, managing the place. Now I actually have time to myself occasionally! And they make such a great team. It really is like working with family."

Yes, it would appear that I could feel guiltier. Stefan's mum continues smiling. Does she ever stop? I can see where Stef gets his positive nature from. "I must go and make my hairdressing appointment," she says. "I'm just waiting for my sister. Where is she?"

"Shall I call her room?" I suggest, happy to break away from the compliments and resulting prickling of my conscience.

"Oh, would you? Thank you. She always was late, for everything. It drove our father mad!"

I ring up to the room and before long, Stefan's mum and aunty are trotting down the Sail Loft steps into town. I hear them exclaim at the bottom of the steps then a grinning Stefan jogs into view, his face adorned with lipstick smudges.

"Erm, I hope that's from your mum, not last night," I say.

"What?"

"Look in the mirror."

"Oh… urgh… Mum!" he exclaims, rubbing at his cheek. "Definitely not last night. It was just a quiet few drinks at the Mainbrace with the boys. Followed by a skinny-dip," he admits, smiling sheepishly.

"You didn't?" I laugh.

"I did… we all did. Did Jonny not say?"

"No!" I can't help wondering if Sam was also involved in this. "I'm just glad I wasn't taking a moonlit stroll along the beach last night."

"Ha! Yes, I think we gave an old man a bit of a shock."

"Bloody hell!" I tut, "Poor bloke. You had a good time, though?"

"The best… the best, Alice. Till today, anyway."

"And did you stay at home? You're not meant to see the bride on the wedding morning, you know."

"I did, but April didn't. She and the kids are at her parents'."

"That's OK, then."

"I meant to say, I hope you don't mind, but Sam stayed at mine."

"Did he?" I guess he must have been part of the naked shenanigans, then. I can't help smiling at the thought.

"Yes, is that OK?"

"Stefan, of course it is!"

"Phew! Now what can I do here?"

"Nothing!" I exclaim. "This is your wedding day. Go and have a look round, if you like; make sure you're happy with the seating plan. We still have to shift the tables and chairs around and dress them all, so don't stay too long. You'll only be in the way!"

He takes a quick peek into the dining room, then the bar, and examines the board with the table plan on it. "It's perfect," he says.

"Great, now get on your way. There is work to do here!"

"I'm so happy, Alice," he dances me around and kisses me on both cheeks. "I'll go out through the kitchen so I can say hello to Jon."

"Lydia's there, too," I say.

"Oh wonderful, I am so happy all my friends are here today."

I smile, and give him a hug. "Have the best day, Stefan. You really do deserve it."

***

156

From that point, it is all systems go. Somehow, while it seemed that there were bags of time, I am still rushing. Jonathan, too, is flat-out. It's hot in the kitchen and it's showing on his face. Lydia is obeying his orders, managing to let the impatience in his instructions go over her head. They do make a good team. I hope they can succeed where Sam and I failed.

Once every last detail is seen to and Bea and I have checked again and again, we lock up and head to our separate homes. Bea and Bob are living in a beautiful big house just round the bay so he is waiting in his car, ready to whisk her away and back to town. He's already suited and looking very dashing, too, his clean-shaven face making him appear younger than his usual stubble does. I wave at him.

"See you in an hour!" I say and scurry off down the hill.

Inside the house, I scoop up the suit carrier and carry it upstairs, unzipping it and laying the clothes carefully on the bed. I have chosen a pair of navy linen trousers and a dark orange silk top, which I will cover with a soft dark blue cardigan while I am back in work mode. The wedding itself is at the chapel on the top of the hill so practical and smart is the order of the day anyway, which fits perfectly with my dual role.

Showered and hair partially dried, I apply a little make-up and I look in the mirror. I bundle my hair into a bun and then fix in the tiny orange flower clips I ordered online. I slip on the dark blue sandals and turn around. I will do. I will have to. My phone vibrates in my bag. It's Paul.

Just wanted to say I hope it all goes well today. I wish I could be there. I'll be back on Wednesday and I'm hoping you're free. I've been thinking about you a lot and I can't wait to see you xx

The words send a little thrill along my spine. I may not have a partner today but it looks like I have a date to look forward to.

Thank you. Wednesday will be perfect. I'm doing nights until Tuesday as Stef and April are away on a short honeymoon xx

While I've got my phone out, I decide to text Sam.

Hi Sam, Stefan mentioned you're coming along later. It will be great to see you. P.S. I heard about the skinny dipping last night. Alice x

I add the kiss, though I'm not sure if I should. A text comes back immediately.

Yes, there was more than one full moon last night. See you later. S.

The brevity of the message, and the lack of a kiss, detract from the humour. I hate bloody text messages, and I hate the tendency I have to dissect them this way. It just feels like a message from a friend, though; and not even a very good friend. But maybe Sam didn't mean it to seem like that. I don't know. What I do know is that I can't spend time worrying about it now. I have a wedding to go to. Another buzz alerts me to a new message, just as I'm putting the phone in my bag. A small, brief hope that it is from Sam brushes my mind but I see immediately that it is Paul.

Hopefully you'll be ready for some fun on Wednesday, then. Can't wait xxx

This makes me smile again. I am looking forward to seeing Paul, and hopefully the thought will keep me buoyed up throughout the day and especially this evening. Also, I'll be working so I should be able to keep busy. I might hardly notice Sam's presence.

15

I arrive at the chapel and see Bea standing with Bob, David and Martin. I go to join them. There are twenty minutes or so until the wedding is due to happen so I'm feeling pretty pleased with myself about making such good time. Jonathan is slightly less so; I see his face, red and stressed-looking, appearing above the grass with just three minutes to go. Lydia is right behind him, looking typically beautiful and unflustered by the whole thing, her long hair streaming behind her in the wind.

It's beautiful up here; my favourite place in the world and where I always imagined I would like to get married. The town stretches away to one side and I can see the Sail Loft sitting grandly on the hill, alongside its equally regal neighbours. I can just make out the red flowers by the front steps. I feel proud looking at it, and thinking of it all dressed up for this wedding.

I grin at Jonathan but he grimaces at me and bends forwards slightly to catch his breath.

Stefan has been here for some time. He stands with his best man, his cousin Pedr, muttering quietly to him. Pedr laughs and puts his hand reassuringly on his arm. Surely Stefan can't be in any doubt as to today? He and April already have two children together; if that's not commitment then I'm not sure what is. His mum and aunty stand nearby; dressed in near-identical yellow-and-blue floral dresses. I wonder if they planned it this way or if they walked out of their rooms only to bump into each other, for a brief moment imagining they were looking in a mirror. The family resemblance is obvious between them, even down to their determined clutching of their skirts up here against the headwind. I'm glad that I wore trousers.

"Is this making you two nervous?" I ask Martin and David.

"Not one bit," says David, putting his arm around Martin's waist. "I can't wait."

Martin smiles. "He knows I'm not going to jilt him," he kisses David on the cheek.

"You're too scared to do that," David laughs.

I look around at the people gathered here: April's mum, holding Reuben by the hand, and April's sister, holding Annabel to her chest. Annabel, oblivious to it all, is asleep to the world, her innocent little mouth puckered open and cheeks rosy in the fresh air. She is wrapped in a shimmering white blanket. I smile at them and April's mum gives a little wave back. Then there is a general murmuring and faces all turn in the same direction. I follow their gaze, to see the wedding car draw into the car park at the bottom of the hill. The parking attendant pulls back the gate with a flourish and the car drives slowly up as far as it can, stopping at the widest point, where the path then narrows and nothing wider than a pushchair could make its way along.

The driver gets out, replete with cap and suit, and lets April's father out first. They walk together, laughing at something, to the other side of the car and the driver opens the door. There is a small collective, appreciative gasp as April appears, resplendent in a long, simple white dress, then stands tall and waves up at us all, a huge smile on her face.

"Mummy!" Reuben cries and April's mum grips hold of him to save him from flying down the hill.

Oh god, here we go again; I'm choked up at the sight of Stefan's beautiful wife-to-be, and from the absolute adoration Reuben has for his mum. His grandma crouches by him, pointing to April and her dad as they make their way up the hill.

The celebrant expertly positions us all to either side of the chapel door. There will be room inside only for her, the bride and groom, their children and immediate family.

As April arrives at the top of the path, Stefan steps lightly down to meet her, and kiss her.

"Hey, you're not married yet!" somebody calls out.

"I think it's safe to say that horse has bolted," David responds and everybody laughs, except for Reuben, who is now looking for a horse.

"Ladies and gentlemen," the celebrant begins, "because – luckily – it is such a beautiful day, this lovely couple have requested that their ceremony is all held in the open out here by our wonderful chapel…"

She is certainly going for it with the positivity but everybody is smiling. Clumps of bystanders stand respectfully back, delaying their own trip to the chapel for now. They, too, are smiling.

All around me, it seems, are happy couples. Bea and Bob; David and Martin; Jonathan and Lydia. Of course, that's not really the case; both Stef's mum and aunt have come alone, as have many of Stef's cousins, and April's sister. But despite the evidence to the contrary, I still feel like I stand out; the solitary loner.

Still, this day is not about me and I soon push those

futile, self-pitying thoughts aside. Instead, I watch and listen to the ceremony. See Stefan's eyes on April's; their absolute conviction in the words they say.

April's sister and one of Stefan's cousins read two short, beautiful passages. Both full of love and adoration, as Stefan and April clearly are for each other.

The ceremony over and the register signed, they kiss in the sunshine then walk hand-in-hand, laughing, down the hill to the car, Reuben – who has clearly used every ounce of self-restraint in staying with his grandma for the ceremony – clinging onto his mum's hand.

The three of them travel together to the Sail Loft and the rest of us make our way on foot, April's sister retrieving a pushchair from the parking attendant for Annabel, who has just woken up and looks surprised by her location and the number of faces crowding round her, smiling and saying silly words to make her smile.

"Sorry, Lydia, but I'm going to have to steal your boyfriend," I say, grabbing Jonathan's arm. "Come on! We've got to get there before the happy couple. The driver's meant to be doing the scenic route so we should have time."

"I'm coming with you," Lydia insists.

"Brill, thank you, Lydia – but can you at least have the decency to pretend the run's made you out of breath?"

"Of course, old thing."

"Mental note taken – I'll come back to you about that later," I threaten. "There's no time now, though."

We stride ahead, winding our way as politely as possible through the crowds of holiday-makers, who all seem to be going the opposite direction to us, reaching the little warren of steps which will take us up to the top of the town, if they don't kill us first.

"Can't talk anymore," I gasp, and I concentrate on climbing the steps, not even able to check on Jonathan's and Lydia's progress, my breathing laboured and my thighs complaining.

At the top, which I do eventually reach, I have to stop. Lydia is right behind me, Jonathan some way behind her. His face says it all while Lydia's is a sickeningly becoming shade of pink.

We wait for Jonathan to reach us, then wait for him to recover enough to walk to the hotel. Luckily, there is no sign yet of the wedding car. I go from room to room, throwing open the doors from the dining room and bar onto the veranda, while Jonathan preps the serving staff. There is a table just inside the door, adorned with more delicate flowers, holding flutes of champagne, and glasses of elderflower pressé.

I turn the sound system on. Stefan and April have painstakingly put together a soundtrack for the whole day. This first song is *Somewhere Beyond the Sea*, and it is just drawing to a close when the first of the guests begin to arrive. Predictably, it is the younger ones first, followed by Bea and Bob who are walking with Stef's mum and aunt, and April's parents. I take the pushchair from Annabel's sister and slide it out of sight behind the reception desk, just as the wedding car arrives and a huge cheer goes up.

From then on, it is manic. I am overseeing the serving staff, and making conversation with the guests, as well as checking with Stef and April regularly that all is going as it should. The canapés are devoured, and the champagne drunk, much more quickly than expected, but we open the bar and the guests seem content to drift out onto the veranda and take seats in the sunshine, which is a blessing as it gives me time to double check the dining arrangements.

"I feel so bad that you're working," says Stefan, finding me in the dining room and kissing me on the cheek. He looks so handsome in his shirt and tie; his jacket has long been cast aside due to the heat of the day.

"Don't be daft!" I say, taking his hands in mine. "If I can make this wedding day go well then that's the best present I can give you."

"Does that mean you haven't bought us anything?" he grins.

"Cheeky bugger! Now go and enjoy your day."

"I am enjoying it, Alice," he says earnestly. "So much."

"Good. You deserve it."

With Stefan gone, I go into the kitchen. Jonathan is beavering away, shouting instructions left, right and centre.

"What can I do, Alice?" asks Lydia.

"Do you know what you can do? You can go outside, get a glass of champagne, and relax. You are here by invite, not as a paid member of staff. And I bet there's not much champagne to be had at uni."

"No, that's true," she admits. "But I think I'd rather stay in here. I don't really know anyone very well out there, apart from Stef."

This is a little glimpse of the old Lydia. I see Jonathan turn briefly round at these words and I smile at him. He smiles back. I really hope this means that all is well between them again. Let them be the exception to the rule and make their relationship work.

"OK, then follow me," I say to Lydia. "Let's just double-check the seating plan and the places match up, and then perhaps we should think about getting everybody seated... does that work for you, Jonathan?"

"Yep, I think so... it's now or never," he says grimly.

Happily, the meal goes without a hitch. The speeches go on for a while, and baby Annabel has clearly had enough. She begins to cry, while Reuben goes from table to table, procuring the little bags of wedding favours which are scattered around. Ties are undone; top buttons, too. In some cases, even the top buttons of trousers, to take the strain of the three-course banquet which Jonathan's pulled off.

There are glasses and coffee cups to be collected, and a myriad of sparkling chocolate-mint wrappers which glitter on the tables. I grab a bottle and bang a spoon against it, ensuring everybody's attention before I've had a chance to doubt myself.

"Ladies and gentlemen, I trust you've all enjoyed your fabulous dinner from the Sail Loft's very own chef, Jonathan." There are cheers and clapping around the room. "Now, I'd be very grateful if you could make your way out onto the veranda, where you can enjoy the beautiful view while we make this room ready for the party! Feel free to take out your wine glasses and any bottles which still have anything left." More cheering. "But before you do so can you please raise your glasses one more time for my wonderful colleague and friend Stefan and his equally wonderful wife April."

I smile from ear-to-ear as the room stands as one, raising their glasses and clinking them together. "To Stefan and April!"

Happily, they then make their way good-naturedly outside and we are able to transform the room from dining room to disco. Meanwhile, the kitchen is awash with suds and ringing with the sounds of the dishwasher.

Glasses are being polished and replaced behind the bar. I make sure everybody has a break and something to eat before it all goes crazy again. Jonathan, however, refuses. "There isn't time!" he says, and I have to leave that decision to him. He enlists Lydia's help and between them they finish the huge bowls of salad, unwrap the cheeses and then cover them with muslins, and lay out all the trays of cold meats and vegetables, loosen the lids of chutneys and pickles. It will be like one giant Ploughman's Lunch, laid out in the bar area. I haven't had a chance to eat, and it's making my mouth water.

"Here," Lydia says, pulling a plate from the oven. "We saved you this." She also pours me a glass of champagne. "One won't hurt," she says. I take both gratefully. "You are amazing. I'm going to sneak off to the office for ten minutes, if that's OK."

"Of course! I'll come and get you if necessary."

"Thank you." I back out of the kitchen door and head into the office. My mind is awhirl and the peace of the wood-panelled room is very welcome. This is a special day and I'm just happy it's gone according to plan so far. It's hard, trying to pull this off at the Sail Loft, which is not built for big events. Christmas and New Year are difficult enough. I think of Amethi; the purpose-built hall, and the grounds. As I'm imagining all the things we could do there, the door opens and in comes Bea. I start suddenly and I must look guilty.

"You are allowed a break!" she laughs.

"Ha, I know. Thank you," I say, wondering if betrayal is written all over my face.

"Lydia said I'd find you in here. And I don't want to take too much of your quiet time. I just wanted to say thank you and tell you what an amazing job you're

167

doing. I don't know what I'd do without you, Alice."

If I didn't look guilty before, I definitely should do now.

"And I also wanted to let you know that Sam is out there." My heart isn't sure whether to skip or sink. "With David and Martin."

I thank my lucky stars that I'm working. I feel really awkward still about what happened that night with Paul turning up as he did. Sam seems fine but I know that if it had been the other way around; I'd been wanting to help him then some other girl turned up and sorted it all out, my nose would be put well and truly out of joint.

I manage to avoid the social side of things for as long as I can but once the buffet is eaten and cleared away, and the wedding disco in full swing, there really isn't a lot to do. Deep inside the kitchen four pairs of hands are clearing and cleaning, but even Jonathan isn't there anymore. He and Lydia are on the dance floor together, laughing and holding each other tightly. I smile at the sight then see Sam's eyes on me. He smiles slightly uncertainly. I go over.

"It looks like it's been a great day," he says, and gestures to the door. "Do you fancy a drink out here?"

"I'd love one," I admit and I follow him to a table, where an open bottle of red wine sits, along with a half-full glass and a clean empty one.

"I saved you a glass," he says.

"That's... that's really nice of you." I'm so tired that this small act of kindness could reduce me to tears. He pulls out a chair for me to sit down, and then pours me a glass of wine.

"Cheers," he clinks his own glass against mine.

"Cheers," I echo.

Darkness has crept in whilst I've been inside. The solar lights along the stone balustrade have come to life and the town is peppered with brightly-lit windows and streetlamps. Even the sea is twinkling, fishing boats biding their time till the tide is high enough for them to come home.

"How's your mum, Alice?"

"She's fine, thanks. Much better now."

"That must have been scary," he says.

"It was. It was awful. But by the time I got there I'd heard from Dad so I knew she was probably out of the woods. I really appreciated your help you know, Sam."

I feel like we are both skirting round the subject of Paul. I almost bring it up but decide to slide onto another, slightly safer, topic.

"Julie and Luke's turn soon," I say, gesturing to the party going on inside the normally calm dining room. Bob appears to be swinging a delighted Bea around the room while Stef's mum and aunt prove they're pretty nifty movers and David and Martin smooch near the window.

"Yep," he says.

"Have you been working on your best man speech?"

"Nah! There's months yet!"

"It'll come round quickly," I say.

"I guess so."

"And is this it now, are you back from Wales?"

"I am – I don't have to go back till September next year."

"I heard you got the placement you wanted."

"Yep!" he beams proudly. "Cornwall Marine Trust took me on."

"I bet Sophie's over the moon, too."

169

"Yeah, although she's not so bothered about hanging out with her old dad these days! She's loving high school, got herself a whole new bunch of mates. She was invited tonight but she didn't want to come."

"That's a shame, I was hoping to see her."

"She'd love to see you, too."

"And is Kate OK?" I hate this slightly stilted way of conversation but it's the best I can do.

"Yep, she's happy. Got more hours now, at the Pilates place. Still with Isaac, too."

"Well, that's got to be a good thing as well." So it seems that of all of us, it's just me and Sam that are single. Well, that is assuming that he hasn't met anybody. I don't feel I can ask him that, though. And I don't think I want to know the answer. It's strange to think he's back here, for a whole year – in fact, more than a year. What will it be like, bumping into him around town? I suppose his work's going to take him all over the county, though – and then of course if Julie and I pull the whole Amethi thing off, I won't be living in town anymore anyway. I look out towards the sea again. I will miss being right next to it but I know I won't be far away.

"Do you fancy a dance?" he asks.

"Yeah, go on then!" I take a swig of my wine and stand up. I think for a moment that he's going to take my hand but instead he gestures towards the open door. I walk into the Sail Loft, aware that Sam is right behind me. I feel his presence at my back. Stefan and April cheer us as we make our way onto the dance floor and we are soon engulfed in a group of friends, dancing to *Uptown Funk*. I smile at Sam and he grins at me and I think we are going to be alright.

Later, as the guests disperse and the hotel reverts to its usual calm self, ghosts of past occupants creeping slowly back along the stairwells and corridors, checking that the madness has passed and it's safe to return, I chat to Lydia as we pull the dining room back to its previous order, removing flowers from tables and placing stray glasses on trays to be returned to the kitchen.

Sam has long since gone, kissing me on the cheek and congratulating Stefan and April before disappearing into the night. I wanted to follow him. I wanted to explain to him about Paul; not that there is much to explain, but I still feel there are things left unspoken which need to be said.

I'm at work, though, and at a wedding. I can't just drop everything. Instead, I turned back towards the dining room and sat with Stefan's mum for a while. I ended up telling her about my mum, and the heart attack, and found I was very close to tears.

"There, there," she said, putting a kind hand on mine. "It's a horrible time. But you are a good daughter and your mum is lucky. Stefan, too, having you to work with."

If only he knew I was going to desert him.

The wine, and the day, had taken their toll on me. Those tightly wound emotions were threatening to spring loose. I made my excuses and stood up. Gradually, the guests took their leave. Reuben and Annabel had been spirited away to April's parents' house at about 10pm. Stefan and April left for their hotel not much later. I can't say I blame them; I know neither Annabel nor Reuben sleep well.

"We just want an unbroken night's sleep!" April had laughed. "So much for a romantic wedding night."

"Ah, but it is romantic, isn't it? Just you and Stef together. No interruptions," I said.

"I suppose it is. Thank you, Alice. I was so scared there'd be a disaster today but it's all gone so well and I couldn't have asked for anything better. Thank you so much."

April welled up and this seemed to give me the perfect opportunity to allow a few of my own tears a little freedom. I hugged her tightly. "It really has been my pleasure. I love you and Stef, you know, I really do."

"We love you too!" she sobbed, then we both found ourselves enveloped in a huge Stefan-hug, which sent the tears fleeing, replaced by laughter.

I send Jonathan and Lydia off just after midnight, as Jonathan at least will be back here in the morning, cooking breakfasts. Bea and Bob leave next and I go round the downstairs rooms, drinking in the quiet and calm and switching lights off. Aside from the excess of flowers, and the boxes of glasses neatly packed away in the kitchen, it is like nothing out of the ordinary has gone on here.

Taking a deep breath, I walk out of the front door. I too need to be back here early in the morning. At the bottom of the steps is a figure. I almost gasp when I realise it's Sam.

"Thought I'd walk you home," he says.

"How long have you been waiting?"

"Oh, only an hour or so. Had to hide in the shadows so David didn't spot me or he'd be jumping to all sorts of conclusions."

What kind of conclusions? I want to ask but I'm too shy.

"You must be shattered," he says.

172

"Like you wouldn't believe." We start to make our way down the hill.

"And you're back here in the morning?"

"Yep."

I am so happy he's waited for me. I'm running all sorts of scenarios round in my mind. A thought of Paul flits through but I know that, while I like him, and I'm excited by his interest in me, if I am honest I'd drop it all for Sam.

Our arms brush against each other.

"Alice," he says.

"Yes?"

"There's something I've got to tell you."

I stop, my heart beating fast. He stops, too. Looks at me. I look up at him into those eyes. His face is so familiar. I've seen it in my dreams for years.

"I've been seeing somebody, back in Wales."

16

Shit. I try to smile. I falter.

"Oh. Right. Somebody on your course?"

"Yes."

I think fast. I bet she's young and gorgeous, and she's studying marine biology too, so they share the same passions. They'll be perfect for each other. I try to will back the lump in my throat.

"It's nothing serious, Alice. And now I'm back here, anyway. And she's up in Scotland." That much, at least, is a relief.

"But are you still seeing her…?"

"I'm… I suppose so. I don't know. I might go and visit her. I want to see some of the coast up that way, anyway."

"OK. Well, thanks for telling me."

We've reached the top of my street so I can justify my next move, which is thanking him for walking me back then dashing off down to the house as fast as I can.

"Alice…" I think I hear him calling me but I don't look back. I try to fit the key into the lock but it won't go in. On my third attempt, it does, and I let myself into the dark house. Julie must be at Luke's. It's just as well really because once I've shut the door I collapse, back to the wall, onto the floor, and I sob, long and hard.

What right do I have to be upset, though? We're not

together any longer. And I've been seeing someone, too. Although, having said that, we've really only had one date – if you don't count the drive up to see Mum in hospital, and I don't. When I finally pick myself up, I take a good, long look in the hallway mirror.

It's over, I tell myself. *What Sam and I had is over and it's time to move on.*

I crawl into my bed, groaning as I set my alarm for just three hours' time. Bea and Bob are staying at the Sail Loft tonight and Bea had offered to be up for the guests but I said no; she's paying me to be the manager. And I really pushed for Stefan and April to be able to hold their wedding at the hotel. I feel responsible.

With a heavy heart, I close my sore eyes, but it's some time before I get to sleep. The day's events appear to carousel around my mind and I can't help a small smile at the thought of Stef and April. All in all, it was a fantastic day and I know I should feel proud. It's just that niggling thought of Sam with somebody else which won't let me rest.

***

Fortunately for me, the rest of the week keeps me on my toes. Even by Wednesday, the day I'm meant to be going out with Paul, my world has changed, but mostly in a good way.

Monday sees a major milestone. The first I know of it is from a call on the hotel phone.

"Hello, Sail Loft?" I answer in my best telephone voice. In reality I am still jaded from the lack of sleep after the wedding but whoever's on the phone doesn't need to know that.

"Alice!" I'd recognise Julie's voice anywhere. "I tried your mobile but you're not answering. Why aren't you answering?"

She sounds breathless and excited. I laugh, "You know I have it on silent at work. I pull it from the desk drawer. "Twelve calls? Are they all from you?"

"Yes, yes they are because… we've been accepted. It's official. Sally rang to say the owner's back from wherever they've been and has spent the last couple of days going through everything with their solicitor, and we're good to go."

"Oh, my…" I feel breathless, like my feet have been swept from under me. It's real, what Julie and I are going to do. "Shit!"

"I know!" Julie laughs. "What time are you finishing tonight? We need to celebrate!"

"I'm not," I remind her. "I'm stuck here now until Wednesday."

"Wednesday night, then."

"Ah, I, erm, have a date with Paul." I rush these last few words.

"Do you? That's brilliant. Although, I have a bottle of champagne in my hands and I need to drink it with you."

"OK, OK, let me think… maybe you could come up here later. Maybe I can have a glass."

"That's not going to cut it, and you know it! Thursday night, lady, no excuses."

"I can't wait till then!"

"I know, don't worry. And we've got some paperwork to go through ourselves before then as well. I can bring it up to the Sail Loft tonight anyway, maybe we could have a very sedate celebration and get through the boring stuff then go for it on Thursday!"

"OK," I laugh. "It's a deal. Oh, but if Bea's about, be cautious, will you? I haven't told her about this yet."

"You're going to have to now."

"I know," I sigh but despite a slight feeling of trepidation at the thought of telling Bea, I am so excited. And nervous. And scared. My stomach feels pinched in on itself. I'm glad I've got work as a distraction. Just as I'm putting my phone away, it buzzes. It's Paul.

Just checking we're still on for Wednesday. I've booked us a table somewhere nice. I hope that's OK and not too presumptuous xx

Great. Something else to be nervous about. But actually, the words make me smile and I quickly reply,

Not presumptuous at all. Do I have to get dressed up? X

Wear whatever you feel comfortable in. You'll look gorgeous whatever you're wearing xx

I am really not used to this kind of thing. Is he too smooth for me? Or just really nice? I must admit, his words make me feel good. Perhaps this is just what I need.

Pizza Hut, then? I'll make sure I'm wearing my best tracksuit x

And my words still stand. You'd still look gorgeous xx

Be still, my beating heart.

When Julie comes round that evening, thankfully Bea and Bob are back at their own place and, with most of Stef's relatives returned to Sweden, it's just his mum and aunt at the hotel for the night, and they've gone out to the theatre. We've a full house again tomorrow so I need to make the most of this quiet time.

Julie and I sit at an outside table, a pile of papers in front of us. We smile at each other, the smile becoming a grin, then a full-on cackle of laughter as we allow what is happening to properly sink in, and feel real.

"I can't believe it," I say.

"Nor me!"

"You know I'm going to have to take you and Luke up on that offer, until I can get things straightened with the bank?"

"Yes, that's fine. You know it's fine."

"I still feel weird about it."

"Just treat Luke as a bank. That's wrong, I don't mean it that way – but this is a loan as it would be from a bank or anybody else."

"OK." I don't feel completely happy about it but with the money from my flat, I've a good deposit to contribute, and I've made peace with the fact that I have to do something uncomfortable in order to do something else which I hope is going to be amazing.

Julie has brought the champagne anyway and we end up drinking it all. Its cold, fruity bubbles remind me of Stef's wedding on Saturday. How much has changed since then!

"Sam told me he's been seeing somebody," I say out of nowhere. Julie looks genuinely surprised.

"Has he? That's the first I've heard of it. How do you feel?"

"I don't know now. On Saturday, when he told me – well, the early hours of Sunday, I suppose, I was shattered by it. But I guess I was worn out from the wedding and everything anyway," I finish lamely.

"You and I both know it's more than that, Alice. But yeah, being knackered probably didn't help matters! I'm sorry. Did he tell you anything about her?"

"Yeah, well not much," I admit. "He said it was nothing serious. And she's in Scotland now."

"There you are, then. And he's back here. He'll be falling at your feet in no time."

Her words remind me of the time I slithered out of the undergrowth, twisting my ankle, right into his path. It seems a lifetime ago but it is just two years since then.

"No, it's OK. I know I have to move on. Shit, I had moved on! Although it was easier when he was up in Wales, I must admit. But it's years now, Julie – twelve years since I met him and eighteen months since we split up last time. I have to accept it."

Julie's looking at me, not entirely convinced, but she smiles. "And you do have that date with sexy Paul on Wednesday."

"I do." I can't help but smile back. "He is sexy, isn't he?"

"Er, yeah!"

God knows what is in store for me with Paul. He's a world away from anyone I've dated before. I think of Geoff, who I went out with soon after my first relationship with Sam. He liked to take me out; buy me things, but he also liked to control me. I am not getting that impression from Paul, though. I think he just likes taking me out because, I suppose, he can. And he's older so maybe it's a generational thing as well. I'm not one of those women who expects to be treated; doors to be opened for me, but I must admit it's quite a nice thought and a very pleasant break from everything else which is going on in my life.

"Anyway," I say, "we also need to sort out your hen do, and you need to fill me in on all your wedding preparations."

"I don't know what to do!" Julie exclaims. "I don't know if I really want a hen do. Luke's having his stag in London, so they'll spend hundreds of pounds, maybe thousands, and have an amazing time. But, I know this isn't really me, I just don't feel like that."

"Well, you don't have to have one."

"I know. And I think what I'd really, really like to do is just have a night away with you, my bestest friend."

"Really?" I ask, touched beyond words by this. Julie is far more of a party animal than I am.

"Really. A great hotel – great food, a pool and a spa. In the next three months, I've got to move house, finish planning the wedding, get things going here," she gestures to the paperwork. "Oh, and actually get married! I think a relaxing night away with you will be the best thing ever."

"You don't think we'll be sick of each other, with all the work stuff?"

"Probably!" she laughs. "But I think that makes it even more important that we take time to do something fun together, away from all this. I know our friendship can withstand anything but there are going to be times when we're pissed off with each other. Or just stressed about something that's happened. We need to promise now that whatever happens with Amethi, our friendship comes first."

"Friendship first," I agree, knocking my glass gently against hers. We sip our drinks then sink into silence for a while, gazing at the view which has become so familiar. Contemplating the future.

17

In the morning, after breakfast, I sit with Stefan's mum and aunty for a while.

"Were you born in Cornwall?" Astrid – Stefan's mum – asks me. She is small and slightly plump, with sparkling blue-grey eyes. Her sister, Ingrid, has a matching pair. In fact, the two of them are so alike they could be twins.

"No, I wasn't. But for some reason I've always felt at home here. I used to come on holiday with my parents and sometimes my cousins, when I was little. Then I spent a few months down here before I started university, with my friend Julie."

"Oh yes, Julie," Astrid says. "She was the one here last night? She is beautiful."

"She is," I agree. I've long since got over the fact that it's my friend's looks people will always comment on. I remember Julie at school, with braces and geeky glasses. Now she is tall and striking and the glasses have been replaced by contact lenses.

"But so are you, Alice," Astrid says but I feel she is just being kind. I smile. "You're a beautiful person," she finishes. Ah yes, the 'beautiful person' thing. 'You've got a great personality'. These are the things I used to hear when I was growing up and, nine times out of ten, the boys I would like were only interested in Julie.

"Thanks, Astrid," I smile.

"No, no – I mean you are beautiful inside and out.

Stefan has told us so much about you. He is very much a fan of yours."

"And I am of his," I say. "But now, I must get on."

I'm trying to calm my nerves; trying to find things to do until Bea arrives. I have no idea what she is going to say. Will she be delighted for me, or just feel I am letting her down? Us businesswomen really should stick together, and it's not like Julie and I will be Bea's competitors; the people we're hoping to attract won't be the same people considering the Sail Loft.

I pop into the kitchen to say hi to Jonathan.

"Things seemed good between you and Lydia," I suggest.

"Yeah, we actually had a really great weekend. Despite having about two hours' sleep. I think the romance of the wedding helped."

"She was a great help here," I say.

"I know, she was amazing, wasn't she?" I notice Jonathan can't help smiling with pride. "Will she be able to work here in the holidays?"

"I… I should think so. Erm…" The question has thrown me. The next holidays are Christmas and New Year. Bea, Stef and I have been making plans to ensure this is the biggest and best yet. It will follow directly on from David's and Martin's wedding, which is 22nd December. Only, I guess I'll need to be concentrating on Amethi by then; Julie and I hope to have the place up and running for the first guests early in the new year.

Breathe, I tell myself, as I have to do increasingly often these days. *Just breathe.* My worries over where I am going to live have been replaced by how the hell Julie and I are going to get our business going, and what if nobody wants to stay, or what if people come and they hate it?

Breathe.

I go into the office and I call my mum. She's at work.

"Can you talk?" I ask her.

"Yes, I've got a few minutes. It's hard work, this part-time thing, though; I feel like I'm trying to do as much as ever, in half the hours."

It sounds like Mum could do with breathing, too. "Mum, they're not working you too hard, are they?"

"No, they're not. They are being great. It's me that's the problem."

"You are a bit all-or-nothing," I say. "You can't be the same as before, though, Mum. You're not old, but you've been ill. You need to make sure it doesn't happen again. I'm so glad you're coming down here this week. A bit of Cornish sunshine should help you relax a bit."

"I know, we can't wait. Your dad's excited, you know what he's like! But I'm guessing you're not phoning to give me a lecture. Well, I hope not, anyway."

"No," I laugh. "No, I just wanted to tell you, everything's going through with Amethi."

"That is wonderful!" she says. "Have you told Bea yet?"

She always knows. "No, I'm waiting for her to come in. I'm going to tell her today."

As if she is also psychic, at that very moment I hear the front door open and Bea's familiar footsteps.

"She's here," I hiss. "I've got to go."

"OK, well good luck. And remember, you are perfectly within your rights to do this."

"I know. Thank you, Mum."

I sit back in the chair, then lean forward on the desk, whizzing the mouse around the mouse pad until the

184

screen comes to life. The door to the office opens.

"Hi, Alice," Bea smiles widely. "How are you? Not too shattered, I hope?"

"No, I'm fine thanks, Bea. It was a bonus being quiet last night – I got a few hours' sleep and feel a bit more normal this morning."

"Are Ingrid and Astrid enjoying their stay?"

"Yes; they seem to be, anyway."

"And has David rung you?"

"Erm, no. Should he have?"

"Well, he said he was going to."

"Is he OK?"

"Yes, he's fine, Alice. He was meant to let you know, though, he's given the go-ahead to get the house on the market. Sorry to just drop it on you like this. David was meant to ring you last night."

"Oh," I say. "OK." *Shit, shit, shit, I have to do it now. Just do it, Alice.* "Actually, Bea, I have something to tell you, too."

"Oh?" She looks up from the pile of post she's been flicking through.

"It's… there's no easy way to say this." Her face is concerned. I have to get the words out now. "I think I'm going to have to hand in my notice."

"What?" Shock is written all over her face but she is already at work to try and smooth it over, regain her composure. "Not because David's selling the house?"

"No!" I say quickly. "Nothing like that. It's – well, it's a long story."

"I'm listening."

"In a nutshell, Julie and I are going into business together. We want to start running some holiday lets."

"Oh," she looks relieved, "well, that doesn't mean you

have to leave here, you know. You could get somebody to manage them on your behalf."

"But it's a little more than holiday lets," I say, and I explain our idea.

"I see," she says, but nothing more.

"What do you think? I mean, you don't think it's going into competition with you, do you? And I hope you know how much I'll miss this place. And you, and Jon, and Stef. And how grateful I am to you…"

I am aware I am babbling. I need to stop.

"Have you found a place yet?" she asks.

"Er, yes, we have. It's not far from town, but just out at the edge of the moors."

"Right, and have you put in an offer yet?"

"Yes, it's… it's been accepted."

"Bloody hell, you two move fast," she says and I am still none the wiser as to her feelings on the matter.

"What do you think?" I ask.

"I think, it's a great idea in principle. It's going to be a lot of work."

"I know. We've been working it all out. We've got a business plan, and funding. And we know roughly what we want to do for marketing. And the best thing of all is that there's a place for me to live there."

"Do you really want to do that?" she asks.

"Live on site? Well, I wasn't sure at first, but it is a lovely place. And, well, you did it here, didn't you?"

"Yes, for twelve years. And this place became my life. I didn't have one relationship in all that time, you know."

Bea has said to me before that she didn't want a relationship until she met Bob; that her ex-husband had messed her up and she'd thrown herself into work instead. But she's also said to me that she had a few flings

186

and that she ended things before they could become anything like relationships. Still, I am the one fighting for some kind of forgiveness here, so I swallow these thoughts.

"I know," I think the best thing to do for the time being is to bow to her greater knowledge and experience. "But that doesn't mean it will be the same for me."

She smiles, as though she knows better. "And what about your friendship with Julie? What if it all goes wrong, or she doesn't pull her weight. I know how flighty she can be."

Now I'm feeling annoyed. "Well, she did a great job when she worked here, and you must have thought so too or else why did you let her come back to work for you?"

"Yes, well," says Bea, clearly unable to come up with a suitable answer. "OK. You've obviously made your mind up. You'd better put it in writing, with a date, and you can help me look for another manager."

She is obviously hurt, but her comment about Julie has put my back up. "Fine, I'll get that sorted sometime today. And I'll work on an advert for you."

"No, don't bother. I'll do that. I know what I'm looking for. In fact, I'll get started now. Can I have my desk back, please?"

And that's it. I log out of the computer, my cheeks burning and my mind whizzing. I hadn't really expected it to go like this. I thought she might be upset but I thought she might also be interested, and supportive. She's ambitious and hard-working, and so am I. She's always said we are alike. Surely she should be happy for me that I'm taking the initiative and acting on my ambitions.

I decide to give her some space and I take a tour of the

hotel, checking all the vacant rooms are ready for today's influx of guests and allowing the hot tears to spill onto my still-burning cheeks.

When I come downstairs, Jonathan steps out of the kitchen. "What's up with Bea?" he asks. "She came in here just before she left. She seemed pretty pissed off about something."

"She's gone?" I ask. I am at once relieved and upset that she didn't bother to say bye to me.

"Yep, said she'll be back later in the week. That seemed weird, she's normally in every day, isn't she? Are her and Bob OK?"

"As far as I know. Look, have you got time for a coffee?"

"Yeah, sure. What's going on?" He looks worried. "We're doing OK, aren't we? The business, I mean."

"Yes, of course. It's nothing like that. Look, let's get a coffee and take it outside. I've got something to tell you."

***

Luckily, Jonathan took it much better than Bea.

"Well, that's great," he'd said. "So exciting! I wish I could come with you. I don't suppose you need a chef...?"

"I think Julie's got that covered," I laughed, "but who knows, in the future? Still, I don't think Bea would be too happy if I nick her chef as well!"

"I can't pretend I won't miss you. But you can't stay here forever."

"Thank you, Jonathan." We'd sat together on the gravel path just outside the kitchen door, the sun still finding its way through the myriad of thick greenery to

188

dapple our faces. This whole week has been so hot, the precious shade around this side of the Sail Loft is a blessing at times.

Stef, too, takes the news pretty well. I sit in the office with him and share the news. I am back in Bea's leather office chair but I no longer feel relaxed in it. Like she is going to burst through the door any minute and oust me from her seat.

"Ah, Alice, I always knew you were destined for better things."

"Not better," I say. "Different."

"Well, you can't stay here forever," he says, his words echoing Jonathan's. I only wish Bea felt the same. I haven't heard from her since yesterday, although I've had to contact her about a couple of work things. I have emailed her, and left a voicemail. She's going to have to speak to me soon. Even if it's only to accept my resignation. The one good thing about all of this is that I haven't had much time to dwell on Sam and his possible new girlfriend. And today I have a reason to feel excited, too. I've got a date with Paul and I am determined to enjoy it.

With the handover complete, I say my goodbyes and I head off into the balmy summer afternoon, skipping around groups of dawdling tourists. I have no time to dawdle. I must get ready. Paul is picking me up at seven and I do not want to be late.

This time, I've selected my clothes without any help from Julie. I must be growing up. It's a proper, grown-up restaurant too, by the sound of things. I'd texted Paul earlier:

Without sounding too much like a girl, what should I wear tonight? X

His response was quick:

I've got to be honest, one of the things I like about you is that you're a girl. I would be hoping for an entirely different end to the evening if you weren't. xx

He gets my heart racing, I must admit. And it feels like he is the perfect antidote to Sam. I know I have to let that go now. Maybe it's true what some say, about other people having a role in your life – perhaps Sam and I being together was meant to be the catalyst to come down here. To leave the dreary comfort of the World of Stationery and throw the dice again.

Not that I think Sam's purpose on this earth is to enable me. Maybe I helped him get to where he is now; I hope I supported him in his decision to leave Cornwall for his studies. I certainly tried to. I can't deny I miss him, and I miss Sophie, too. I kind of… nearly… miss Kate as well. She was a pain in the arse, but as it turned out she was far less so than she seemed. I'm quite fond of her, really.

But what am I doing, dwelling on the past? I need to shower and slip into the dress I've chosen; it's not new but like all my dresses it has barely been worn. Once I'm looking in the mirror, I think I made the right choice. It's a deep, satin-shiny blue, with straps just wide enough to conceal those of my bra. I pair it with some very, very slightly heeled dark blue sandals, and pull on the cardigan I had for Stef's wedding. Too much blue? I grab a red bag, and pull some colourful chunky beads from my drawer. There, a dash of colour, and not a moment too soon as I hear the noisy engine of Paul's flash car outside, and the firm sound of the handbrake.

He is at the door, hand ready to ring the bell, but I am too quick.

"Hello!" I say, keen to get going, to skip the nerves before they hit me.

"You look gorgeous," he says, his eyes running over me. I feel self-conscious, very aware of this appraisal.

He looks pretty good himself, in a dark green shirt, open at the throat, but only by a couple of buttons, and a pair of probably very expensive jeans. His shoes are brown, shiny and pointy – never shoes I would choose for a man, and I must admit I'd never have envisaged choosing a man with those shoes, but here he is, and I'm happy to see him.

"Are you ready?" he asks, opening the passenger door and gesturing towards the seat with a flourish. The roof is down again and when he slides into the car he passes me the blanket from the back seat.

"You've got this down to a T," I say, then, "What does that even mean? 'Down to a T', I mean. Sorry, I'm babbling. It's been a long day."

He just smiles at me. "Well, hopefully I can help take your mind off it. You can sit back and enjoy the ride."

He starts up the engine and the car exclaims joyously. We can't go fast through the town streets but people step back, out of the way, to let us through. There are a lot of glances at the car, and at us, and I find myself wishing that we could get out of town faster. From Bea's warning words, I know people will talk if they see me out with Paul.

"Who gives a shit?" he laughs when I voice this concern to him.

"You've got a point," I have to agree, and I love his attitude. I just wish I could share it.

Soon enough, though, we are out of the tiny, twisty streets, and off over the dusty moorland roads, heading to the other side of the county, which is not as far as it sounds. It's a noisy ride again so we don't speak much. It's the perfect chance to sit back and let the rush of air blast the negativity away. With each twist of the road, I cast something else aside. Bea's coldness. Sam's new girlfriend. Concern about starting a business. Worries about Mum. Tonight, I'm out with Paul and I'm going to bloody well enjoy it.

The sun is still high in the sky when we draw in through some grand, unmarked gates.

"What is this place?" I ask.

"It's a private members' club," he admits, half-sheepish and half-proud. "I just thought, I belong to this place and I never use it. There's a health club, a golf course, a pool, guest rooms…" He leaves that thought there for a moment before continuing. "Also, of course, a restaurant. One of the best chefs in the county, too. Your friend Julie excluded, of course."

"Ha! Too right."

He pulls the car across the crunchy gravel, smoothly tucking it in next to what I think must be a Bentley, though I am no expert.

"Hang on," he says, as I go to open the door. He's quick to get out, and is round at my side, letting me out of the car and holding his hand out to me. He gives a half-wave to an older gent, who is putting some golf clubs in the boot of his car. I feel very out of place but I take a deep breath.

"Shall we?" Paul asks, and he keeps hold of my hand as we walk together towards this grand old mansion, built of huge creamy bricks, two sphynx-like figures flanking the steps up to the doorway. Before we even get there, the thick oak doors are pulled back on either side.

"Good evening, sir… madam," an older man who I can only describe as a butler smiles at us.

I pull the sleeves of my cardigan over my hands. I feel like I should be wearing evening dress. But Paul is wearing jeans, of course. I am just going to have to bluff this one out.

"Thank you," I smile, and Paul and I walk through a huge room, fires burning at either end despite the sheer heat of the day, and on towards some more doors, which are open onto the dining room.

"Paul Winters," he says to the lady who greets us.

"This way, sir," she smiles at him and leads us efficiently towards a table by the window. I look out over the sculpted gardens, behind which sits woodland and behind that the sea.

"This is beautiful," I say.

The lady smiles at me. "It is. I love working here."

"I'm not surprised!"

She smartly pulls my chair out, and I sit while she hands Paul and me menus.

"It's not too much, is it?" This is the closest I've seen Paul come to looking unsure of himself.

"No," I say. "It's really not. If the staff were snotty and unpleasant then it would be totally different but they're all smiley and friendly, and nobody seems to be looking down their nose at me."

"Why on earth would they do that?" Paul asks and his

eyes meet mine, quite sincerely. I feel myself blush. "It's so good to see you again, Alice."

"You too."

"And your mum? Is she OK?"

"She's fine, thanks. In fact, she and Dad are coming down on Friday for a few days."

"That's good," Paul smiles. "You can't help but relax when you get down here."

"That's just what I've been saying to her! She knows, though; we used to come down to Cornwall for holidays when I was a kid. I've got her and Dad to thank for my love of the place, really."

"And so what's going on with work? This business idea...?" He breaks off as a young waitress brings us a bottle of water. "Could we see the cocktail menu, please?"

"Of course."

"Would you like one?" he asks, that earnestness back on his face. "No pressure. I just thought you might like to see what they do."

"I'd love one," I smile. "That sounds lovely. It's just a shame you're driving."

"It's not a problem. I am quite happy to drive and let you relax."

When the waitress comes back, I order something with gin, elderflower and prosecco. Paul orders an orange juice. "I might have a glass of wine with dinner," he says.

I sip my drink. "You were asking about work," I say. "Well, there's actually a lot going on."

"Oh yeah?"

I fill him in on Amethi. I leave out the part about Julie making an offer without consulting me; I feel protective of my friend and I don't think it would cast her in a good light. I move on to how it's all progressed, and finish with Bea's reaction today.

"Oh, shit. Poor Bea."

"Poor Bea?" I ask, the drink having gone slightly to my head.

"Yes, and no, not because I think you should feel bad about it. You're doing the right thing, I promise. But I guess she is just gutted you're leaving her. I know what it's like when you find the right person to work with. You don't ever want to lose them. But she'll come round. She can't expect somebody like you to stay there and work for her forever."

Somebody like me? I want to ask but instead say, "I hope you're right."

The waitress comes back at this point and I realise I have barely even glanced at the menu.

"I could order for us both, if you like…?" Paul suggests. I remember laughing with Sam at a man ordering for his wife, when we were at Glades Manor in Devon. But this doesn't feel the same, somehow. And actually, somebody taking on the decision-making for a while seems like a relief. I nod my head.

"OK, great, it's just that I know the chef does this really beautiful vegetarian dish with noodles, but it's not on the menu. Is it something you'd like, do you think? Loads of fresh summer veg, and chilli."

"It sounds gorgeous," I say.

"Could we have that, for our main course?" he asks the waitress, smiling at her. "And for starters: olives, rosemary bread, dipping oil, samphire, and artichokes, please."

My mouth is watering already.

"No problem," the waitress collects our menus and

turns smartly, striding off to the kitchen.

"Sorry, I don't mean to be such an old man, ordering for you. It's just I looked into the vegetarian dishes and I know the menu today isn't great. But I dug around a bit and asked some friends of mine what they'd suggest. This noodle dish is meant to be the best. I know it doesn't sound very exciting but…"

"It sounds lovely," I say, touched that he has asked around, and also that he's having the same as me.

"Do you want to choose the wine?" he asks. "In the interests of fairness, I mean."

"No, you do it, I honestly haven't got a clue about wine."

"I hope you don't mind if I have a glass? I'll just have one."

"I hadn't thought of that. I don't know if I should finish the bottle off. I have got a day off tomorrow, though," I concede.

"Well, we'll get a bottle and see how we get on."

"OK."

I don't see how much the wine costs but I suspect from Paul's discussions with the sommelier that it's an expensive one. It is brought over, and Paul sniffs it then tastes a little. "Perfect."

I never know what I am meant to be detecting if I am asked to taste a wine, I will always say it's fine. I suspect Paul's pronouncement is from experience and knowledge. I drain the last of my cocktail and look back out at the view. The sun is behind the house now so a very long shadow is being cast over the grounds. A flock of seagulls is making its way slowly across the skyline and shades of pink and purple are introducing themselves to the view.

"This is such a lovely place," I say.

"It is. It's ostentatious, I know… and no, don't try to deny it out of politeness! It's totally over the top. But it's quiet, and private, and I just thought I'd like to spend an evening getting to know you better. And treating you. If that doesn't sound too condescending."

"It sounds bloody lovely," I grin and he grins back.

"Cheers!" he says, and we push our glasses together, eyes locking across the table.

The food is not long in coming and all of the starters are just perfect. The artichokes are chargrilled but there are no burnt bits to pull from between my teeth; the olives are plump and deliciously salty. The bread clearly freshly baked, still warm from the oven. I am so hungry, I realise, and it takes all my will power not to just eat it all in minutes.

Instead, between mouthfuls, we talk. I find myself telling Paul about Sam.

"So he's the reason you're down here?" he asks, his eyebrows raised. He tops up my glass of wine.

"No, not really – well, I mean, he was, kind of. The real reason is Julie." I feel a bit tipsy and need to remember not to drink too much. Paul is still sipping his solitary glass. It's good wine, too. Even I can tell that much.

"She sounds pretty great," he says.

"Oh, she is. She's amazing. You'll have to meet her…" Oh god, am I being too keen?

"I'd like that," he smiles.

"But Sam, yeah – I thought it was meant to be. Love at first sight and all that."

"Sounds like me and Melanie," he says. "We were just a bit younger; seventeen. I really thought it was forever. I didn't realise that people grow up, and change."

"I suppose they do," I say. "But you get on with her OK?"

"Oh yeah. Now, anyway," he laughs and I think of Bea's warning to me. "I'll be honest with you, Alice, I wasn't the best husband. I was away a lot, and then, when we'd drifted what I thought was too far to ever pull ourselves back together again, I had an affair."

"Oh," I say, wondering if I look surprised or disappointed, or like I already know.

"I'm not proud of it. It was about twelve years ago, I guess, and it didn't last but it kind of told me what I already knew. Melanie, too, though she was less keen to admit it. Telling the kids was the worst thing."

"I can imagine." I think of Sophie, and Sam. Once more, I feel like I'm looking into a world I know nothing of. I think I'd like to know, one day, what being a parent is all about. But I'm not ready yet.

"Anyway," he says, "I was really looking for a way I could tell you that, to get it out of the way because if we're going to keep seeing each other, somebody is going to tell you. It's hard keeping secrets round our way. Like I say, I'm not proud of it, but it happened and I can't pretend it didn't."

"Have you had many relationships since?"

"In honesty, nothing serious. But I have seen a few women – nobody local, though. I had my fingers burned there!"

"I'm glad you told me," I say, and I am. And I have also just clicked that he said something about us carrying on seeing each other. I can feel his knees against mine under the table. I like the physical contact. I like the cosiness of our table for two, and the extravagance of this place which he has brought me to. I also like the wine.

Luckily, our main course is with us before too long and I hope that the noodles are going to give the booze some kind of carbohydrate to soak into. I'm not really sure it works like that but it sounds good.

It's hard to eat noodles in an attractive way, though. And nigh on impossible to have a conversation. Paul is right, though – they are absolutely delicious. All of the vegetables; finely julienned carrots, crunchy mange touts, succulent baby sweetcorn, taste as fresh as though they have been picked within the last hour. We sink into a comfortable silence for a while as we tuck into our food. Eventually, though, I can't eat another thing. Paul, too, looks like he's had enough.

"Would you like to sit outside for dessert? It's a lovely evening." The lady who showed us to our seats has appeared as if by magic and she makes me jump.

Paul laughs. "Alice?"

"Why not?" Maybe some fresh air is a good idea. As we follow her out through a small (in terms of this house; huge in terms of a normal place) reception room, Paul places his hand lightly on the small of my back. I do not want him to take it away.

Outside, there are other couples, and some groups of – presumably – golfers sitting at tables, all placed a distance away from each other and tucked cleverly between potted trees which twinkle with fairy lights. We are shown to a small table with two covered benches either side of it, angled so that both face partly towards the sea. I sit on one and Paul sits next to me. He is close enough that I feel the soft hair on his arms against my skin. I shiver.

"Are you cold?" he asks, putting his arm around me.

"No, I'm…" I turn towards him and then he is kissing

me. Under a bower of leaves studded with tiny flowers and twinkling lights, I kiss him back. He smells faintly of aftershave, and tastes of wine and red chillies. His hands are on my back, pulling me to him, and I'm briefly glad of the privacy offered by the carefully placed trees before I am lost in the kiss. Who cares if anyone sees us, anyway?

After a while, Paul draws back and tucks a strand of hair behind my ear. "Alright?"

"Yes," I smile and, without thinking, say, "Why don't you have another glass of wine? You said there were rooms here. And I'm not working tomorrow…"

"Ah, Alice, if only we could." He smiles, and kisses me on my lips, lingering for a moment. "I've got my second-in-command due at my place first thing in the morning, though. Shit, I wish I'd planned this better."

"That's OK," I say and I mean it. I hadn't planned to be so impetuous; but then, I don't suppose that is something you would plan, as a general rule. "Let's just enjoy tonight."

"Of course, but you do know that's not a brush-off, don't you? Really, truly it's not. I would love to stay here with you, take you up those sweeping staircases to a four-poster…" His hand is on my leg now and he's looking into my eyes.

"Sorry to disturb you, sir and madam." The butler-type man has appeared at our table. "But if you were wishing to have dessert, I have to tell you that the kitchen will be closing shortly." He produces two dessert menus and leaves them on the table. Once he's out of earshot, we burst out laughing.

"Saved by the bell," Paul says.

"Or not."

"No, right. Or not."

We share a cheeseboard for dessert and I drink plenty of water to dilute the alcohol. We manage to keep our hands off each other, if you don't count Paul putting his arm around me, and I don't. When we're finished, we walk back through the open door into the reception room we'd come through earlier. The furnishings are plush; huge old polished wood-framed seats and elaborately framed paintings of men with curly white hair and haughty expressions. I smile at a similar-looking man sitting alone at a table but he glances away. I stifle the urge to giggle.

Back at the car, Paul kisses me again. "I really don't want to take you home," he says. "Or rather, I really do want to take you home."

"Another time?" I suggest, feeling suddenly tired and like a good night's sleep wouldn't go amiss.

"Definitely." He kisses me again, firmly and determinedly. Then he starts the engine and off we go into the night; the summer stubbornly refusing to relinquish full control to darkness. There are still strands of light in the star-studded sky. I take some deep gulps of air as we whizz along, though it's difficult to do with the wind in your face.

Town is reasonably quiet when we get back and the house is in darkness. Paul kisses me again.

"Do you want to come in?" I ask.

"I had better not, gorgeous Alice, or I may never get home. And I do need to do a bit of work tonight," he admits. "You wait, this'll be you soon when you've got your business flying along."

"I hope so!" I say. "Well, kind of, anyway. How far is it

to your place?" I realise I have no idea where Paul lives.

"Oh, about twenty minutes' drive; only because the roads are so dodgy. It's actually only about six miles from here. "You'll see it when you come to my party. If you're still coming…?

"I'd love to," I say.

"And I was thinking," he kisses me, "If we can find a way to do it subtly, so we don't get a load of gossip going, maybe you could stay the night?"

"I'd love to," I say again and I kiss him this time, pushing my lips against his. I really want him to stay the night now. But all good things come to those who wait, or so they say. "Goodnight, Paul. Thank you for a really lovely evening."

"It's my pleasure," he smiles. "Make sure you get a lie-in tomorrow morning. I'll be thinking of you when I'm going through work with Simon, and I know which one of you I'd rather be with."

I let myself into an empty, dark house but unlike just four nights ago, tonight I am grinning from ear to ear. The day's warmth is contained between the walls and I feel a tinge of sadness at how much I am going to miss this place, but these are exciting times and I really feel like great new things are just around the corner.

18

"Mum! Dad!" I am so happy to see their faces as they step down from the train onto the platform.

"Alice!" Mum grins and waves, and Dad takes a moment to locate me then does the same. We hug and I wrestle Mum's case off her and lug it towards the little red car.

"Thanks for coming to meet us, love," Mum says.

"It's no problem. Bea insisted on it." It's true, she did – in typical Bea fashion, only it wasn't exactly typical Bea. Her manner towards me is more subdued and I am feeling increasingly guilty. Paul says I shouldn't.

Stand your ground, read his message last night. One of his messages, I should say. **I know I said I could understand that she was upset but she will have to get over it. You're doing this, Alice, and I have a feeling you won't regret it. Don't feel bad, this is your life! xx**

I really love his positivity, and his drive. I don't know if I have met anyone quite like him before, and I can't help but imagine him at work. He must be pretty strong-willed and focused to have built up such a business.

Anyway, enough about Paul. Back to Mum and Dad. I tell them quickly, in the short journey up the hill to the Sail Loft, about the progress with Amethi. I tell them that

Bea knows, too, and that she doesn't seem 100% happy about it.

"And David?" Mum asks. "Have you spoken to him about it?"

Actually, I haven't. I did leave him a voicemail yesterday, but I haven't heard anything back from him yet, which is making me feel uneasy. He is usually prompt at responding to messages. I really hope I haven't upset him as well; he adores Bea and could easily be offended on her behalf.

"I haven't spoken to him about it yet, no, but I'm waiting for him to give me a ring back."

Maybe he thinks I'm ungrateful, that I let him take things slowly with his house sale on my behalf and I hadn't even mentioned the possibility of this new place.

"We can't wait to see this place, Alice," Dad says.

"I can't wait to show you! Julie, too. We thought we'd take you up there after work today. Julie's got the night off, so we can go for something to eat afterwards, too."

"Sounds great," says Mum. "I bet Julie's excited about the wedding. Not long now!"

"No," I say, "it's not." And I'm grateful that I don't have a wedding to plan on top of everything else. Julie and Luke will have the keys to their new house in a few weeks. It is in town, and I feel slightly envious of that, but Julie says she's going to stay up at Amethi on a regular basis, and also that I can stay at theirs whenever they want. "We'll share the load, Alice, and I know you like to wake up by the sea so we've already chosen your room, at the top of the house. It'll be like when we first moved in to David's."

What have I done to deserve such a friend?

Bea greets Mum and Dad warmly but by the time I've returned from taking their luggage up to my room, she's gone out. She didn't appear at all yesterday, which is not like her, and now she's not here to usurp me in the use of the big wooden desk and the comfortable leather chair, I find I am wishing she was. It's been a source of irritation since she came back from America, really – I am the manager but when Bea is about I feel like my wings have been clipped. It's not how she wanted me to feel but having her 'popping in' a couple of times a day really did start to become annoying. Now, though, I'd give anything for her to muscle in on the plans I'm working on.

Luckily, David interrupts my gloom, phoning the hotel landline.

"Hello, Alice! I am so sorry I haven't called before now, Martin and I have been on a jolly… I beg your pardon, a *very important* research trip, to some vineyards up in Hertfordsh… Herefordshire," I heard Martin correcting him in the background. "For the wedding, you know. Did I tell you we're getting married?"

"You may have mentioned it once or twice," I smile, and think as I always do of that sales training from a previous life, where it was hammered into us that people can 'hear' a smile down a phone line. It seems things are OK with David although I am not totally out of the woods yet. Maybe Bea hasn't spoken to him.

"Have you spoken to Bea?" I ask.

"Yes, just put the phone down. She said you and Julie have found somewhere, for your business. That's amazing!"

OK, so David clearly doesn't have a problem. It's almost like he already knew. I suppose, when I think about it, Julie and I have probably told him about this dream of ours. We've spent many a drunken evening together in the last couple of years, talking about hopes for the future and all the other tripe that comes out when you're in the company of your best friends and a few bottles of wine.

David had given up drinking for a while, having relied a little too much on it during some difficult years, but he is settled now and seems able to cope with it.

"Did she tell you there's a place for me there, too? Somewhere to live, I mean?"

"No, she didn't! I guess she knew you'd want to tell me yourself."

"Is she OK?" I can't help asking.

"Who, Bea? I think so. I mean, I know she'll miss you. She thinks the world of you, you know that."

"And I think the world of her."

"I know, stupid! Look, we're all moving on. Bea's got married, I'm getting married, in case you hadn't noticed. And Julie and Luke. And Stefan and April."

"Alright, alright, rub it in!" I laugh.

"I don't mean it like that! What I mean is, we are all doing things with our lives and that includes you, and you mustn't go feeling bad about it, Alice. You can't stay at the Sail Loft forever. Bea knows that."

"You don't know how good it is to hear you say that, David." I send that smile down the phone line once more.

"Well, it's true. Now you'd better be getting along. Bea said your folks are down, too? Say hi from me."

"I will. And don't forget to bring me some of that heavily researched wine back."

"I will, if there's any left. I must stop eating and

drinking before the wedding, though, or I'll never fit into my dress! I forgot to tell you, I'm going to have some personal training sessions. With Sam's ex."

"Aren't I Sam's ex?" I ask.

"You know what I mean! Kate Collins! That is OK, isn't it? You two are mates again?"

"Well, I wouldn't go that far, but only because I never see her. Of course it's not a problem. Sounds like something I could do with, too."

"Great. Because I've paid for a month up front!" I hear Martin's voice again in the background. "OK. We've got to go now, but Martin sends his love. Bye now. Love you, Alice."

"I love you, too."

That phone call, along with my parents' presence, completely lifts my spirits. By the time evening comes around and Stef has taken over the reins, I am bubbling over with excitement, so happy and proud to be able to show Amethi to my mum and dad.

Julie drives, and I sit in the back with Dad. Mum is very keen that I should get the front seat. "I'm not an invalid!" she chides.

"No, I know, but… oh, just get in the front or we'll never get there!"

"OK, OK," she laughs.

Julie waits while we clip our seatbelts in. "Ready?"

"Yes!" we chorus.

"Then let's go!"

On the drive out of town, I turn my head to see the view that I love, across the rooftops, over the sea, disappear as we head along the twisty road. I really will miss being right in the town. I am a little nervous about being all alone out in the sticks as well, but I have to give it a go. If I hate it, I will have to think again. The solicitor said we'd still be able to rent the house out as a residential let anyway. But I find I don't like that idea, either. It feels very much to me that the house should be mine.

As we take the turn into the drive, Dad mutters at the sharpness of the turn, and Mum grips the sides of the seat as we go along the bumpy track.

Will all this put people off? We can't afford to do anything about the driveway at the moment; we have just enough to complete the grounds around the buildings, and buy in the furnishings. We've managed to strike a deal with a hotel up the coast which is being refurbished. We have furniture for all the bedrooms, and some lounge chairs. We will need to buy brand new mattresses and bedding but we can do it. It has to be great, this place. The most comfortable mattresses, top-of-the-range coffee machines and fibre broadband. Luke's been speaking to his rich mates in London, about what they would look for in a holiday home. The great news is that they all seem to love the idea of semi-catered accommodation and apparently some of them are already asking about coming to stay in our first year of business.

I think it's going to be large groups during the quieter months – small business conferences, perhaps some writing courses, that kind of thing, although I have to bear in mind that I set up a writers' retreat for the Sail Loft and I absolutely cannot tread on Bea's feet in any way, shape or form.

In the summer months I envisage our guests being the kind of people Luke's been talking to. They'll have had their winter ski experience, and be looking for somewhere hot and sunny by the sea. It's not guaranteed but at least you have a better chance in Cornwall than in many other parts of the UK. And with the ski-chalet-type catered-for experience thrown in, I think we can make Amethi a place people will want to come back to. This is what I hope, anyway.

As we drive between the trees, I try to gauge my parents' reactions to the place. It's not difficult when we emerge into the clearing and the little cluster of buildings sits neatly before us.

"It is beautiful, girls," gasps Mum, who has a better view from her front seat. Dad leans between her and Julie to see for himself.

"This is fabulous!" he says. "I must admit, I'd been worried it was going to be a ramshackle old place, but this has obviously been taken care of. Which one's yours, Alice?"

You can't actually see my little house from this angle. "I'll show you when we get out," I say. "It's tucked away round the corner."

Mum and Dad wander off to have a look and Julie and I lean on the car, arms folded across our chests, grinning. I can see they like it and the fact that they do is a huge boost; reassurance, if any were needed, that we are doing the right thing. I feel proud taking them into my little house. I am going to furnish this myself rather than use the stuff from the hotel. I sold the things from my old flat to a clearance place. It wasn't worth shipping them down here and I have to admit I'm quite excited about choosing new furniture and fittings.

Mum and Dad follow me around the house and it starts to feel like it really is my place.

"It's beautiful, Alice." Mum smiles and I can see she really does mean it.

After we've left Amethi, we go to the pub in the little village nearby. I have halloumi salad and chips while Mum, Dad and Julie all order the fish and chips. I can't deny they smell delicious. As it's such a lovely evening, we eat outside. I have a pint of bitter shandy and it tastes perfect. The bubbles of the lemonade tingle on my tongue. I sit back in the wooden seat and gaze briefly at the perfect sky; a confident blue with mere wisps of clouds traipsing obediently along the horizon. The vapour trails from two planes criss-cross above my head. I wonder briefly about the people all the way up there; who they are, where they're going.

With Mum and Dad here, it almost feels like I'm on holiday and as sorry as I am for Stefan that his wedding and honeymoon are now over, I am grateful that I get this weekend off. It's shaping up to be a beautiful one, and I want to make the most of this break before the long, hard work of getting Amethi off the ground. Thank god Julie only wants a night away with me, instead of a full-on hen do.

"Will you need to take on any staff?" Mum asks me, "Once you're up and running?"

"I don't know. I'm not sure we're going to be able to at first. I guess we'll just have to see how it goes. It would be nice to have at least a couple of cleaners and maybe some extra hands in the kitchen."

"You girls are going to be worn out!" Dad says. I love the way he and Mum still call us girls. It's not something I get often anymore. I think briefly of the outside feeling I have with Sam and Sophie, Paul and his kids. That I haven't yet been let in on a secret world, open only to those of us who have crossed that line, taken on the responsibility of parenthood. While my parents certainly don't treat me like a kid, I still feel very much their child when I am with them and I wonder if that would change if I had children of my own.

"We will be," I say. "We have to go into this with our eyes open."

"And it's impossible to know what it's going to be like, until we're doing it," says Julie. We've said these things to each other time and time again. But we remain undaunted.

"I have every faith in you," says Dad, "and you never know, you might be able to get some help sooner than you think."

"Yeah, we'll just see how it goes," I say. In reality, I can't see us being able to afford any staff for at least the first two years. I suppose these will be the years which make or break us.

We sit and chat, about work, and Julie's wedding, and Mum's health – or as much as she will allow it. Around us, all the other tables are taken with little knots of people; families with kids, groups of friends. "I love it here," I say, to nobody in particular.

"I can see that," Mum smiles at me. Dad and Julie, deep in conversation about some poem he's recommending for a wedding reading, are oblivious to us and I take the opportunity to ask what I've wanted to since Mum was in hospital.

"Are you OK, Mum?"

"I am. I promise I am. And I promise I would tell you if I wasn't. Or your dad. But it's shaken me up a bit."

"I'm not surprised," I say, putting my hand on hers. "And I'm glad you're thinking about leaving your job. You wouldn't have to give up work altogether."

"I know, but there's something psychological in the

word 'retiring'. I *feel* like I'm giving up. I know, I know it's silly but work's been part of my life for such a long time. I can't imagine being without it."

"Don't forget what Pat told you," I remind her.

"Don't pretend you know who Pat is!" She swipes at my arm. "But well remembered. And she's not the only person that's said similar things. So there you go. But I don't half envy you and Julie, just starting out with this business. I wish I'd been brave enough to try something like this!"

"Well, I have to have got it from somebody, Mum."

She puts her arm around me and pulls me to her side. I breathe in for just a moment; close my eyes briefly; see if I can remember what it was like being a child.

The rest of the weekend goes just as I'd hoped. We eat out, a lot, and swim in the sea. We sit at the Mainbrace in the evenings, watching for a table becoming vacant like three gulls eyeing up a kid eating fish and chips. We also revisit some of the places on the south Cornish coast, where we used to holiday when I was growing up. We did that the first summer I was back, just when I was working out whether I could be with Sam. I remember my anger when I found out he hadn't told me about Sophie, and then him explaining everything to me. Sophie was the result of a short-lived relationship which had ended before Kate knew she was pregnant; in fact, she hadn't found out until she and Sam had got together. Sam took on the role of father; took to it with ease, even after he and Kate broke up.

It was Sophie finding out that Sam was not her 'real' dad that was the catalyst for Sam and I breaking up for a second time but it was me that made the decision. I could see that, what with being in Wales for his course, in reality he couldn't be there for both me and her as we needed him to be. And Sophie had to come first.

While Mum and Dad paddle in the sea, watching the guillemots nose-dive the crystal-clear waters, I remember my birthday that summer that Sam and I were back together; how he'd brought me for a picnic on a secluded little beach down this way. He'd thought of everything; packed it himself and lugged it all down to the sand. I had thought then that nothing so perfect could end.

My phone buzzing distracts me from this futile line of thought.
Paul.

Hi gorgeous, I hope you're having a good time with your parents. Just a reminder that my party's two weeks today and I am really hoping that you can still make it xx

Of course! I can't wait. I'm on the beach, my parents are paddling and I'm just sitting back and thinking. I feel like I'm on holiday x

Good. You deserve a break. Say hi to your parents from me xx

Should I do that? I haven't actually mentioned Paul to them, aside from as the driver who brought me to the hospital that night.

Will do. Hopefully see you before the party? x
God, I hope so. I may have to go to Belgium for a

couple of days but let me check and I'll get back to you. I don't think I can wait two weeks to see you xx

I smile and lie back, not caring that my hair will be infiltrated by sand. The sky is clear above, just the odd seagull drifting lazily in and out of view. Although somewhere at the back of my mind, thoughts of Sam still niggle away at me, I know that I can be happy about other things. Life is taking a new direction now, and it's pretty bloody exciting.

19

I am back to asking Julie what I should wear. It's the day of Paul's party and amidst my friend's haphazard packing of all her worldly belongings – in preparation for her moving in with Luke – I need her to stop and give me some advice.

"Right, let's see what you've got," she says, rummaging through my wardrobe.

"You know what I've got!"

"Yeah, well, I'm just reminding myself. I've got other things to think about, you know. I'm starting a very successful business."

"Oh, that sounds good. I might be interested in joining you."

"We'll see," she says airily, emerging from behind the wardrobe door with a load of hangers, and dropping various garments onto the bed.

"I'm going to miss living with you," I say wistfully.

"I think you're going to see quite enough of me at work, Alice. But I know, I'm going to miss this, too. No time for dwelling on it now, though. You need a killer outfit, and I need to keep packing. But it's soooooo boring."

"I'll help," I say.

"No, don't worry. You need to chill today and besides, you'll be packing your own stuff soon enough. And there's no chance I'll be helping you!"

"Thanks very much."

Julie tuts and *hmm*s over my clothes for a while then disappears into her room. She returns with a teal dress. "I think it's going to have to be this, madam."

"Julie, that's beautiful. I haven't seen that before."

"No, well, I haven't worn it before."

"Don't you want to save it for yourself?" *Please say no.*

"No, it's fine, I promise. To be honest, it's a bit short on me. It should be perfect for you, though, shortarse."

"Ha." I wriggle out of my pyjamas – I haven't quite got round to getting dressed yet – and into the dress. It is beautiful and it's not flouncy or frilly, or flowery.

"I love it!" I say, just as the doorbell goes.

Julie looks out of the window. "It's Paul!" she hisses.

"I wasn't expecting him," I say. "I'll just go down…"

"No you won't, he can't see you in the dress!"

"Julie, it's a party, not our wedding!"

"I don't care. You step out of it and hang it up… and put some clothes on, young lady."

I laugh. "Alright, Mum."

I hear her gallop downstairs and greet Paul enthusiastically. The warm murmur of his voice comes through the floorboards. My heart has started beating rapidly. I quickly throw on a sweatshirt and some cut-off jeans and come down the stairs. I can hear them in the lounge.

"Hi," I say, walking slightly shyly in.

"Hello," Paul's smile is wide and open. I want to go to him. I want to kiss him, but it doesn't feel the right thing somehow, with Julie there.

Speaking of Julie, I can see her grinning at me. I know exactly what she's thinking.

"I'm wearing this to the party; that's OK, isn't it?"

"You can wear whatever you like, as long as you're still

coming," Paul smiles.

"Great."

"Right… well, I'd better get back to my packing," says Julie, who I can tell really wants to stay. She disappears out of the door and when her footsteps indicate she's back upstairs, Paul stands and kisses me.

He puts his hands on my waist and leaves them there. "Still coming, then?"

"Of course!"

"Thank god for that. Listen, I know this sounds a bit pretentious but I've got a car to pick up a few of the guests from out of town, who are staying down the coast. I was thinking I'd like to send it for you first, so you can get to me before anyone else does."

"A car?" I raise my eyebrows.

"I know, I know, it's a bit much, isn't it? But these folks like to be treated, and they're important customers of mine. I thought you might like a ride, as well. And I wanted to see you before anyone else turns up, you can help calm my nerves."

"You don't get nervous!"

"Of course I do! I am human, you know, although I can forgive you for thinking I'm super-human."

"Whatever you say. The car sounds amazing. I'd be mad to pass up on it."

"Great!" he smiles at me, "And you can have a ride back here at the end of the night if you like. Or, you can stay and I'll drop you back tomorrow."

"I'll let you know," I say, and kiss him slowly.

"I hope that means you're going to stay."

"We'll see."

"Ha, I used to say that to the kids. It usually meant yes. Got to get going now, though. So much to do! I'll send the car for you at about six. Is that OK?"

"Perfect."

I walk him to the door, where we kiss again and look into each other's eyes. I love his eyes and the lines that crinkle around them. There is so much good humour there. Although I'm not really sure I want to be at the party, I do know I want to be at Paul's, and I'm quite sure I want to stay over.

As I open the door I hear my name from just down the street. I poke my head out to see a red-faced David, accompanied by a barely-sweating Kate, making his way up the hill. I think 'jogging' would be a little too generous a description.

"Am I glad to see you," David says, then spots Paul just beside me. "Oh, hello," he says between breaths, "I'm David. Alice's landlord. And friend. And this slave-driver is Kate."

I look at Kate, in time to catch what might be an expression of surprise cross her face.

Paul just laughs. "Hi, David. I remember you from the wedding. And Kate, I already know, although it's been a while. How are you, Kate?"

"I'm fine," she smiles. "Just trying to get this one in shape for his wedding!"

"Oh yeah, it's not long now, is it?" Paul asks.

"No," David grins. "And I believe you're having a party of your own tonight."

"I am. Speaking of which, I'd better be on my way. See you later, Alice." He squeezes my hand and I can't decide whether I am grateful or disappointed that he doesn't kiss me. "Nice to see you again, Kate – and good luck with the run, David."

When he's just far enough away, David grins at me.

"Nice!"

"Yes," I say, very aware that Kate is with us. It feels strange, after the bad feeling between her and me about Sam, that I am now seeing somebody else. And it's such early days with Paul, I'd really rather keep things low-key for the time being.

"Come on, David," Kate says, "if we don't get going again you'll seize up. It's good to see you, Alice. Sophie's always asking about you. Why don't you come and see us sometime?"

"I'd love to," I say and I mean it. My feelings towards Kate are so different to what they were and just because I'm not with Sam anymore, it doesn't mean I can't be friends with his daughter and her mum. "Thank you!"

Kate smiles, and prods David. "Let's go!"

She jogs onwards, David slightly behind and whingeing like a five-year-old boy.

***

At six on the dot, the car arrives. It's big and black and shiny. Julie has had to go to work so it's just me in the house, and I've been carrying these nerves around for what seems like hours.

It's now or never, I tell myself, and grab my bag, checking for keys, wallet, phone and the toothbrush and small pack of wipes I have secreted in the internal zip-up pocket.

A man in a suit and a smart cap stands by the rear door, holding it open for me.

"Hi," I say.

"Hello," he smiles. "Are you Alice?"

"That's me."

"Then your carriage awaits!"

I hope none of the neighbours are watching as I slide into the back seat and the driver closes the door. Once in the car, he introduces himself. "I'm Jack, one of Paul's school mates. He said it would be OK to tell you that. To my next passengers, I'm just Driver."

I laugh, feeling slightly more at ease. "This feels a bit weird," I admit.

"I know, don't worry — I've done this before, to help him out. This is my car, though. I do airport runs and other trips for businesses round the south west."

"It's lovely," I say, admiring the shiny, pristine interior. "I don't think I've ever been in such a clean car... besides Paul's, of course."

"Yeah, he is quite a clean freak," Jack laughs. "Anyway, once I've picked up the other guests I'm going to get out of this monkey suit and I'll be at the party. The others won't even know, they'll never expect their driver to be a guest as well."

"Brilliant!" I feel relieved already, knowing it's not going to be all high-flying, scary business people.

We go quiet and I gaze out at the hedgerows and the sky, both muted by the tinted windows. The air-conditioning is on and the car feels sterile, somehow. I would rather open the window, feel the blast of real air, but I will only end up arriving a total mess. Instead, I sit back in the comfy seat and rest my head, practising slow, deep breathing to calm my nerves.

The route seems familiar, somehow, and I realise we're around the same area that Paul brought me to on our first date.

"Nearly there now," Jack says.

I check my bag for the fifteenth time, making sure I still have all my essentials — although how I could possibly have lost any of them during the journey is beyond me – and when I look up, I realise I know exactly where we are.

"No way!" I breathe.

"Impressive, isn't it?"

"Just a bit." But it's not just the size of Paul's house, or the electric gates which are slowly opening to allow us passage, which have struck me. This is the house behind the beach – the place where I speculated about the owners and wrote that stupid message in the sand for them to read.

"Why didn't you tell me?" I ask Paul, who has come down the steps to open the car door for me. In a dark grey shirt and black trousers, he looks every inch as though he belongs here.

He laughs lightly. "I just didn't want you to know then. I don't know why. Sorry, I wasn't messing with you, or not intentionally."

"Well…" I actually don't know what to say.

"I'd best be off, Paul," Jack says.

"No problem." Paul puts his arm around me. "Are you mad at me?"

"No, well I don't think so. But I don't know why you didn't tell me this was your house!"

"I guess I didn't want you to judge me."

"You know I wouldn't do that."

"You thought I'd kept the beach path hidden so nobody else could use the beach."

"Oh, yeah," I say, flushing. "But haven't you?"

"You've got me there! No, well, okay, maybe a bit! Come on, let me show you around."

I feel like I've just walked into an episode of *Grand Designs*. Paul's house is all clean lines and floor-to ceiling windows. In short, it is beautiful. The downstairs is mostly open plan, with a huge fireplace and chimney in the centre, although of course it's far too hot for a fire at the moment. I try to imagine whether it's possible to feel cosy in such a space. There are all manners of artwork adorning the walls, but far more impressive than any of it is the view: framed by trees on either side sits the sea, reaching far away to the distant horizon. A living, breathing, ever-changing work of art, framed by huge sheets of glass, and smaller bifold doors which give way to a large area of decking, below which is the walled garden I had wondered about when we walked down to the beach.

"There was an old, dilapidated building here. Georgian, I think," Paul explains, "but the years, and the unsympathetic weather, had totally ruined it. I'd originally wanted to restore it but a friend of mine, an architect, persuaded me to do this, instead."

"Well, it's absolutely amazing," I say, tipping my head back so I can see all the way to the very top of the house. A staircase is tucked into the side of the open plan space, and up above there are balconies which go around three sides of the building. The fourth side is all glass, facing the sea.

"How do you clean that window?" I ask, thinking that actually, I barely ever clean our normal-size windows back home.

"It's self-cleaning!" Paul laughs.

"What? How does that work?"

"I'm not entirely convinced it does," he says. "A mate of mine who's a window cleaner comes three times a week for the outside, otherwise it's crusted up with sea salt."

"Window cleaners… architects… do you know everybody?"

"Not quite!" he laughs then he pulls me to him. "Excuse me if this sounds cheesy, but I'm very keen to get to know you better."

"A little," I smile, moving closer still. "But you did grow up in the 80s so I suppose it's not that surprising."

"Alright, don't rub it in!" He kisses me now, and my eyes close so his house can't distract me. I kiss him back and I feel his arms tighten around my waist, then his left hand moves up into my hair. His skin is soft and smooth against mine and I detect that aftershave again, which is starting to become familiar.

"What if your guests arrive?" I ask.

"We've got a little while yet," he says. "We do need a plan, though, unless we want everybody talking about us."

"I don't," I say, staunchly.

"No, I'm not ready for that yet, either. I was thinking… how about you pretend you're leaving, but head upstairs? If that's not too presumptuous? You can escape whenever you want to; I hope you'll stick around and enjoy it but I know what these things can be like sometimes. I'll show you where my room is and you are free to head up there whenever you want."

I follow him up the staircase then around the landing, passing three other doors. "Those two are Georgia's and Lenny's, when they're staying with me," he points to the first two. "That's the bathroom," he says, gesturing to the third door, then, pointing to a further door, on the next section of the balcony, "Then there's the guest suite."

"A suite?" I ask. "Can I..?"

"Be my guest... although I wasn't planning on you staying in the *guest suite*," he says quietly into my ear, close behind me. I feel a little shiver run down my spine.

"It's beautiful!" I exclaim. Although at the back of the house, with no view of the sea, the room looks over the driveway and into the trees beyond. There is an enormous bed in the centre, facing the window. There is also a door onto a balcony, and a walk-in wardrobe, a seating area by the side window, and a bathroom three times the size of my parents'.

"Come on," Paul says and leads me out of the room. It seems a huge drop, from the interior balcony to the room below. The chimney, which rises from the central fireplace, is adorned with more artwork. I think I recognise a Ben Nicholson but I don't have time to ask about it as Paul is behind me, his hands on my waist and his mouth ever-so-gently on my neck, whispering unheard words into my skin as he carefully edges me towards his room. He reaches around and pushes the door open. I take a deep breath. It is my dream room. The far wall is all glass, every inch filled with the sky and the sea. The bed is even bigger than his guest room, its covers white and blue, against the warm gold of the wooden floorboards and the white walls. He shuts the door behind us and all is quiet. I can see the waters moving; the tips of the waves, but it seems like the sea is silent. Paul moves closer to me, guiding me towards the window which I see has a Juliet balcony in front of it. Paul presses on the glass and like a magic trick, it slides away.

"What the..." Now, I can hear the sea. And the gulls. The breeze ruffling the trees. A dog barking, somewhere

224

not too far away.

"Good, isn't it?" Paul is at my side now.

"How does it work?"

"Magic," Paul smiles at me and turns me to face him. "Think you could spend the night somewhere like this?"

"Well, I guess, if I really had to." I kiss him on his mouth and then slide my lips towards his neck. There is not one tell-tale prickle of stubble. He holds me firmly then he buries his head on my shoulder. I hear some muffled words. "What was that?"

"I said," he lifts his head slightly, "I'm going to cancel the party. Let's just stay up here, you and me."

But at his very words, we hear a mechanical clanking sound. "Oh no," he groans. "They're starting to arrive."

From the window at the back of the room, we see a car appear between the trees. Paul quickly kisses me. "There's the TV, tucked away behind that picture. You just press this button," he shows me a remote control, "and it will appear."

"This place really is magic!" I laugh.

"It's a bit over the top, really, I know. But there's no going back now."

"I love it!" I say. And the nerves are kicking in now about this party. Who will I talk to? Who will I know? The thought of being able to escape to this haven is a huge comfort. The thought that Paul will be joining me later, even more so. How I'll get up here and round those balconies unnoticed is another matter, but I'll do my best.

Paul pulls the window back into place and all is peace and quiet once more. He kisses me but I can tell his mind is already on other things. "I'll go and greet the guests," he says. "You come down when you're ready, you can always say you've just been to the bathroom. It's back round there, next to Georgia's room. The one with the sailing boat on the door. And don't worry. Jack will be here, and Rachel – that's his wife – she's really nice and good company. She's usually looking for somebody normal to talk to so I'll introduce you as soon as I can. And you'll know a few other people from around town."

"And I can escape up here whenever I want to?"

"Yes," he says, and kisses me quickly once more. "But I really hope you'll enjoy the party, too. If not, though, you could feign illness, pretend you've called a taxi, then sneak off up here. But don't you go falling asleep before I've had a chance to find you." He flashes me his best smile then he's gone.

I practise using the remote control, surprised when the first button drops down a blind which was hitherto concealed in the ceiling. I press the same button and the blind mechanically folds up, pulled back into its hiding place. My second attempt is more successful and the large abstract painting Paul showed me also disappears into the ceiling, revealing the most enormous TV. It switches on and I panic. It's loud, and it's showing some kind of car race. I hurriedly switch it off, and I hear voices downstairs, then music. My palms are sweaty. I suddenly feel like I don't know what I'm doing here. And I really don't want to go downstairs. Can't I just stay here? Have a little sleep in the oversized bed, which looks incredibly inviting? Watch the changing face of the sea? But I know I can't. I am Paul's guest, not Goldilocks, and this is his world. I need to be part of it.

I slowly open his bedroom door then I walk, my back close to the wall, along the balcony, very, very quietly. It looks like people are heading straight out onto the decking, which is a relief. I make it, unseen, to the bathroom by Paul's kids' bedrooms, and I go in. It's spotless, and as stylish as everywhere else in this house. A corner bath is flanked by frosted-glass windows, which flood the room with light. I lock the door, and look in the mirror. A light comes on as I move to turn on the taps, wanting to cool myself down with some water on my wrists. I look at my reflection, the artificial light casting a slightly strange glow on my skin and highlighting thousands of tiny hairs I am usually unaware of.

"Right," I say to myself. Then, "Right," again.

I flush the toilet to make my visit to the bathroom authentic, only to realise that I actually want to use it properly now. I wait a while before flushing it again then I wash my hands and before I have time to think any more, I am unlocking the door and descending the stairs. I see Paul glance across and cast a quick smile my way, mid-conversation with a regal-looking white-haired lady in a black sequinned dress. I check out the other guests and I'm relieved to see a real mixture here, appearance-wise. I nervously sip my champagne, not sure where to look or who to talk to. It's a relief when I spot Jack, no longer the driver, his cap and suit jacket cast aside, looking much more relaxed in a blue shirt with its sleeves rolled up; standing with a woman who I guess must be Rachel. I gratefully accept a glass of champagne from a waitress who I guess must have been in the kitchen previously. I realise I haven't even seen a kitchen here. I make my way over to Jack and Rachel, smiling politely at an older gentleman as I pass by.

"Hi," I say boldly.

"Alice!" Jack says. "I was just telling Rachel she might have some company tonight."

Rachel smiles at me. "I hate these things! But I love

Paul, and he sends a lot of work Jack's way."

"Yep," Jack agrees. "There'll be all sorts here tonight – local aristos, Paul's high-flying mates, and god knows who else, but the food's usually good, and there's free booze, so who's complaining?"

"You!" Rachel says. "Because now I've got somebody to talk to you can go and do some networking."

"Do I have to?" Jack groans.

"Yes!"

I laugh as Rachel gently pushes her husband in the way of a small knot of people. He walks up confidently and puts a hand gently on one of the men's shoulders. The man turns, clearly recognises Jack, and allows him into the group. Jack casts a woeful glance back in our direction then he's swallowed into the conversation.

"Have you been to many of these parties?" I ask.

"Too many," Rachel says. "It was great when the kids were little as I could use them as an excuse not to be here but now they're old enough to look after themselves."

"How old are they?" I ask politely.

"They're thirteen and fifteen," she says, "But you don't want to talk about my kids all night. And neither do I, no matter how much I love them! Paul tells me you're starting a new business, with a friend?"

"That's right," I say, surprised how pleased I am to think that Paul has been talking about me.

"That's brave. You must have a strong friendship."

"We do," I say, and tell her a bit about Julie.

"You sounds like me and my mate Bella, only she's in New Zealand now."

"You must miss her."

"You have no idea, I would love it if she came back. I run a business, too; I sell flowers."

"From a shop?"

"No, though I did start out that way. It's more of a wholesale thing now."

"Really? I might have to take one of your cards, if you have one." I can picture our places at Amethi, fresh bouquets sitting alongside welcome hampers on our countertops.

"Of course," she reaches into her bag and pulls out a neat case. "Here. Have you got one to swap?"

"No, not yet." The only cards I've got are for the Sail Loft and I don't suppose I will be giving them out much longer.

"Well, I hope your venture goes well, and your friendship survives!" she laughs. "I'm sure it will. I love the way Jack works with Paul, and some of their other mates, too. It's quite a nice little business community round here, you know. You and your friend will have to start coming to the networking meetings."

"That sounds like a great idea."

"Look, there's a couple of seats over there, shall we set up for the night? I'll grab us another couple of glasses, and I'll also grab anybody I see passing who might be good fun. We should just about survive that way."

"That sounds great," I say, relieved and relaxing already.

As the evening drifts on, Rachel and I talk about everything from our parents to our school and uni days and I find myself telling her about Geoff.

"God, how awful!" she says. "Paul and Jack had a friend like that… *have* a friend like that, I should say. And maybe I'm being a bit unfair. He wasn't controlling with his wife like Geoff was with you, but he has got lots of mental health issues, poor guy, and his wife left him eventually. Lucky for him, he had a bit of cash behind him, or at least he did when Paul bought his house. I think he's doing better now, he's left town and started a business somewhere else. I think he might have even got a new girlfriend."

"That's good," I say, wondering if it is really. I often think about what would have happened to Geoff if he hadn't killed himself. Would he have straightened himself out? Could that ever be a possibility? What if he'd got a new girlfriend… I'm pretty sure he would have done. How much more damage might he have caused?

"Yeah, I think it is. Urgh," Rachel shivers, "I don't know if I should feel sorry for her, though. I think that Paul's helped him out quite a bit. Sorted him out with a counsellor, made him go to the sessions, on more than on occasion, I think, he's really bailed him out…" She stops, mid-sentence, as if she's just remembered something. "Anyway, you don't want to hear about this. I imagine you'd rather forget about the whole Geoff thing altogether."

"Yes," I admit, "I would. But I just have to accept it's happened and get on with things."

"That's a lot easier said than done, I'd think. Great that you're seeing Paul, though. He's such a good bloke. I know all this looks flashy," she gestures around the place, "but he's not, really. He does enjoy the finer things in life these days, I suppose."

"Yes," I laugh, "and I'm just about to start leasing a place to live from my own business! A tiny, but lovely, little cottage."

"It sounds perfect… size isn't everything, you know!"

At that point, I hear my name and I recognise Angela

and Tom Southeby, from the spa hotel in town. "Hello!" I say, rising to kiss them both.

"We didn't know you'd be here," Angela says. "And we were sorry to hear that Bea's losing you at the Sail Loft. She's very disappointed."

I feel like Angela is fishing for more information. "Yes, I'll really miss her, and the Sail Loft, but I can't stay there forever. It's Bea's place, really."

"Oh yes, it is. I remember when she was starting out, just a year after Tom and I got the Harbour, wasn't it, Tom?"

"Hmm? Yes," Tom is the archetypical quiet husband to the overbearing wife.

"She's done so well with the place. And we are so happy she's met Bob. What a dish," Angela giggles.

"He is lovely," I agree, feeling sad that things aren't great between Bea and me at the moment, and hoping I can make them right again. I had hoped she and Bob would be here tonight but Paul said they'd been otherwise engaged. Some more people Angela and Tom know join us, then I am free to make my excuses and leave. Rachel is nowhere to be seen so I wander to the edge of the balcony, looking down to the beach below, which I can just make out in the darkening evening. Now that it's August, it is noticeably far earlier when the daylight fades away. We're lucky it's still so warm, though, and being outside feels right. The night breathes around me and I feel an urge to escape; run down that shady path and onto the cold, dusky sand, sinking my bare feet in and letting the waves bite at my skin.

"Everything OK?" I hear Paul's voice at my shoulder, and I turn and smile.

"Yes," I say, wanting to kiss him but knowing I can't.

"Me too," he smiles intimately, although I haven't spoken the thought aloud. "Later," he promises. "And it's great to see you chatting with Rachel, but don't forget our escape plan when you need it."

"Don't worry, I haven't!"

Seeing my empty hand, he passes me his glass of champagne. "Have this," he says. "And I'm really sorry but I need to go and be the gracious host. Will you be OK? Do you want me to introduce you to anybody?"

"I'm fine," I reassure him, seeing Angela Southeby's eyes on us. I smile and raise my glass to her. I realise I'm feeling a bit drunk.

Paul turns to see who I'm smiling at. "Oh god," he groans, "Gossip Central."

"She's a nightmare," I agree. "Don't worry, you move along. But is there anywhere I can get a coffee?" I ask quickly.

"If you go and ask at the kitchen, they'll get you one," he says, looking slightly concerned. "You sure you're OK?"

"Yes, I think I just need to pace my Dutch courage drinking! Don't worry, just point me in the direction of the kitchen. And go and flirt with somebody else to throw Angela off the scent."

"I don't want to flirt with anyone else," Paul says. "I just want to take you upstairs and…"

"Watch it," I say, "I'm pretty sure she's an expert lip-reader."

"OK!" he laughs. "But I can't wait till later."

I see a door at the far side of the living space which I hadn't noticed before. I walk across, realising I'm feeling really quite light-headed. The clattering noises and shouted orders from the other side reassure me I have found the kitchen. Should I knock on the door, or just open it? Luckily, one of the waitresses comes out, a tray of canapés in hand.

"Can I help you?" she smiles.

"Oh yes, please, if that's OK. I was just hoping to get a coffee. And a glass of water?" I say hopefully.

"Of course, let me just shout through to somebody. You don't want to go in there," she says, "the chef's a nightmare!"

"Ha, my best friend's a chef and I know better than to venture into her territory," I smile.

"Could you hold this a sec?" She hands me her tray and pushes the door open. Through the door, I'm impressed to see a military-precision operation and the kitchen itself is as modern as the rest of the house. I want to go in and explore the gadgets and wizardry I am sure Paul has in there. The worktops and cupboards are expensive wood, and a huge stove stands on the far side. The tiled floor is Cornish slate, reminding me of Amethi.

"Can you get this lady a coffee?" the girl asks.

"And a water?" I remind her politely.

"And a water!" she shouts then takes the tray off me, grinning. "They'll be with you in minutes. One of the perks of being the boss's daughter."

"The...?" I ask but she is gone. So I've just met Georgia. I really hope I didn't seem too drunk.

I take my coffee and water outside, happy to see Rachel safely installed in our original place.

"Hi Alice," she says, "I'm afraid Jack and I are going to make our excuses soon. Can we give you a lift anywhere?"

"Erm, no, I…"

"Say no more!" she smiles, and kisses me. "It's been lovely meeting you and I hope we get to see you again soon."

"You too," I say.

Jack smiles and waves at me and the two of them disappear. I am happy sitting tucked away at the edge of the gathering, hearing the sea below and downing my water, then sipping my coffee, the two combining with the warm, gentle breeze to clear my head.

When I'm feeling a bit better I realise that I don't really want to be here anymore. I can't see Paul anywhere but I check my watch and it's nearly half-ten. A respectable time to get going, I think. I leave my glass and cup on the table then head as discreetly as possible inside, smiling at people as I politely squeeze past them.

Damn! Angela and Tom are in the house, Paul helping Angela into what might well be a real fur coat. They all turn and smile at me.

"Alice!" Angela says again. "Are you alright, all on your own?"

"I'm fine!" I say. "Well, actually, I don't feel great."

"Oh," Angela's face is all false concern. "Something you've eaten, perhaps?"

"Erm," Paul looks a bit annoyed. "We've got one of the best chefs in the county here, thank you."

"Oh, yes, of course, Paul. I am sorry, I didn't mean to suggest…"

"No, of course not," Paul says, his face suggesting he thinks the exact opposite.

"How are you getting home, Alice?" Angela's expression is all fake concern.

"I'll call a taxi," I say, suddenly seeing the wrong turn

this conversation is about to take.

"We can give you a lift, can't we, Tom? Can't have you waiting round for a taxi when you're not feeling well."

"Oh, well, no…" I flail for something to say, looking at Paul, and at that moment the kitchen door opens nearby.

"Georgia!" Angela exclaims and, sure enough, here is Paul's daughter to join our little group. "What a marvellous party! You and your friends make such wonderful waitresses. But we're just about to go and we're giving Alice here a lift. She's not well, I do hope it's not food poisoning."

Paul's expression sits between anger and panic. Now his daughter is here, how can I possibly get out of this? My stomach sinks rapidly as I realise there is no way out. I am not staying here tonight, in Paul's perfect house, or sleeping in his ridiculously comfortable bed, or… I can't even think of it.

"I'm sorry to hear that," Georgia says politely. "It's nice to see you, Angela and Tom, and nice to meet you, Alice, but I need to take these drinks outside."

"Do you mind if I take one?" I ask.

"I thought you weren't feeling well, dear?" Angela asks.

"One more won't hurt," I say and I down my drink, much to her disgust. Now she's scuppered my evening, the least I can do is be sick in her car.

20

Julie's non-hen night comes around quickly. Suddenly, Amethi has begun to eat up much of our time outside of our normal work, topped off with the final arrangements for the wedding. I can see now why people might want to employ a wedding planner. It's a constant trickle of late responses, checking and changing dietary requirements, caterers and kitchen staff, bar staff, seating, to make sure that everybody will be catered for; not to mention the bloody seating plan, which I will be glad if I never see again. Only I know I will be seeing it again, for the next two weeks, and possibly for the rest of my life, in my nightmares.

As Sam is best man and I am chief (only) bridesmaid – I refused to be maid of honour as it just makes me sound old – we are going to have to spend time together, and be seated at the top table, too. I just hope nobody is insensitive enough to make any remarks about the bridesmaid and best man copping off.

He's been up in Scotland a couple of times recently and I've tried very hard not to ask questions of Luke and Julie, as I don't want to put them in an uncomfortable position.

Julie doesn't care about that, though, of course. "Look, I really think it's something to do with his work or his studies, I haven't heard anything about this supposed new woman of his. Luke may have done but I find it hard to believe that he'd be able to keep anything quiet from me."

"Well, don't ask him. Please. Promise you won't. What Sam does is completely up to him."

"Hmm," grumbled Julie. "What if I want to know?"

"If you knew something and I didn't, there's no way you wouldn't tell me."

"I suppose," Julie admitted. "OK. But if you want to know, just say the word. I can be quite forward when I have to be."

"And not just when you have to be," I muttered.

"What was that?"

"Nothing."

So this night away is much-needed and much-appreciated. I feel us both relax as the little red car chugs into the grounds of a beautiful old country house. The leaves have become golden and tawny, clinging to the branches with as much strength as they can muster, dangling teasingly above their fallen comrades.

We are deep inland, or as deep inland as it is possible to be in Cornwall. The hotel is surrounded by thick woods, the car park tucked away from the main house in a neat clearing, so that when you arrive at reception no vehicles can be seen. There are women strolling through the lobby in thick white dressing gowns and so far not a man in sight. The receptionist smiles at us.

"We've a booking in the name of Alice Griffiths," I say, "for a twin room, just one night, full spa package."

"I've got you right here," she continues smiling. "I'll just get you checked in then you can have your room cards and away you go. The spa's through the door in the corner, down the stairs. The restaurant is through the door next to it. Complimentary coffee, tea, herbal tea and light refreshments are in the spa lounge and available all day."

How many times a day does she have to reel all this off? I wonder, grateful that the Sail Loft is not a spa hotel and starting to wonder how my spiel for Amethi is going to go. We're thinking of trying to book it out as a yoga retreat if we can. It was Kate who gave us the idea; she was at David and Martin's when Julie and I dropped off some wedding magazines the other day.

"You're looking well, David," I said while Julie was busy talking flowers and cakes with Martin. "I can see your work's paying off, Kate!"

"Hey, it's my hard work, thank you," David objected.

"Of course," I said, smiling at Kate.

"I'm hoping to get some more clients like him," she said, "I've decided to quit the clinic. It's just a bit too much, with me and Isaac being together and working together. In fact, I think we're going to move in together after Christmas."

"That is great news," I say, my thoughts going immediately to Sophie and Sam, and wondering how they feel about this. "I bet you could build up some clientele, though. What about starting some classes again? You'd got quite a following before."

"I've been thinking along those same lines," Kate said. "If I can get a balance between personal training and classes, I reckon I could do OK. I want to get more into yoga, and I bet I could get a few people interested in classes. And now Soph's getting older, she's a bit more self-reliant."

"Well, you could think about using the space at Amethi." The words were out of my mouth before I'd had time to think about what I was saying.

"You could do retreats!" David said excitedly.

My first reaction was to back-pedal but Julie eagerly took up the idea. "That would be perfect!" she said. "That communal space, Alice, that would be great. You'll have to come and see it, Kate."

"I'd love to," Kate smiled.

The conversation quickly turned to specialised yoga retreats and personal sessions for guests who are staying – or morning classes for businesses using our facilities. As the ideas flowed, I could see that it might just be a great thing, for Kate and for us.

So it is all coming together, but today I must switch off. Today, and tonight, are about Julie, and our friendship, and her happy-ever-after, which is, of course, really just the beginning.

We trundle up to our room, exclaiming at the charms of the grand old building. There is a faint whiff of chlorine on the air and we are both keen to get changed and into that spa. Our room is gorgeous; good-sized twin beds beautifully made with crisp white covers. Old oak furniture, polished to within an inch of its life. The bathroom is more modern, housing a spa bath and a huge 'rain' type shower.

We admire it all then get into our swimsuits and dressing gowns, now part of the army of identikit spa ladies, make-up-free but glowing from the steam room and sauna, and the sheer exhilaration of having this gluttonous, extravagant time with friends, folded away from the pressures of work, relationships and family life for just a small snapshot in time.

We look round the place then lie back on adjacent sun loungers by the window, a generous slice of sunshine falling thickly on our bare legs and across the luxurious robes, reading from a menu of treatments and selecting three each.

"I'll see you on the other side," I say to Julie as we are led into separate rooms by girls who must be a similar age to Lydia. I often wonder what it is that appeals to young women like this, about having to knead and relax other people's soft, flabby flesh, and become almost intimately acquainted with all shapes and sizes of bodies. But today I am not going to question this too deeply.

Instead, I lie face-first on the couch, feeling my body sigh as it is coated with slippery, wonderful-smelling oils, and gradually treated bit by bit to a half-painful but ultimately stress-relieving massage, to a soundtrack of soothing music. In time, I must doze off, as the next thing I know, I am being asked gently if it's OK to work on my feet now.

"Yes," I murmur blissfully. "That will be fine."

After the full body massage and the foot massage, I am treated to a facial and Indian head massage and after that I feel like I could just go and crawl under my duvet and sleep for the rest of the day. Instead, I lie in the dimly-lit relaxation room and pull a soft blanket over me. Julie arrives shortly after this, and lies on the settee next to me. We smile a greeting but neither of us speaks for some time.

After a while, I start to feel revived. I get a glass of water and fetch one for Julie, too.

"Thanks," she smiles and sits up.

"I feel like we need to be making the most of that pool," I say, "but I don't want to wash any of these oils off me."

"I know what you mean. Let's get some lunch then we'll swim this afternoon."

"Excellent idea."

We spend the rest of the day swimming or lying in the sauna, the steam room, the jacuzzi, or back on the loungers. Both having brought books with us, we are happy to either be reading or lying back and just wallowing in the feeling. It's striking that most of the other guests – and they really are all women, it seems – are happy to do the same, with just one group of slightly irritating chattery types.

In the evening we have a bottle of champagne in the bar, by a crackling fire. It really hasn't been that cold yet this year but still there is something just right about the fire, and the autumnal scent on the air.

We eat from the bar menu, washing down bites of roasted pepper and goats cheese paninis with the dregs of the champagne, and ordering another bottle. By ten we are full, we are merry, and fully satisfied with the day. We both agree there is no shame in being in bed by eleven – even on a hen night – and wander back arm-in-arm to our room.

"This has been exactly what I needed," Julie said.

"Me too. And I'm absolutely honoured to have spent your hen night with you. The only guest."

"The only one I need," Julie slurs slightly.

"I can't believe that after tomorrow we won't live together anymore!" As of Monday morning, Luke and Julie will be officially cohabiting – getting in two weeks of sin before they are married.

"Don't," Julie puts a clumsy finger to my lips and we both crease up with laughter. It takes an age to get the key card to work, as we try unsuccessfully to cease our merriment and look like the proper grown-ups we are meant to be. An older couple smile at us as they pass by.

"Bet they think we're lesbians!" Julie says in a less-than-quiet whisper as we fall into our room.

"No chance, you could never pull somebody like me."

"Ha! You wish."

"That doesn't even make sense," I say and we find ourselves in hysterics once more.

I magnanimously – try saying that after sharing two bottles of champagne – allow Julie first use of the bathroom and I am not kidding, when I've come out myself she is fast asleep.

I smile at the sight of my friend, and allow myself a moment to think how lucky I am to have her and how many good times lie ahead. It's all too easy, forcing myself to be realistic and acknowledging the possible pitfalls in starting this business, to forget about the possibilities and the great things which may come about. The reasons we decided to do this in the first place.

Relaxed I may be but, lying in bed listening to my best friend breathing deeply just a metre or two away, my mind turns over for a while. I've told Julie I'm fine with seeing Sam but I don't really know if that's true. The last communication I had with him was a few weeks back, not long after the failure of Paul's party I wasn't actually sick in Angela and Tom's car, in case you were wondering).

Hi from Scotland. I hope the sun is shining in Cornwall.

Oh, he's in Scotland, I'd thought. Was he trying to make a point?

I believe it is sunny, I'd replied after a moment or two's thought. **But I'm stuck inside, creating**

spreadsheets. I'm meant to be learning this new software Luke's installed for us but I just... can't... be arsed.

Ha, I didn't bite at the Scotland reference.

Sounds like my afternoon, he typed back. **I'm stuck inside comparing data on native crustaceans.**

Fascinating!

I knew you'd be interested. How's the business going?

I love it! It's a bit scary but so exciting. You know I'm leasing my own house from myself (and Julie)?

Luke said. That's a stroke of luck.

I know. I can't believe it, really, though I think I'm going to miss being in town. Can't look a gift horse in the mouth, or something.

This was the longest conversation of any type that Sam and I have had since the day of Stefan's and April's wedding. I knew I should be working but I was enjoying myself. I was disappointed, then, when Sam cut it short.

Definitely. I'll let you get on with your work, though, and I'd better crack on with mine.

OK. See you at the wedding if not before.

Yep.

And that was it. I'd felt elated at our messaging, even though it was pretty mundane stuff. It kind of liked the mediocrity of it, like we were finding a new footing. I unlocked my screen and carried on filling in details of papers, magazines and freelance journalists to contact about the launch of Amethi.

Meanwhile, all had also gone quiet on the Paul front. He'd rung the day following the party, first thing in the morning.

"I am so sorry," he said.

"What for?" I asked, rubbing my eyes and realising that I may have had a disappointing night but I had at least had a good ten hours' sleep.

"I should have thought of something – been quicker off the mark. But with Georgia and everything…"

"I know," I said. "I was the same. I just didn't want things to get weird, what with your daughter." Foiled by another daughter. "Why didn't you tell me she was working there, though?"

"I don't know," Paul admits. "When Georgia does things like that for me she normally likes to do it incognito but normally it's for clients from out of town. I hadn't thought that she would know some of the people there, or that I should maybe have introduced her to you."

I wasn't convinced by these words; and I also thought that was fine. We had, after all, been on only two real dates, not counting the car journey to the hospital, or of course the party. Why would he want to introduce me to his daughter?

"I'll make it up to you, I promise."

"Great." Was I just tired, or had something changed? "Listen, I've just woken up. Can I give you a call in a bit?"

"I've been up for hours!" he said. "Best part of the day." Now that was something my dad said. Not that Paul is anywhere near Dad's age, but he is a dad himself, of course. And perhaps it was beginning to dawn on me that I am just not cut out for ready-made dads. I can't deny I'm drawn to Paul, and I had really wanted to stay over at his place that night, but there I was, unexpectedly alone in my very own bed, having enjoyed ten blissful hours' sleep. I couldn't truly say I was disappointed.

Since then, we've been out a couple of times; once to a nice little bar on a beach up the coast and once for a walk, followed by a lovely pub lunch. It was notable that the spark seems to have dimmed.

Paul, in what I have come to realise is fairly typical of him, tackled this head-on. We were sitting back in our seats, appetites sated. I'd been thinking about what we'd be doing after our meal; would Paul want me to go back to his? Would I want to? His words took me by surprise.

"It put you off, didn't it? Meeting my kids – or at least one of them."

"No, well, OK, in honesty, yes a little. But not because I didn't like Georgia," I added hastily. "She's lovely."

"She is," he smiled. "Does it make me seem old to you, though?"

This was the closest I've seen to Paul doubting himself. This little glimmer of vulnerability made me warm to him even more.

"No, I promise it doesn't. You're not old, you're only in your forties!" At this, he gave a slightly wry smile. "But I suppose it made me realise that we're at very different stages of life. And I know that makes me sound horribly serious about everything but I guess I know that I want a family of my own one day. And," I borrowed a bit of his directness, "I know that won't be what you want. On top of that, between the Sail Loft and Amethi, I am exhausted."

"Even more reason to have some fun," Paul said, putting his hand on mine and grinning. "But really, Alice, I know where you're coming from."

"I'm so boring, aren't I?" I asked, squeezing his fingers.

"No, you're not, you're very sensible."

He drove me back home and we kissed in the car but he didn't come in. We haven't actually seen each other since then. I miss him, and that excitement he brought into my life.

It's time to be strict, though. Alongside our work worries, Julie and I agreed to leave relationship talk at the door of the hotel. I switch the soft bedside light on, grab my book and snuggle down under the duvet, pulling the bottom corners free so that my feet don't feel so restricted. After just a few pages, I feel my eyes closing and I am dimly aware of the book falling closed on my hands, then the next thing I know it is morning.

After a leisurely breakfast, Julie and I head back to the spa, allowing ourselves a good half-hour's reading to allow for digestion, then our morning follows a similar routine to the previous afternoon. All too soon, it is lunchtime and then time to get going. I pick up the bill, despite Julie's protestations.

246

We take a long, wistful look at the place before we retrieve our baggage and head back to the car, and the world beyond those golden-leaved trees.

21

When we get back from the hotel we are straight into reality and spend most of the afternoon and evening finding, losing and packing Julie's possessions. Luke ferries boxes back and forth to their beautiful new house until all that is left is an overnight bag and Julie's bedding. We are exhausted. The three of us share a bottle of red wine in the garden, all of us quiet and contemplative. It is a still evening and warm enough to sit out, though I feel a very slight chill across my skin. I think of all the time Julie and I have spent in David's house – our arrival as slightly nervous eighteen-year-olds, so many years ago, when we'd found seasonal work at the Sail Loft and had high hopes for the best summer ever, away from school and parents. David was a stranger then and I remember my first impressions of him – struck by his good looks only to have my hopes dashed when I discovered he was gay.

The second time we came down here, just two summers ago – Julie escaping her failed relationship with Gabe and me keen to do something new, shake off my steady, reliable existence (and secretly, of course, wondering if I might find Sam again). I remember the arguments, too: me casting doubt on Julie's relationship with Luke; her telling me she'd let on to Luke that Sophie wasn't Sam's biological daughter – and our subsequent fear that was why Sophie had run away. This was the night which led to my breaking up with Sam, but it wasn't Julie's fault.

Aside from the arguments, which may have been big but definitely few and far between, we have had some of the best times in our lives so far while we've lived here together. Whether it has been shared meals, parties, or just lying around watching crap TV, Julie and I have rarely failed to have a good time.

"I can't believe we won't be here anymore," she says suddenly and Luke takes her hand. "I mean, I'm excited about the future, obviously, but this has been the best fun."

"I know," I say, happy to think her mind has been wandering along similar lines to mine and that she is not wholly preoccupied with the wedding and moving in with Luke. "I love this house. It felt like home immediately when we came back to it."

"We've been so lucky," Julie sighs.

"And we still are," I say. "I am really sad to be leaving, too, but I guess we just have to face the future and get on with it."

"I hope you don't think Julie marrying me is something she just has to get on with!" Luke laughs.

"No, I didn't mean it like that, I…"

"It's OK, Alice, I was only joking, I know how special this place is to you two. And it's special to me, too. But you two, well, this is where you came together, isn't it? Where you've made huge changes to your lives and started again. And there's no going back to our eighteen-year-old selves, but that summer was a really stand-out one. Unforgettable."

It was, totally unforgettable. Over the ten years that followed: all the way through university; my relationship with Geoff and the hard times which came after it;

getting a job; buying my flat; through all these times, I never forgot that summer in Cornwall, and never quite shook that wish to be back here. I hadn't thought Julie was serious when she'd suggested we do it but she tapped into something which had never gone away; a yearning nestled deep down inside me.

"Thank you, Luke," I stood and kissed him. "You are amazing."

"You are," Julie agreed, her shining eyes fastened on her husband-to-be.

"And now, I am going to say goodnight. I have an early start in the morning. And I don't think I can feel any sadder about this or that any good can come from staying up now!"

Julie stands and we hug for a long time. When we pull back, we both have tears in our eyes.

"Onwards and upwards," she says.

"Onwards and upwards." I kiss her on the cheek and go inside, placing my wine glass in the sink. In the warmth of my bedroom, I draw the curtains, lingering for just a moment to take in the view of the street. I remember that night when Luke's mum died, when I saw the dark figure walking disconsolately through the pouring rain, towards this very house. Sam. I also remember sitting here, hoping desperately that Sophie would appear, thinking of all the unimaginable things which might have happened to her. Knowing that it would all be my fault because Sam had trusted me and I had betrayed him. I still feel sick when I remember that night and even though Sophie turned up safe and sound – and it turned out to be Kate's indiscretion which had caused her to run away – it made me realise that I couldn't expect Sam to put me before Sophie. It broke my heart, and his too.

I brush my teeth, wash my face, then climb into bed and switch the lights off. There is so much to look forward to, I know, but just for this moment I need to look back and remember it all. With Julie moving out and on, my remaining time in the house will not be the same. It feels very much as though an important chapter of our lives is ending tonight.

22

I awake to the rain pattering against my window pane. For a good few weeks now, it's been dark when my alarm has gone off, but this is the first rainy start I have had to face. The house is quiet and it has been for two weeks.

It's been strange not having Julie around, although not as strange as I thought it might be. I guess she and I are often out at different times, with our opposing working patterns, and Julie has also often been at Luke's dad's when Luke has been back from London. I wonder briefly how it feels to Luke to have left London behind but he says he was more than ready to make the break.

Today, though – for one day only – Julie will be back. And she'll be here in just an hour or two. Before she gets here, there is much I have to do.

I start with a long, hot shower, singing to myself as I push conditioner through my hair and slide bubbles across my shiny skin. Then I wrap my hair in a flimsy towel – I miss Julie's soft, fluffy towels almost as much as I miss her – and put on my jogging trousers and a hoodie.

Down the stairs I go, casting a glance at the rain-spattered stairwell window. The weather is not showing any mercy yet and there is no sign of morning in that moody sky. The odd light on in other houses is comforting, knowing I am not the only person up right now, but they are not about to embark on one of the most emotional days of their lives.

While the water boils in the kettle, I hoover the hallways, dining room and lounge. I make sure there are enough chairs because this morning the house will be full of people. Julie and her mum will be here; Charlene the hairdresser; Julie's cousin Lucy and her girlfriend, India. I asked Bea if she wanted to come but she said she'd have to meet us at the wedding. She seems to have accepted that I'm leaving the Sail Loft, and she even asks me questions about Amethi from time to time but things have never really returned to how they were before.

I'd envisaged that after the initial breaking of the news, Bea might get behind me and Julie, and we might even be able to ask her advice on a few things. I just don't feel comfortable doing that, though; I can sense that she is still upset. Sometimes it annoys me as I am completely within my rights to be moving on – and I honestly think she will be happier taking more of an active role at the Sail Loft again (Bob may not be so happy). Sometimes, though, I just feel sad. She is an important person in my life and I want her to know that.

I have agreed to stay on till 31st December – to see Christmas and the New Year. I really don't know how I'm going to do it all as well as finish the preparations for the grand launch of Amethi as a fully-functioning business but I could certainly do with the money and in honesty I'm quite keen to be here for one more Christmas at the Sail Loft. I will just have to swallow back the stress and trust that between us all we will make it work. That first Christmas, Bea was not around, and Stefan was with his family. This year, the three of us can share the load. Likewise with Amethi, it is up to me and Julie to make it work. None of it is my responsibility alone and when I make myself realise that, I feel far better about things.

I sit and drink a coffee in the dining room, looking out at the rain and noticing gradual shades of daylight enter the sky. I am so nervous about today that it might be me who's getting married but the nerves are mostly on Julie's behalf, and partly to do with seeing Sam again.

I haven't been able to shake thoughts of him over these last few weeks. Paul asked if I wanted to go out last week but I told him I was too busy. Which is true − I am ridiculously busy − but it seemed a convenient excuse.

"Are you mad?" Julie had said when I told her about it during one of our fleeting get-togethers. "He's drop-dead gorgeous and loaded!" But she had a twinkle in her eye.

"You're right, I think I might just chuck it all in and see if I can get him to marry me. Then I'll never have to work again."

"Great plan."

"I just think it's a bit futile," I said. "He is, as you rightly say, drop-dead gorgeous, but he's at such a different stage of life to me. And yes, I know, it can just be fun, but I don't know... I see you and Luke and everything you have together and I think I'm better off hanging on and seeing if I might find that with somebody. And you know, I want kids. Not now," I hastened to add, "not yet, but I don't think that seeing somebody who already has a family − and an almost grown-up one at that − is the best idea."

"Still, it wouldn't hurt to spend a bit more time with Paul. See what it's like staying over at his space-age palace!"

"Ha! I won't pretend it's not tempting. We'll see."

I didn't bother saying anything about Sam. It's something which will just have to fade away with time and hopefully, after Luke's and Julie's wedding, I won't have to see him for a while, which might make it easier.

I swallow the sugary dregs from my coffee cup. "Forget it all," I say out loud to the empty room and continue my preparations for Julie. I make a load of sandwiches, and set out coffee cups, champagne glasses and plates. I cover tiny cakes and Florentines with foil and set them on the side. Bringing down a mirror from my chest of drawers, I glimpse a little patch of blue in the sky through the window on the stairs. My heart gives a tiny skip.

I don't know where all the time goes but go it does because, soon enough, Julie is knocking at the door. I let her in and exclaim at the sight of her zipped-up dress carrier, then I kiss her mum on the cheek. Julie is not as close to her mum as I am to mine but nevertheless I can tell this is an emotional day for Cherry and can practically feel the nerves popping off her like tiny fireworks.

"Come in, come in," I usher them in, which feels weird as really it still feels like this is Julie's home. I make a fresh pot of coffee and hand a cup to them both and we all sit on the edges of our seats, unable to relax.

I look at Julie. She is make-up free, as she always should be in my opinion, and I don't know if I've ever seen somebody look more truly the definition of 'glowing' before. I've also never seen her look so nervous.

Luckily, the doorbell goes and Charlene comes in, bringing a blast of autumnal air and a few stray leaves with her. "Ooh, sorry," she giggles, "can you show me where you want me?"

I take her into the dining room and get her a drink. "Mother of the bride first?" she asks.

"Sounds like a plan," I say, and I fetch Cherry through

from the lounge.

I return to Julie and we can hear Charlene chatting away to Cherry, who sounds like she is soon at ease.

"So how do you feel?" I ask my friend.

"I just want to get on with it!" she says. "I know that sounds awful. I don't mean I want to get it out of the way – but I can't bear all this waiting around!"

"I know, I'm the same and it's not me getting married." I check my watch. "Only four hours to go."

"Four hours!" Julie exclaims. "Why didn't we set the time for 10am?"

"It'll fly by, you'll see. You've got to get changed, get your hair done, do your make-up. Speaking of which, what's the correct order to do all these things? Make-up first?"

"Yes… I think so, otherwise I might get it on the dress. Then I guess I put the dress on, otherwise it might mess my hair up. Oh, I don't know!"

"Shh," I soothe. "Let's get a glass of something to calm your nerves, shall we?"

"Yes. But I can't be drunk when I'm getting married."

"You won't be! Look, we'll have a glass now, have something to eat, then we'll do your make-up and all that, OK?"

"*We* won't be doing my make-up. *I'll* be doing my make-up!" she scolds. "There's no way I'm letting you near it, Miss Natural Look."

"Ha, fine," I say, "I need to get myself ready, anyway. But let's get that bottle open, shall we?"

We head through to the kitchen, bypassing Cherry and Charlene, who appear to have really hit it off. Cherry looks almost shyly at us, sitting there with her hair pinned up all over her head. I remember her from our school days, and how nervous I used to be of her. She seemed so tall and confident, and sure of herself. Now, having not seen her for some time, she looks older, and softer. I can see the strong resemblance between her and Julie, with their high cheekbones and deep, dark eyes.

"Champagne?" I ask and both of them exclaim their assent. Fetching the bottle from the fridge, I hand it to Julie to open, only her hands are shaking. "Here," I say to Cherry, "would you do the honours?"

"I'd love to, thank you, Alice."

The cork flies out with a pop and bubbles spill over the sides of the glasses but we don't care. We push all four drinks together merrily.

"To Julie!" I say.

"To Julie!" Cherry and Charlene respond.

"And Luke," adds Julie.

"And Luke," I agree.

As we are finishing our glasses, Lucy and India arrive, so we have another glass with them.

"See," I say to Julie, "I told you time would fly."

I uncover the food and tell everyone to help themselves. Cherry stands and Charlene removes the jacket from around her shoulders.

"You look beautiful," I say to Cherry.

"Ha! Thank you, your turn now," she says, going to kiss Lucy and India, and take a plate.

I sit back and let Charlene do her thing; answering her questions but not quite feeling up to chatting. I don't really know what I want done to my hair so I let her decide.

"I think we'll straighten it," she says. "Then pin it up. Maybe a few loose strands so it doesn't look too perfect. Does that sound OK?"

257

"That actually sounds perfect for me! I don't really do neat very well."

"OK, well, leave it to me," she says. "What colour's your dress, by the way?"

"It's called Midnight Blue."

"That sounds gorgeous. Perfect for this time of year, too."

"I do love it and I'm very grateful Julie didn't get me the meringue she'd been threatening me with!"

I sit and close my eyes for a while as Charlene hums to herself and chats with Julie and her family. Her touch firm as she combs and tugs at my hair then runs it firmly through the straighteners. Finally, I can feel her pulling bits into place and piling it up at the back of my head.

"That looks amazing, Alice!" Julie says.

"Here," Charlene holds a mirror up behind me so I can look in my bedroom mirror and see the way she's folded and pinned my hair, which looks shinier than I have ever seen it. There are just a few loose strands falling round my face.

"I love it," I say, "Thank you so much, Charlene."

"Not a problem!" She pulls the jacket from my shoulders. "Now, Julie, you can't escape it any longer!"

I take the opportunity to eat a couple of sandwiches, then go upstairs to get into my dress. I need to be available for Julie after her hair is done, even if she doesn't want my help with her make-up.

I pull on my dress and struggle a little with the zip but when it's on, I'm pleased with the result. Opening my curtains, I see the rain has truly cleared away and although the pavements and road are still glistening, there are dry patches beginning to appear. I take a last glance in the mirror then remind myself it doesn't really matter. This day is not about me.

Downstairs, Charlene is putting the finishing touches to Julie's hair – a handful of tiny, delicate cream flowers tucked in and around the curve of the glimmering, glistening chignon.

"That looks absolutely beautiful," I breathe and both Julie and Charlene turn to me. I can't tell which one looks more pleased with herself.

There is a knock on the door. It's Jamie, the official wedding photographer and one of Luke's and Sam's friends from school.

"Mind if I come in?" he asks. "You look lovely, if I may say so."

 You certainly may! Come on, Julie is decent … I think we all are. Everybody decent?" I call. "Jamie's here!"

He comes in and takes photo after photo, of the room, the table covered in hairdressing paraphernalia and plates with half-eaten sandwiches. "Enough!" Julie says as he snaps a series of pictures of her. "I'm going to get my dress on."

While she's upstairs with Cherry, we all sit quietly, making half-hearted attempts at conversation. Then I hear her familiar tread on the stairs. My head turns and so do Lucy's, India's, Charlene's and Jamie's. From where I am sitting I can see Julie's bare feet, the ends of her skirt lifted above them as she steps carefully down the stairs. A moment later, she is in the doorway and I don't have to wait for the wedding itself to feel that familiar catch of my breath. I gasp, and feel shaky. Before me is my best friend, standing self-consciously but beautifully in the doorway; a genuine vision in her long, simple wedding gown, its dusky pink making her skin look darker than ever. I can see that everyone in the room feels the same; with the exception of Jamie, who has resumed his incessant camera-clicking.

"Well, what do you think?" Julie asks, half bashful and half impatient.

"You look…" I say but feel a lump in my throat which cuts my sentence off.

"So…" Lucy clearly has the same problem.

"Beautiful," finishes India.

"Ha! Good," Julie says, mock-arrogantly. "This is the effect I was hoping to have. Now where's my drink?"

We open a further bottle of champagne and there is just time for one more glass each before the wedding car arrives.

"We'd better run!" Lucy says, kissing Julie on the cheek and grabbing India by the hand. "See you at the wedding!"

Jamie continues taking pictures and the house seems to close in on us protectively as Cherry and I fuss about getting Julie's shoes and wrap, and sorting ourselves out. We say very little but we all stand up straight at the same time, look at each other and smile.

Click.

"Perfect," Jamie says.

***

I walk ahead of Julie, nervously eyeing the people to either side of me. Mum and Dad are at the end of one of the rows, beaming from ear to ear. I see Bea and Bob, and David and Martin, at the other side of me.

The wedding is in a clifftop hotel, where the reception will also be held. The room where the wedding is boasts huge glass windows, offering a tantalising view across the neat green lawn and the sea beyond.

But nobody is looking at the view. I turn my focus to the front of the room where I see Luke, standing tall and dignified and more handsome than I have ever seen him, in a dark blue suit. In the seats behind him, I can see the backs of Jim, Luke's sister Marie and her boyfriend Alan, and, of course, Sam.

The row behind that holds Sophie and Kate, with Isaac. Sophie turns and smiles excitedly at me. I return the smile and then I am at the front, where Julie's brother Lee sits in an otherwise empty bench. I stand to one side and I look back to see Julie walking hand-in-hand with Cherry. My friend did not want to be given away but she wanted her mum with her as she walked up the aisle today and the sight of them together makes me well up again. Oh my god, I'm going to be a nightmare. Just wait till the speeches.

As Julie and Cherry reach me, I smile at them and kiss Julie on the cheek then I sit down and Cherry sits next to me as Julie and Luke move together and he takes her hand. The look he gives her could never be reproduced, no matter how many photos Jamie takes, but it says everything anyone could ever need to know.

The first reading is by Lucy. *It's All I Have to Bring Today* by Emily Dickinson; it is short and unbelievably sweet.

"It's all I have to bring to-day,
This, and my heart beside,
This, and my heart, and all the fields,
And all the meadows wide.
Be sure you count, should I forget,
Someone the sum could tell,
This, and my heart, and all the bees
Which in the clover dwell."

The second reading is, unexpectedly, by Sam. It's a poem by Simon Armitage called *Let Me Put It This Way*. I love it. I had thought Marie was doing this one but I see her mouth 'thank you' to Sam as he stands up. I notice he can't look at his audience. It makes me want to stand up there with him. But I don't.

When he's finished reading, for the briefest moment Sam looks at me before he takes the piece of paper and hurries back to his seat. He looks shy and I see his shoulders hunch slightly self-consciously then relax as the celebrant begins to talk again. I just want to go over and put my arms around him.

Before we know it, Julie and Luke are married. They speak their vows to each other never once breaking their gaze. When the celebrant tells them they are married, Luke sweeps Julie into an all-encompassing embrace and kiss and we all clap and cheer. I am glad of the excuse to release some of the emotion which has built up in me today.

Following the service, we all head into the bar while the ceremony room is deftly turned into the dining room. The smartly dressed young hotel staff scurry around behind the semi-closed doors and I stand with my parents, sipping sharp-tasting lemonade and watching the goings-on.

"You look lovely," Mum says.

"I feel tired!" I laugh. "I'm also a bit nervous."

"Why are you nervous?" Dad asks. "Oh, is it Sam?" he says, a bit too loudly.

"Shh!" I scan the room, hoping that neither Sam nor any of his friends are nearby. "Well, maybe a little, but it's actually because I've got a surprise up my sleeve…"

"Oh?" says Dad.

"You'll see."

I stick to the non-alcoholic drinks, thinking I will have a 'proper' drink later. The effects of the earlier champagne are long gone; in fact, this morning feels like it was days ago. As we head in for dinner, Luke winks at me.

Once all the guests are seated, Sam stands and bangs a small gong. He is just five seats away from me, with Luke and Jim, and Julie and Cherry, between us. Sophie and Kate are on the same table as Mum, Dad, Bea, Bob, David and Martin. I look at them all and smile. My palms are sweating.

"We thought we'd do things differently today," says Sam, "so that we can enjoy our dinner without any of the pre-speech nerves. So I believe that, as best man, it's my duty to start things off."

I swallow nervously, self-conscious as I wonder whether I should be listening rapt to my ex-boyfriend or if people will perceive it as my still being in love with him. In the end, I can't help listening anyway, and laughing as he recounts some of the stupid things he and Luke used to do. Then he gets to the serious bit.

"But despite being a total idiot, Luke has always been my best friend. We met at primary school and I don't think we've ever really fallen out. Then, when we were eighteen, Luke met Julie one summer when she and her bridesmaid, Alice –" he broke off for a moment and our eyes met briefly "– came down here for a few months. I knew Luke was in love, but it took another ten years for Julie to feel the same way about him." There is a smattering of laughter at this. "I don't think Luke ever forgot Julie in those intervening years and I remember the night when he met up with her again, down on the beach. It was obvious he felt the same way as he had done all those years before. I am so happy for both of them that they found each other again and I am absolutely sure that they have a long and happy future together. All that remains is for me to ask you to raise your glasses and toast them both. To Luke and Julie."

"To Luke and Julie," we echo, standing, raising our glasses and taking a sip.

As everybody settles in their seats, Sam remains standing and so do I. I take a deep breath.

"Now, I know this isn't exactly by the book either but today, the bride's best friend would also like to say a few words."

Julie looks at me, not sure whether she should be horrified. Luke grins. I stand. My heart is in my throat.

"Thank you, Sam," I say, glancing nervously at him as he sits down. I envy him the relief which is obvious as he takes a drink from his glass of wine. I address the room. "As Sam said, this is not exactly the way things are normally done. But I just couldn't let today go without saying a few words. Like Sam and Luke, Julie and I have known each other since school. Unlike Sam and Luke, we've never done anything stupid or embarrassing." I am relieved to hear a little laughter at this. "So, sorry to say, I don't have any stories to entertain you with. I just really wanted to stand up here and tell you all what a wonderful friend Ju…" Oh no, I'm choking on my words. I can't look at anyone. I give myself a moment. Take a deep breath. "What a wonderful friend Julie is. We often get to hear from the best man at weddings, who will tell us about their friend, or brother, or whoever the groom is to them, and what they mean to them. We also often hear from the bride's dad but that is not always the case and today is an example of that. So in lieu of a proud father, Julie has me – her very proud friend. She has been an inspiration to me in so many ways as we've grown up and I feel like we are still growing up, and she is still inspiring me. She pushes me and she makes me brave when I might never have been. If it wasn't for her, I would probably still be selling stationery, still doing Pilates every Monday and running every Wednesday… so, come to think of it, she's probably had a detrimental effect on my health and fitness levels." A little more gentle laughter. "But really, being an only child, having Julie in my life is like having a sister. I couldn't love her more and, like Sam, I am absolutely certain that she and Luke are meant to be together. Julie, I love you." I look at my friend and see she is in floods of tears. We manage a smile at each other. "To Julie and Luke," I manage to squeak, raising my glass before I sit back down on my chair, overcome with the release of nerves and the emotions of the situation. Cherry smiles at me then I feel a pair of familiar arms embracing me and Julie's face is next to mine.

"Thank you, Alice," she whispers in my ear and our tears mingle on my cheek.

23

Once the speech is over, I sit back and enjoy Luke's, then Julie's, then tuck ravenously into my dinner, and began to enjoy the wine as well. By the time coffee is being drunk and the shiny silver wrappers being pulled from the chocolate mints and discarded, ties, tongues and waistbands around the room are being loosened.

"Alice," Julie appeared at my side.

"What is it?"

"Your mum said I should make the time at least once today to just stop and take it all in – otherwise it will fly by in a whirl."

"Sounds like Mum!" I grinned.

"So that's what I'm going to do. Can I sit with you for a moment and we both do it?"

"Of course!"

She pulls her chair up next to mine and holds my hand. We both look around the room and I imagine what it feels like for Julie, and for Luke, to have most of the people they care about gathered here in one place, to help celebrate their love.

I catch Mum's eye and she smiles at me. She clearly knows exactly what we're doing. Dad, meanwhile, is in deep conversation with David. I see him topping up both their wine glasses. Sam has moved over to sit next to Sophie and she's laughing at something he's saying. Kate and Isaac are talking to Martin.

At each table, people sit smiling and chatting. The room is filled with the hum of conversation and ringing with laughter.

"This is not a bad moment to capture," I say.

"My god, it's amazing," breathes Julie. "Thank you again, Alice, for the speech."

"It's my pleasure. I didn't want to go on about Amethi but you know that's our next big adventure."

"Too bloody right!" Julie lifts her glass to mine and we push them briefly together, looking each other in the eye. Whatever happens in my life, I must never forget how lucky I am to have this woman for a friend.

Shortly after this, Julie is whisked away by Jamie for outside photos so I wander over to Mum and Dad.

"That was wonderful, Alice," Dad says. "I bet Julie loved your speech."

"Thanks, Dad. I just felt like it would even things up a bit if I did that."

"It certainly did," he says.

"So what were you chatting to David about?"

"Oh, this and that," Dad is laying on the nonchalance a tad too heavily and I can tell there's something going on but Mum smoothly swoops in.

"I love your dress, it's as beautiful as you said it would be. And your hair! How many hours is it going to take to unpick those pins?"

"I don't want to think about it! Maybe I'll keep it like this forever."

"That might be easier."

"Alice!" Sophie spots me from across the table. Sam is still next to her. He smiles at me, too.

"Hi Sophie! Are you having a good day?"

"Yeah, Julie looks so beautiful!"

"I know. But then, she always does."

"But extra, extra beautiful today. Will you let me try some of your champagne? Dad won't let me!"

"Well, I definitely don't think I should, then."

"You're only eleven, Sophie."

"I'm nearly twelve."

Ever since I've known Sophie she's been 'nearly' the next age on.

"Six years too young to drink alcohol legally."

"Well, Mum says I can at home, have a little taste, if I want to."

"OK," I can see Sam isn't one hundred per cent delighted by this but what choice does he have?

"What's this?" Kate's clearly heard her name mentioned. "Is she trying to con you into letting her have some wine? What I actually said, young lady, is that it's legal for parents to allow their children to have a small taste of alcohol in the safety of their own homes." Sophie looks caught out. "Great speech, Alice," Kate says. "If I had a friend make a speech like that about me I'd probably marry them!"

"I'll bear that in mind," I smile.

I see Dad is in conversation with David again. I look at Martin and he rolls his eyes. Sophie, meanwhile, has engaged both her parents' attention now.

"Are you having a good time, love?" asks Mum.

"Oh yeah, especially now the speech is out of the way."

"But it's a bit strange being here with Sam..? And I guess that's Kate – the ex, Sophie's mum?"

"Yeah, that's Kate."

"She seems very nice. And her boyfriend. Isaac, is it?"

"She is very nice. And Isaac, yeah."

"And you're wondering what on earth is stopping you and Sam from being together now. Well, actually that's what I'm wondering. I'm just guessing you are, too."

"I don't know, Mum. We've tried… twice. And it didn't work."

"What about this new man? This Paul?"

"Oh, I don't know. He's nice. Really nice. But he's already had his family. Made his fortune. And we're really very different."

"It's none of my business, really," Mum says, "but I've never seen you happier than when you were with Sam. And Sophie clearly adores you."

"I love her, too." *And Sam.* The words remain unspoken. "Maybe this conversation is better had another time. It's Julie's day today."

"You're right. Just as long as you're OK."

"I am, Mum. I promise."

"Good."

One of the best things about the evening is that I feel like I know at least half of the people here. And the whole thing is so relaxed. Julie and Luke have booked a local band, Ska Dust, who are just excellent. I find myself dancing with so many different people, although Sam and I pretty much manage to avoid each other. At one point, I see him talking with Kate, and Bea – they make for a strange trio, I think, and I am sure that I see the three of them cast a couple of glances my way.

Whatever, I think, smiling at Sophie, my current partner. I am having too good a time to think about it. Then I notice that Bea is nowhere to be seen and Sam and Kate are now deep in conversation while Isaac stands nearby, smiling and nodding his head to the music. He's clearly not bothered, and I guess Sam and Kate must have much to discuss, with shared responsibility for a *nearly* twelve-year-old girl.

I dance with Julie and Luke, and Cherry joins us, at which point I make my excuses and head to the bar. I am very hot, my feet are aching, and I need a drink.

"Ginger beer, please," I say to the barman then have to shout the request above the music. I sit on a stool and take my shoes off. Bloody heels. Remind me never to wear them again. They're just not practical for dancing, either.

"I'll get this," says an all-too-familiar voice.

I turn and smile at Sam. "Thank you."

"No problem. I'll have a single malt please, mate." He doesn't look at me immediately but takes the stool next to mine and looks at my bare feet. "Painful shoes?"

"You should try them!"

"No thanks." He makes an attempt at a smile but I can tell there's something on his mind.

"Are you OK, Sam?"

"I'm fine. I was just talking to Bea. And Kate."

"Oh yeah?" Why are my hackles rising?

"I didn't realise that bloke who picked you up was Paul Winters."

"Yeah, that's right. Do you know him?" Stupid question. Obviously he doesn't or he'd have recognised him.

"No, but I know of him. And I know a bit more about him now, too."

I can feel my face flushing. I don't say anything for a moment then, "And is there a problem with Paul?"

Suddenly I feel protective of the man I've been dating. And I think back to Bea's gossip that day in the office.

What's she been telling him?

"No, not a problem as such. But are you still seeing him?"

"Why?"

"Oh nothing, it's none of my business. Sorry."

He's grumpy about something, though, I can tell. And now this conversation has begun I don't think I can let it just tail away.

"Go on, Sam. What's the problem? There's obviously something."

"No, sorry, let's save this for another day. This was stupid." He downs his drink in one and gets up to go.

"Sam, you can't just start a conversation like this and then leave it! What's the problem?"

"Nothing. Nothing's the problem."

"OK." I shrug. I feel annoyed and I don't want to feel like this at my best friend's wedding. The music has stopped now and the singer announces that's the end of their set. Sam orders another whisky while I sip my ginger beer and watch the band pack up and the DJ take to the decks.

"Maybe you should find out a bit more about your boyfriend, that's all," Sam mutters.

"What was that?" I almost say that Paul isn't my boyfriend but actually I don't think that's any of Sam's business. I want to know what Sam is on about.

"Just… oh, nothing." The whisky goes the same way as the one before and he gets up, leaving me bemused. What the hell is he on about? I slip my protesting feet back into my shoes, determined to find Bea and question her as it seems to me that her chat with Sam preceded this strange situation.

Before I get the chance, however, my heart sinks. The

DJ is summoning Luke and Julie to the dance floor, for their first dance and, in his innocence, follows this request with another: "And let's see the best man and bridesmaid up here, too."

Everybody cheers and I have no choice but to do the right thing. Sam and I look at each other, walk through the merry party-goers, and reluctantly meet on the dance floor.

Next to us, Julie and Luke dance smoochily. The track they've chosen is Elbow's *One Day Like This* and it feels as though Sam and I have no choice but to hold on to each other, for the full three minutes, forty-five seconds of the radio version. Behind us, Jim and Cherry dance good-naturedly. Gradually, the dance floor fills up and the pressure is off. But I don't want to let this go. "What was that about?" I ask through a kind of half-smile which probably looks like a grimace.

"Just ask your boyfriend."

"He's not…" I say but I think no, it's none of his business.

"Just spit it out, please, Sam."

"Fine. You know he's the one who sold you that place?"

My mind is blank for a moment. What's he on about?

"What place… what, you mean… Amethi?" Somewhere in my mind, something clicks. A vague memory of the same slate tiles in Paul's kitchen, that are in the buildings at Amethi. But no, that can't be right. Why would Paul have kept it from me?

"Yes," he says, "*Amethi*. Obviously trying to buy you."

"Don't be stupid," I say and I can see the anger on Sam's face at those words.

"I'm not being stupid. The man obviously thinks he's better than us mere mortals."

"What…?" I feel really angry now and I don't know if it is more at Sam or Paul. I will have to ask Paul about this, but tonight is not the time.

Sam's arm is still around me and I want to push him away but I don't want to make a scene.

"Even if this is true, and I'd like to know how told you it by the way, what's the problem?"

Also, I think, if Paul really did do this but didn't tell me, how is he trying to buy me? But I can't quite get that thought straight in my head yet. The immediate problem is the man in front of me, my ex-boyfriend, who somehow seems to think it's OK to cast judgement on me. We dance in silence to the end of the song and then go our separate ways. I can see Julie clock our looks but I just wink at her and smile in what I hope is a convincing way. I do not want her day being spoiled by this.

I wander outside to get some fresh air and think through what just happened. How ridiculous. I feel like we've argued about something which is actually nothing to do with either of us. Why is Sam annoyed at me?

Outside, it's chilly, and I wish I'd brought my coat. The balcony is largely populated with smokers. I want to find a quiet corner away from everyone, where I can let the outdoors work its magic and I can return to my friend's wedding, as happy and jubilant as I have been all day.

"Alice!" My dad is out here, too, it turns out, with David. What is going on? Are these two having an affair? "We've got some news for you. Great news. Well, I hope you'll think it is."

"OK…" I say.

"We're buying David's house."

"You and David?" I know what Dad's saying, though. I'm just being facetious. "Are you kidding me, Dad? You and Mum?"

"Yes, me and your mum. We're moving to Cornwall!"

Thoughts of Sam and his strangeness momentarily forgotten, a huge smile spreads itself across my face and I hug Dad, and then David, in turn.

"I take it you do think it's good news, then?"

"Dad," I say, "that is the best news I've had in ages."

24

I have quite a sore head the day after the wedding – even though I stopped drinking early on. It was absolutely exhausting and I am very glad to have the following day off work, to recover.

Aside from trips to the bathroom and to the kitchen for supplies, I am planning to spend all day in bed. Mum and Dad have gone to Falmouth for the day so I know they won't be dropping in, and Julie and Luke are on their way to their Maldives-based honeymoon. I have the luxury of a day of peace and time to myself. I am determined it will be my chance to get my head straight.

I've woken annoyingly early – one of the side-effects of the hours I keep at the Sail Loft. However, it's been possible to doze since then and I've drifted in and out of sleep and some weird dreams, for about three hours.

My bridesmaid dress is folded over the back of a chair in the corner of the room, heels cast gratefully aside in the hallway, as soon as I got in last night. I lie back, letting my eyes take in the details of this room. I can't believe it will soon be Mum and Dad's! It's such a strange thought and perhaps I have a slight tinge of jealousy or something; after all, this place is mine. Only it's not mine. It's David's. It's been a much loved home to me and Julie for two years, though, but who better to take it on next than my own parents? And, best of all, it means we'll be living close together again.

"You're not annoyed about it, then?" Mum asked last night.

"No! I think it's brilliant. And I'm so happy you'll be close by. Does this mean you're giving up work? I guess you have to, otherwise it would be a hell of a commute," I laughed.

"Well, yes, I'll be giving up my present job, at least. I did wonder whether you and Julie might need a hand with your business… at least in the early days, until you get things running like clockwork. But no pressure. I do not want you to think that we're all of a sudden going to be everywhere you turn!"

"I'll talk to Julie but I'd say we could do with all the help we can get right now. Maybe you can help us with some of the advertising and PR."

"I'm sure I can. But we're not planning to move until the new Year and I've given in my notice at work to leave on 31st December. We don't want to rush the move and we've lots to do before we leave."

"That's the same date I'm leaving the Sail Loft," I say. "It's going to be hard for you, isn't it? Leaving, I mean."

"Like you wouldn't believe! The house, our friends… we've lived there a long time, and it won't be easy. But I don't know, when we come down here it feels so right. It must be your influence. And our friends will be jostling to come and visit us."

"I'm so excited about it, Mum."

"Then that is all I need to hear. I'm very glad, Alice."

We hugged and I felt a sense of calm helping to smooth over the anxiety Sam had managed to create within me.

The sale is going ahead soon but Mum and Dad say I can stay in the house as long as I want. "Even after we've moved in, if you like."

"Well, I think by then I'll be ready to be in my new place," I say.

"Alice doesn't want to live with her parents again, Phil," Mum nudges him with her elbow, laughing.

"I'm just – I don't like the idea of you living up there on your own," Dad admits.

"I'll be fine, Dad, but thank you. And once we've got a steady flow of guests, I won't be up there on my own."

"But they'll be strangers."

"It'll be fine!" I say, hugging him. "But it will be good to know that you're just a couple of miles away."

The thick curtains are still closed so I open them to reveal another beautiful blue-skied day. I am so happy for Julie and Luke that the weather managed to sort itself out yesterday. I can't believe that this time yesterday morning, I was getting ready for Julie's arrival. Now she's married and the big day is over. Does she feel an anti-climax, I wonder. Or is she just happy that the day went so well? Perhaps she is just looking forward to her break away with Luke. I can't say I blame her. She said she'd wait, until we're sorted up at Amethi, but I wouldn't hear of it. "What difference is a week going to make, Julie? Go on, you'll never feel the same 'just married' feeling again. Go on, it's not fair on Luke if you don't, either."

I would love a week somewhere hot and sunny and remote, myself. I picture a secluded beach; a warm sea teeming with tiny, colourful fish. A sunbed, a cocktail, a book… I can but dream. A day in bed will have to suffice for now.

I run through that weird conversation with Sam again; in truth, it has not been far from my mind since it happened. And that painful dance we had to share.

Urgh. But what did he say? *Obviously trying to buy you.*

It doesn't make sense. Neither Sam's anger nor that Paul would keep it quiet that he was the one who sold Amethi to Julie and me. I guess I am going to have to speak to him about it but not right now. I remember Sam's arm around me as we danced. The anger in his eyes and something else, like hurt. Why on earth would it matter to him if Paul was the owner, anyway? I don't get it.

Time for breakfast, I think, hoping that I can push these thoughts away again, for a while at least.

The house seems so quiet. Even though it's been just me for a couple of weeks now, I suppose I haven't had a lot of time here. And yesterday it seemed full of life and people. I groan at the sight of the plates and glasses still sitting dirty from the previous day then smile at the sight of a tiny cream flower which must have come loose from Julie's hair. I stoop and pick it from the floor, placing it on the windowsill.

While the kettle boils, I wash everything up. Tidying wasn't on the menu for today but I will relax better knowing that all is in order downstairs. I warm an almond croissant and take a handful of raspberries from the fridge, dropping them into a bowl. Then I fill the coffee pot and I warm some milk. Finally, I put it all on a tray, which I carry carefully up the stairs, casting an admiring glance through the stairwell window. I have a feeling Mum and Dad are going to love it here.

For now, though, the place is still mine. I dust off the bedroom TV and switch it on, then slide back into my beautifully warm and soft bed. The duvet gives me all the comfort I need as I pull it around me and just lie for a few moments, basking in the luxury of a whole day to myself.

I flick through the TV channels, eventually settling on some re-runs of *Friends*. Perfect.

Despite the coffee, I catch myself nearly dozing off from time to time but clearly something in me isn't going to allow this to happen as I jolt quickly back to my senses. I'm ill at ease and I know it is because of Sam. And possibly Paul. I need to get to the bottom of this. Reluctantly, I sit up and retrieve my phone from my bedside drawer. There is a lovely message from Julie:

We're just about to catch our flight. I am so happy, Alice. Thank you so, so much for everything you've done for the wedding, and for me over the years. I don't want to sound patronising when I say this but I am so sure that your day will come, too. I can't wait for the honeymoon but I also can't wait for us to start our very own business. It is going to be amazing, I just know it. See you soon, my friend. I love you very much. Xxxx

I find my eyes tingling as I read the words. The emotions of yesterday are clearly still very much there. What an honour to see my best friend married to her perfect man. I don't mean Luke is perfect; who is? But he and Julie are perfect for each other. Of that, I am sure.

She will be in the air now though, so I won't reply just yet. I must get this over and done with.

"Alice? How are you?" Paul sounds pleased to hear from me.

"I'm fine thanks, how are you?"

"Oh, I'm OK. But tell me about the wedding. Did Julie have a great day?" I feel like he's talking as though he knows her but I also know this is just him; he remembers things about people, and is very charming with it. I wonder if he deliberately puts on a phone smile. It sounds like he's smiling now but he may not be for much longer.

"It was fantastic thank you," I can't deny my enthusiasm. "Well, most of it."

"Oh?"

"Yeah, I…" Suddenly doubting myself, I wonder if this whole thing is just ridiculous, in which case he's going to think I am mad. But I must know. "This is going to sound a bit strange, but are you the person who sold Amethi to me and Julie?"

Silence for a moment.

"What makes you ask that?" he says, not denying it.

"Is it true?" I answer his question with another.

"Yes," he sighs. "It is. But I didn't want you to know."

"Well, that's…" What is it? I don't know. Is it unbelievably kind, or astoundingly patronising? As if Julie and I can't manage things ourselves.

"How did you find out?" he asks.

"Sam told me."

"Sam? Your ex? How did he know?"

"I think we both know there's no keeping secrets round here," I say, still trying to figure out my feelings about the whole thing. "But I think that Bea may have told him."

"Ah."

"Did Bea know? Did you tell her?"

"No. I didn't know that she was aware of any of it. I suppose we've got people in common, going back years. Look, Alice, I know how it must seem. First, putting that covenant on the house…"

"You made that up?" I gasp. That hadn't even crossed my mind.

"Yeah, well, I could tell you were struggling and I… I've been very fortunate in my life, not that I haven't worked hard for it, but I want to be able to help other people a little where I can. I could just see you were brimming with excitement, and I think that your business idea is excellent. I wanted to help you make it happen."

"But don't you see that as your…" What am I, or was I? His girlfriend? Not exactly. He knows what I'm saying, though.

"I do see, I saw it from the start. Which is why I didn't want you to know. Look, I only bought that place to help a mate out. He was struggling, he'd split up with his wife. He needed a fresh start. I thought maybe I could do it up a bit for holiday lets. But it's not what I do. And then you told me all about your plans with Julie and I could just sense your enthusiasm and vision and drive, all bubbling over. As soon as you said you'd found your perfect place, it all clicked in my mind. But I could also see that, if you wouldn't let Luke help you, there was no way that you'd let me."

"Oh, Paul…" I stop, trying to assemble my thoughts and feelings into some kind of order. I'd begun this conversation in annoyance, bordering on anger. I find all that has gone, though. "That's actually one of the nicest things anybody's done for me."

"Ha!" His laugh is short, sharp and full of relief. "I thought you were going to crucify me for it!"

"Well, I wasn't sure how I felt about it, to be honest. And I'm still not sure I'm comfortable with it but I know you've just been unbelievably generous and supportive and I don't think I can be angry about that."

"So we're OK?"

"We're OK," I confirm.

"Thank god for that! But I need you to know, you don't owe me anything. You know that already, of course, but what I mean is *I* don't think you owe me anything. I helped because I wanted to. I didn't expect anything in return and I know how you feel about us, and the future, and all of that."

"Oh, Paul." I find I am reluctant to confirm what he's saying. I am really not sure right now that I want to end things between us. How the hell have I been so lucky as to find this amazing man? And am I really going to just let him go?

But I don't have to answer just yet as Paul continues, "I know, your heart's not in it. And quite frankly, Alice, it shouldn't be with any man right now, it should be right in your business, till it's making a profit. But that's not for me to tell you. I can't help wondering, though, what Sam's problem is with all of this. Why did he feel the need to tell you? Is he jealous?"

"I don't know about that. I don't really know what his problem is," I admit.

"People are complicated, Alice. You already know that. It might be worth talking to him, to try and work things out. After all, you called me straight about this."

"I did. You're right." But this somehow easy, I don't feel like talking to Sam will be so straightforward. "Thank you, Paul."

"You're very welcome, Alice. Please keep in touch, and let me know if I can help with anything. And if you change your mind…"

"I'll let you know." I'm smiling now.

"I'm kicking myself that I never got to make you breakfast in bed."

He still has the ability to make my stomach turn somersaults.

"I think," I say reluctantly, "it just wasn't meant to be."

25

The holiday lets are ready! It took every inch of Julie's persuasive skills to stop me going as far as actually making the beds.

"The first guests won't be here till mid-January, and we want to make sure the bedding smells freshly washed for them. If we put it on now, it will get dusty and maybe even become a cosy little hiding place for spiders or something."

"Oh, OK," I said, "but it would look sooo nice."

"You're right. Maybe we should make up a couple of the beds, for the photos. But we have to take it all off again and get it laundered, OK?"

"OK," I said, pulling a sad face.

"You're an idiot!"

"I know."

The pictures do look great. We managed to find a sunny wintry day for the shoot so that the light is streaming through the windows, showing the rooms at their best. The grounds have been properly landscaped, although it's not exactly the ideal time of year to do this, and a good spread of shrubbery planted.

We've also got a website now, created by Luke, which shows off the gorgeous photos and focuses strongly on the 'exclusivity' angle.

While Mum sees out the last few weeks of her job, Dad has been sending press releases to as many magazines, websites and newspapers as he can find. He's got a spreadsheet recording it all and he is very happy about it.

We have two weeks left of this year and it certainly feels like it's been a long one. Three weddings so far, with one to go. Mum's health scare. Falling in love with, and taking on, Amethi – and in the process, making the difficult decision to leave the Sail Loft. What I would really like now is a break but there is no time to rest on my laurels. My last day of the Sail Loft is the final day of the year, and my first full day of Amethi is January 1st, when we also have our launch party. We did question whether it was a good idea when everybody would have new year's hangovers but hopefully it will keep the drinks bill down. We are actually holding it in the communal space, as we've taken to calling the hall on site, and we're so excited about showing prospective guests and clients around.

But – that is for the future. The present is David's 'hen do', which is happening tonight. He has invited me, Julie, Kate, a couple of friends from work and, of course, Bea.

"Oh my god, I'm such a stereotype!" he said. "All my friends are women."

"No they're not!" I scolded. "You could easily have had a stag do. It's just that mean are idiots – present company excluded – and you'll have a far better time with us."

I don't know how I feel about being out and about with Bea. At work we're both being very professional; civil with each other and making sure that everything is done as well as it has ever been. The guests are happy and we have a full house for the Christmas and New Year celebrations. I am glad I don't really have time to think it all through; I know I feel hurt by Bea's attitude towards me, and her telling Sam about Paul and Amethi. I have no idea why she'd do that; what did she hope to gain from it, or was she just exercising the gossipy side of her nature? The thing I can't bear to contemplate is that she was doing it to hurt me, knowing that Sam would react badly and knowing how I feel about him.

Still, tonight I must put a brave face on it once again; I'm not ruining David's hen do for anything.

Julie comes to call for me at what will soon be Mum and Dad's house. They exchange contracts at the start of January and then Mum and Dad will be moving here! Bloody hell, if I thought this year was busy, I have a feeling the next one is going to be twice as bad.

I pour two gin & tonics to get us started and we sit in the lounge, reminding each other to stop talking about work, only to discuss the finer details of the arrangement with the florist, or the bakery, or Kate's yoga sessions and retreats.

"OK," I laugh. "We're as bad as parents talking about their kids. We should have a night away again, like we did before your wedding, where work talk is absolutely banned."

"That's an excellent idea. We should do it twice a year, so our relationship doesn't go stale."

"Shit, we really do sound like a married couple!"

"Speaking of which…" Julie stands, draining her glass, and I follow suit. We pull on our thickest coats and head out into a town decorated with twinkling, dancing Christmas lights. As the cold kisses my cheeks, I feel a deep warmth from being here.

"You made it!" David exclaims from his seat at the large table by the fire. His cheeks are flushed and his eyes glowing.

"Of course, you dimwit," Julie says, kissing him.

"As if we'd miss this!" I agree.

"I'm so excited," he says. "What have I done to deserve to be so happy?"

"Probably nothing," I tease. "This is all some great error on behalf of the universe, but make the most of it anyway."

"God, I think you're right," he says. "Best hope the universe doesn't notice. Now, get one of these down you." He pours two long, dark drinks from a pitcher on the table. "Long Island Iced Tea. Chin, chin."

Now, I love Long Island Iced Tea but it does seem to have quite an effect on me. Still, this is David's hen night and when in Rome and all that…

There are two seats next to Bea. Julie diplomatically takes the one directly beside her, and I sit beside Julie, giving my boss and erstwhile friend a fairly brief greeting. I see Kate opposite me and greet her slightly more enthusiastically. I wish things weren't like this with Bea, but what can I do?

As it turns out, Long Island Iced Tea has the answer. Four glasses in, when Julie strolls off to the toilet, leaving a trail of admiring glances in her wake as usual, I slide onto her chair and edge closer to Bea.

"Hi," I say.

"Hi."

"Emotional night, your brother's hen do."

There is a small smile on Bea's lips. "Yes, traditionally a watershed moment in a family's life."

"Oh Bea," I kind of sway towards her. "Why aren't we friends anymore?"

"We're friends." Her stiff exterior suggests otherwise.

"Come on," I cajole. "You hate me because I'm leaving you."

"This isn't the time or the place," she tries.

"Course it is," I slur slightly. "I'm leaving the Sail Loft in a couple of weeks and I… and I…" Oh no, here come the tears. "I don't want to."

"Of course you want to," Bea's expression has softened slightly. "You're about to embark on something really exciting! Why would you not want to?"

"Because I love it there. You and Stef and Jonathan, you're like family to me."

"And you're like family to me, too. To all of us. That won't stop when you're not working with us." I am sure Bea's eyes are glistening. I am also aware that I am meant to be annoyed with her but right now I can't really remember why.

"I'm sorry, Alice," Bea says and now I can see her eyes are definitely wet with tears. "I haven't been very supportive. David's told me off about it, you know. I just felt really shocked when you told me you were leaving. I knew it would happen one day but I had no idea it would be so soon. I just wish you'd told me what you were planning. I could have helped you, or advised you. I suppose I felt like you'd been plotting behind my back."

I'd never thought of it like that. "I would never do that, Bea!" I cry although even in my drunken state I can see that the evidence points to the contrary. "I didn't want to tell you until I knew that it was definitely going to happen. I thought you'd be annoyed with me, for being ungrateful and untrustworthy."

"Oh Alice," she says, "as if! It's just, when you told me, it was like a kick in the teeth, like *you* didn't trust *me*! I would have loved to have helped you and Julie, if you'd let me. You must know that." Her face falls. "I regretted saying that to you about Paul, you know. I thought that it made you feel differently about me and maybe that was part of the reason you decided to leave. I shouldn't have said anything but I really did just want to make sure you didn't get hurt."

"Why did you tell Sam about Paul selling me and Julie the business?" I must take this chance to get this straight.

"I'm so sorry about that, too. I genuinely didn't mean to cause you any problems. I actually thought that you must have known all about it."

"No," I say, "Paul didn't want me to think he was trying to buy me."

"Wow," Bea takes this in. "That's really kind of romantic!"

"It is," I can't help smiling at the thought of my lovely benefactor.

"I hope I haven't caused any problems for you and Paul. He's a good man."

"You haven't," I reassure her, "but he wasn't for me. Not because of what you told me," I add hastily, "just because I know what I want from life. And he's already got most of it sorted for himself. I feel like we're at two different points in our lives and I don't think I've got the energy to put into something which hasn't got a future. If I'm honest, I don't really think I'm over Sam yet."

"I wouldn't give up on Sam, Alice, you know. The way he reacted about Paul – although I wish I'd kept my big mouth shut – why would it have bothered him, if he wasn't still into you? And remember what you said, about that night when your mum was in hospital? How Paul managed to step in when Sam couldn't? It must be hard, seeing somebody else do these things for you."

"Oh Bea, I've missed you. I wish we'd had this talk months ago. We are a pair of idiots." I hug her. "I love you, Bea."

"I love you too, Alice." She blows her nose.

We are both sniffling like a pair of little kids. From the other side of the table comes a cheer from David. "Thank God you two have put things right, I was going to have to bang your heads together otherwise."

Bea and I rearrange ourselves so we can look across at him. "You've made my night," he says. "More cocktails!"

I groan.

Later, David suggests we leave our wonderfully comfortable and warm fireside seats to go out into the cold December night, to the beach.

"Yes!" I say, "Great idea!"

Nobody else seems to agree, judging by the mutterings and protests around the table.

"Come on, you lot, it's my hen do," David says and so we shrug on our coats. I survey the group and see that really we aren't dressed for the beach. Kate, for example, is wearing a very figure-hugging strappy dress and spiky heels. Thankfully, her coat will keep her covered but I don't fancy her chances getting across the sand in those shoes. Nevertheless, she seems quite excited about the idea. While Julie, Bea and David skip arm-in-arm down the street, attracting smart remarks and laughter from those they pass by, I tuck my arm into Kate's.

"Mind if I walk with you?"

"Of course not! How are you, Alice?"

"I am having a great night," I hiccup merrily.

"Good," she says, "Me too."

"Do you know, Kate, how much I am looking forward

to working with you?"

"You've clearly had too much to drink!" She grins at me.

"No, really, I mean I am terrified about running a business, but getting to work with you and Julie, it's going to be so good."

"You don't need to be terrified." Kate seems remarkably sober, or is that just through my Long Island Iced Tea-tinted glasses? "It is going to be fantastic. Just wait and see."

"Thank you, Kate, that's so nice. You're so nice."

She laughs. "You're so drunk."

"Are you not?"

"No, not really. I mean, I've had a couple but Isaac's tee-total and I kind of think my body's had its lifetime's quota of booze already. Do you remember me telling you I used to drink every night?"

"I think so," I actually remember it well.

"Well, that is a thing of the past," she says proudly.

"Because you're happy now?" I suggest.

"Yes, I think so."

I squeeze her arm with mine then I'm shocked and embarrassed to find tears are running down my cheeks.

"Hey, are you OK?" Kate makes us both stop on the street while the others make their merry way onwards, down the cobbled street which shines under the streetlights.

"Yes," I snivel. "I think I'm just pissed. But, everybody's so happy together. And I'm really, really happy for all of you, I promise. But…"

"Oh, Alice," Kate says, pulling me to her.

We stand, hugging for a while. She smells like Sophie. I choose not to say that in case it sounds weird.

"I fell out with Sam," I say.

"I know," she soothes, "but it's all in the past now. And you know it wasn't your fault. And Sophie's fine. More than fine." She smiles as she thinks of her daughter.

"I don't mean that!" My voice is sharper than it's meant to be. "At Julie's wedding, I mean. I fell out with Sam then."

"I didn't know that. I thought you two were OK. You were dancing."

"Under duress," I laugh bitterly, feeling slightly more clear-headed for the fresh air. Disembodied whoops and cheers reach our ears. I guess they've arrived at the beach. "No, he was annoyed at me about something."

"What about?" Kate asks, standing back slightly so she can see my face.

"It's a long story, but I've been seeing this bloke…"

"Paul," she fills in, and I remember she and Paul knew each other.

"Yes, Paul." I smile. "It's nothing serious, in fact we're not seeing each other anymore." I am half aware that something is going on in Kate's mind but I am on a drunken roll and I really want to tell her everything. "It turns out he was the man who owned Amethi."

If I am expecting Kate to look surprised, she doesn't. Was she privy to that conversation between Sam and Bea, as well? I remember them all standing together, talking, and weren't they looking at me? "Did you already know that, Kate?"

"Yes," she says quietly, "I did."

"But what's the big deal? I don't get it. So what if we bought the place from Paul? I spoke to him about it and he was lovely. He's just tried to help me out, that's all. Why is Sam so pissed off about it?"

"I'm not sure," Kate says thoughtfully, "but I know Paul, he wouldn't have done this unless he wanted to, and God knows he can afford to, so I wouldn't worry about it, Alice. Maybe Sam just feels a bit redundant, like he can't help you in the way that Paul can."

"That's what Bea said."

"I'd say she's right. I don't really think Sam's feelings for you have gone away so it must be hard seeing you with another man."

"I was never really with Paul, as such. We just had a few dates."

"Well, you obviously made quite an impression on him, Alice."

"But…"

"Sam?"

"Yes. Sam."

"Bloody hell, Alice, you and I have an awful lot in common. Now come on, chin up, we're on David's hen do. Let's get down on that sand and throw all our worries into the sea!"

This is not the Kate I thought I knew. The first time I met her was on this very beach, with Sophie but while her daughter was busy collecting sea creatures, Kate didn't seem very involved. Then there was the time we met at the beach – which is when I realised the link between her and Sam, which I don't really want to think about right now. She spent most of the time sunbathing, while Sophie and I built sand castles and moats. Tonight, though, when we get to the top of the slope down to the beach, Kate pulls off her shoes, then her tights, putting them in a neat pile at the bottom of the slope.

"I hope nobody nicks them," she laughs.

I take off my own boots, and socks, even though they'd

probably be OK on the beach. Solidarity, though, sister.

In the moonlight, I can see the figures of David, Julie, Bea and the others, dashing to and fro purposefully. What are they doing? Kate and I take each other's hands, without thinking, and exclaim at the sensation of the sand on our feet. It is bitingly cold, and the wind from the sea strikes us but it feels amazing.

We run, breathlessly laughing, to the others and as we get closer I see they all seem to have sticks or stones and they are using them to write in the sand.

"Grab a stone or something," David shouts to us.

"We're doing sand art!" Julie calls happily.

All over the sand are hearts. Huge ones and tiny ones. Each member of the group seems to be happily in their own little world, creating these symbols of love.

"This is going to look amazing," I say.

"If the tide doesn't wash it away."

"I'll get up early," Kate says. "Try to get some photos if it's clear. The tide's on its way out now so there should be time."

"You are great," I say and I hug her again before we set about our own artistic endeavours.

Not far away, the sea rumbles and crashes; white foamy waves glowing in the light from the moon. Up on the headland is the chapel, carefully angled lights illuminating it against the sky, where clouds take their turn in the limelight as they pass before the moon. Up along the roads in town, Christmas lights dance merrily.

This time next year, Mum and Dad will be living here. Amethi will be nearly one year old. Assuming it doesn't just dive and die immediately. We do have bookings, though, taking us into June – with lots of gaps to fill in the meantime. It's not time to relax, and I'm not sure it ever will be, but right now I have to seize this moment. My friends laughing and shouting, the wind from the sea making them billow with life and excitement.

"Julie," I say, catching my friend's arm. "Thank you."

"For what?" she takes my hands and dances me around until I feel dizzy.

"For making me come down here! I'd be at some World of Stationery office party right now, if it wasn't for you."

"In that case, it is my pleasure. Love you, Alice."

"I love you, too."

At this point, David interjects, taking one of my hands, and one of Julie's, then the others join us and we dance in a circle, spinning progressively faster, until the moon and the chapel and the Christmas lights become a blur, spinning around our dizzy heads and eventually we collapse in a heap, arms and legs jumbled up and helpless laughter emanating from the ungainly pile of bodies.

26

On the morning of David's and Martin's wedding, I wake early and open the curtains onto darkness.

Bea has closed the Sail Loft for two days; something previously unheard of, and the wedding is not until this evening so there really is no need to be awake now but there is so much going on in my mind, it is pointless trying to sleep.

I remember the morning that summer when we'd come back down here, when I couldn't sleep, and snuck out early for a walk. Though it was the summer then and quite different to the cold mid-winter, I feel the urge to do the same thing again. I pull on my underwear, then some leggings, then jeans over the top. A vest, a long-sleeved t-shirt, a hoodie and my coat. I fill a flask with hot coffee, putting it in my rucksack along with a blanket, a day-old pain au chocolat and a fat, bright orange.

My gloves on and my hat pulled firmly over my ears, I fasten my walking boots and I creep out of the house, wondering if this is a really stupid idea.

The streets are silent, aside from my footsteps, which sound incredibly loud. I walk first down to the harbour where the creaking of masts and clinking of metal chains on the boats is somehow eerie and magical at the same time. I walk all the way along the harbour, looking into the dark depths of the water, hoping to see some sign of life; fishermen loading onto their boats, or the sleek, oily head of a seal ploughing nose-first through the waters. So far, though, there is only me.

I make my way back, tiptoeing around the foot of the town to the smallest of the three beaches. There, I am joined by the thin, reedy piping of a baby gull; unseen but heard nevertheless. There are snatches of daylight now; thin strips of sapphire blue mixed with oranges and golds, seeping into the dark velvet of the night sky. The moon seems translucent, bidding a distant farewell till tonight, by which time David and Martin will be married.

Up the steps onto the island, breathing hard as I approach the chapel. There, I sit on the cold stone blocks which serve as seats; rest my back against the thick wall, catching my breath and looking out across the town. There is the Sail Loft – lights off, catching its own breath before diving headfirst into the Christmas celebrations.

The town looks like it is still sleeping; catching its breath in this winter's pause. As my eyes scan the view; the houses and flats, the shops and hotels predominantly still in darkness, the Christmas lights flick on, all at once, as if by magic. I smile at the sight. But I can't sit here all day.

Down the other side of the island, onto the long surfers' beach, trudging across the sand but keeping my boots on. Now is not the time for cold, soggy feet. I push on, up the slope at the far end to the coastal path, the sky opening up before me now; seagulls rising, calling, to greet the day.

The path is rugged and slightly muddy so it's hard going but it feels so good to be here. I know exactly where I am going. Further along, into the dark tangle of shrubs and bare brown stems, stalks and seed heads. And there it is. The tiny stone shepherd's hut, run-down as ever but seemingly no worse for wear than twelve years ago. Tentatively, I push the little door aside and enter the cold, damp room. Water drips rhythmically from the ceiling onto the earth floor. I touch the walls, trying to feel something. Self-consciously (even though there is only me to witness it) trying to connect with the past.

I pull a blanket from my bag, and my flask, and I make a little nest, which I sit on while I drink a cup of scalding, sweet coffee and eat my pain au chocolat. It's dry and flaky in my mouth, which is grateful for the sharp, juicy orange that I tuck into next, trying and failing to pull the peel away in one long spiral.

This is the place I sometimes see in my dreams; although it doesn't always look quite like this, I know it's this place. I remember the stormy summer day when I was just eighteen, when Sam pulled me in here, away from the torrential rain. Then the time I came back here and managed to twist my ankle, falling inelegantly at a surprised Sam's feet. I will be more careful this time, I think.

When I come out of the hut, it is to a rising sun, still low in the sky; the night has slid away to reveal a perfect winter's day. A small part of me hopes that I will see Sam on the path but I know it's ridiculous.

Walking back along the path to town I pass other walkers – mostly out with dogs – and some early-morning runners. Without exception, they smile and wish me a good morning. It makes my heart sing.

Back in town, I go to Joe's and order a full vegetarian breakfast. I plan to fill my stomach, go home and take a good, long nap. It's warm and cosy in the café, the windows steaming up slightly. I sit alone by the window and tuck greedily into my sausages, hash browns and beans, mopping up the smooth yellow yolk of two eggs with my toast.

I wake in the early afternoon to my alarm going off. My first thought is the Sail Loft but I'm aware that the light is all wrong for the morning and after a few moments I remember what day it is. I pull off my clothes and step into the shower then I dress in the trousers and top I've bought especially for the occasion. David and Martin have requested that we try to look Christmassy so my top is a deep, dark red, and sparkly and I have a red tinselly hair decoration to add to the festive feeling.

A hot, short coffee followed by a shot of grapefruit juice ensures I am fully awake. I dry my hair and put it up, struggling with the decoration until I'm happy with how I look. Then I go back down the stairs and wait for my lift.

"Get in!" shouts Julie from the back seat of Luke's car. I smile at my friends and do as I'm told. It's only a short drive but we need the car to get to the reception afterwards.

Outside the registry office, I see Bea, Bob and David. Martin is apparently inside with his parents and his brother. David's teeth are chattering.

"Are you OK?" I ask him.

"Yes, I don't know if I'm cold or just ridiculously excited," he says.

I hug him. "I hope you have the best day. You really, truly deserve it."

"Thank you, Alice," he says, eyes shining and cheeks pink.

"Hi, Bea," I say.

"Hello, Alice," she kisses me. "I'm so glad I closed the hotel!"

"I bet. You can really enjoy today, now."

Bob kisses me. "Bea's really pleased you two are friends again; she felt like a total ass, you know," he whispers conspiratorially.

I squeeze in beside Luke, with Julie. Martin stands at the front of the room, looking nervous but smiling at his mum, who is fussing over his buttonhole.

There are about thirty people here and the room is humming with anticipation and good humour. As a non-denominational place, there are no Christmas decorations; no Advent candles as there might be in church, but everybody has done their bit to look festive. Mine is not the only tinsel-based hairpiece, and the room is awash with shades of red, green and gold. There is a definite whisper of festive magic in the air as the room goes quiet and the music starts to play. Bob rushes in and takes his seat at the front, next to Martin's dad, who smiles and claps him on the shoulder. Martin stands up straight at the front, his brother next to him. Then Bea and David appear at the doorway and, although there is no dress to gasp at or wonder over, I'm struck by that familiar lump in my throat and sudden tears at the sight of my friend embarking on one of the most emotional experiences of his life. Martin and David smile at each other and hold hands. Martin's brother sits down, as does Bea. I can see she is trying not to cry.

This time, I am to do one of the readings and I'm smiling inside because I know which one it is and over this year I've learned these short words off-by-heart. I walk slightly nervously to the front.

"From *Romeo & Juliet*," I begin, unable to look up and scared I am about to cry.

I continue,

"My bounty is as boundless as the sea.
My love as deep; the more I give to thee,
The more I have, for both are infinite."

I smile briefly then, suddenly very self-conscious, scurry back to my seat. I am shaking. Luke puts his arm around me. "Well done," he says and kisses me on the cheek.

The rest of the service is beautiful and Martin and David exit the building to the serendipitous sound of church bells ringing across the town and a flutter of snow-white confetti. We wave them off in their smart wedding car then the rest of us follow on in a procession, up out of the town; past the shops with their Christmas displays, the streets dripping with glittering, sparkling lights, and the church with its star shining brightly on top of its tower, out onto the coast road. We listen to Christmas songs all the way, admiring and laughing at the over-the-top decorations adorning some of the houses we pass; singing along with Tom Jones and Cerys Matthews to *Baby, It's Cold Outside*, and the Pogues and Kirsty MacColl's *Fairytale of New York*. After fifteen minutes or so, we arrive at the village where David and Martin live, and find our way to the community hall.

I know David and Martin have been up two nights running, decorating this place, and gasp is followed by admiring gasp as people enter. I am keen to see it for myself but manage to wait my turn. It is beautiful. There are small, potted trees and swathes of cream cloth across the walls, all dotted with tiny, star-like lights. Tables have been placed around the outsides of the room so there is plenty of space to mingle and, later, to dance. Soft

301

classical music is flowing through the speakers and in the tiny kitchen, some of David's and Martin's friends and neighbours are preparing food or ladling out mulled wine or spiced non-alcoholic cider to hand proudly to the guests.

Dinner is a buffet, which only adds to the Christmassy feel. I sit with Julie and Luke, and Martin's brother, his wife, and their three-year-old son. We each go up two or three times to the buffet table, and with the attentiveness and care of our friends' amazing army of willing helpers, our glasses are never empty. With a full stomach and a warm, boozy feeling, I pull open one of the nets of sugared almonds and nibble a couple as I sit back to listen to the speeches. Bea has us in tears with her description of her little brother but it is Martin's dad who blows us away.

"It seems some people still can't get used to the fact that a man can love another man," he says in his strong northern voice, "but who is anyone to say what's right or wrong? I can speak for Michelle here as well as myself when I say that Martin has never been happier than since he met David. And David, well, he's like a third son to us. There is no reason why the two of you can't do everything you want in life and it seems to me that your resilience and the adversity you've faced at times will only make it more likely you'll achieve your dreams. I wish you both all the happiness and love in the world."

Shortly after David has finished thanking everyone for sharing their day, and Martin for making him the happiest man alive, the evening guests start to arrive. Because the wedding itself was late in the day, it feels like everything has happened in no time at all. The neighbours are smilingly clearing everything away but I know they're ready to party, too. There is so much goodwill in this room, it would feel like Christmas whatever time of year it was. This is a very different wedding to the one Martin and David had originally planned but in all honesty I can't think how anything could top it.

I am happy to see Stefan and his family arrive, closely followed by Jonathan and Lydia, who look happy and intimate as they hang up their coats and share a quick, smiling kiss. I am deep in conversation with them when my heart beats a little faster at the sight of Sam at the door, accompanied by Sophie, Kate and Isaac.

"Alice!" Sophie cries and she runs up and hugs me, oblivious to any awkward feelings between her dad and me. I listen to her holiday plans, and how she and Amber are going shopping in Truro the next day. All the while, I have half an eye on Sam, who is at the kitchen serving hatch, which is now acting as a bar. He hands drinks to Kate and Isaac then he walks over to me and Sophie.

"Here you go, Soph," he gives her a bottle of apple & mango J2O. "Hi, Alice."

"Hi," I say. I can't seem to find any other words. He looks lovely, his face slightly flushed in the sudden heat of the room after the cold, sharp night air. I try to work out if I am annoyed with him still, or just unbelievably happy to see him.

"Would it be OK to have a chat later?" he asks, his eyes on mine.

"Yeah… sure," I say. I feel my fingers grasping my glass a little tighter but my eyes focus on Kate not far behind Sam, grinning at me and raising her glass. I raise my own glass in an answering salute then she calls Sophie and her daughter skips happily over, lifting and kissing her mum's hand in joyful, uninhibited affection.

The room is being prepared for a ceilidh. All the guests are gathered around the edges, merry chatter and laughter filling the air. Somebody bumps into me, pushing me towards Sam, who catches my elbow. I look at him and decide I might as well grasp the nettle. "Do you fancy coming outside for a bit?"

Sam looks surprised but shrugs. "Why not?"

We find our coats in the lobby and he helps me into mine. Retrieving our glasses from a small shelf, we head out into the cold. It is deeply dark already but the outside of the hall has been decked with hundreds of multi-coloured fairy lights and above us the sky is clear of clouds. The moon casts a magical light around us, making the frosty paths and road twinkle like they have been scattered with glitter. The scent of the sea is strong on the air, though from here the source is nowhere to be seen. I shiver and pull my coat around me.

"Bleeding cold, isn't it?" says Sam.

"Yes," I say, continuing boldly, "but I guess that's not what you wanted to talk about."

"No," he admits, looking into his glass. "I wanted to say sorry. For being such an arse, at Luke's wedding. I don't know what I was thinking."

I stay silent.

"Well, I do, actually," he continues. "I know you must think I was jealous of Paul, and that was a part of it if I'm honest. But it's none of my business, what you do with your life, or who helps you get to where you want to be."

"I've worked bloody hard to get to where I want to be," I retort. "And Paul may have helped a little but it's not like he's given us Amethi. We've had to beg, steal and

304

borrow – well, borrow and beg at least –" I give a small smile, "to get that place."

"I know, I know. Oh, this is all coming out wrong," he groans. "There's more – so much more to this."

"Then tell me."

"Paul Winters…" he begins, as if he can't bear to say that name.

"Yes?" I ask, impatiently.

"Well, he had an affair when he was married."

Not this again, I think.

"With Kate."

Shit. I don't say anything. This is a lot to take in. My mind flashes back to the time Paul and I saw Kate with David. They knew each other, but I didn't think anything of it. I recall the conversation with Bea, or rather her warning to me. Did she know who that affair had been with? And Paul confessing to me – it was about twelve years ago. The words 'nearly twelve' pop into my head.

"He's Sophie's dad!" I exclaim without thinking. Sam winces. "Sorry, I mean, you're Sophie's dad. In every way," I quickly try to mend my error but I'm in shock.

Sam gives a small smile. "Thank you, Alice, and I leapt to the same conclusion as you. And that is probably the real reason I was so pissed off. I knew Kate had been with a married man before she was with me but I hadn't given it much thought. Then something twigged in my mind, that he'd been called Paul, the same name as your new boyfriend. I did a bit of asking about, which I really shouldn't have done and Kate's given me a proper bollocking about it. I'm so sorry, Alice, I just couldn't bear the thought of you being with Sophie's natural father and then when Bea said that about him selling Amethi to you, it just triggered something in me. I guess the whisky probably didn't help."

"OK," I say slowly. "This makes a bit more sense now, I think. You're sure Paul's not..?"

"Yes, I'm sure, thanks to Kate. She said she had a chat with you at David's party the other night, and worked out what I was thinking. She says I'm wrong. She also says I'm an idiot for not asking her about it." I can't help smiling at this. Sam continues, without looking at me, like he has to get his words out, "She says she had broken up with Paul before she was pregnant. She met somebody who was working down here, and he was long gone before she knew she was pregnant."

"Bloody hell," I say.

"I know. It all happened that summer, when we met. Kate met this bloke who was skippering a yacht, and she fell for him but he left and, as you know, I thought you'd left me, too. By the time Kate realised she was pregnant, we'd been seeing each other for a few weeks."

"Shit." I can't think of anything to say, I'm trying to take it all in, piece everything together. I'm glad Paul isn't Sophie's dad – that really would be far too weird. I look at Sam, wishing he'd look at me.

"So I guess I just wanted to apologise to you, Alice. My head's been a mess. I already felt threatened by Paul, when he gave you that lift, when your mum was ill, and I couldn't help. I felt useless. Then when I started to put everything together...."

"Incorrectly," I offer.

"Yes, incorrectly," he smiles slightly but still doesn't look at me. "I realised who Paul was, and that you were seeing more of him, and I was jealous. I would have been, even if he hadn't been the bloke Kate had a relationship with."

"But you've been seeing somebody…" I begin, not really sure which part of all this to focus on.

"That was nothing," he smiles wryly. "Less than nothing. I kind of made more of it, to see what you'd say. I have been up in Scotland, for work, and I have seen Tracy while I was up there, but just as friends. It was never anything more than that, really."

"Oh."

"Let me finish, please, then you can tell me I'm an arsehole and you can go back and enjoy the party."

Finally, his eyes meet mine and I can see his earnestness. The air seems to be getting colder but it is fresh and clean. The branches of the trees which surround the hall move slowly on the gentle wind, revealing different patches of starry sky. I don't have any wish to return inside right now.

"So, I thought Paul could give you everything I couldn't. Then it turned out that was entirely true as he was the person you bought your new place from, and the cherry on the cake was that I thought he was Sophie's real dad. I felt like I was falling apart."

"Oh, Sam." What a mess. I think I can understand why he's been the way he has lately. And a little part of me is jumping for joy that he wasn't really seeing that other woman.

"Kate's set me straight today, about quite a few things," he says drily. "I feel like she's really sorted herself out this last year or two. But that's not the point," he pushes himself back on track. "The point is, Alice, I love you. I have never stopped loving you. It's no excuse but it's why I've behaved like such an idiot. And I know it didn't work out before, but Sophie's older now, and she loves you, too. You must see that. Besides, Kate is with Isaac and

Sophie's accepted that pretty well. I'm back in Cornwall for now then I've got nine months left in Wales next year, Alice, but that's nothing."

"It's enough time to have a baby," I quip but immediately regret it. It's my nerves, trying to bring some levity to this situation.

Luckily, Sam smiles. He tentatively puts a hand on my shoulder, and he looks at me, his eyes flickering over my face as if trying to read my feelings there. He moves towards me hesitantly then kisses me on the lips, holding my gaze when he moves back again.

"Sam," I say, "I've spent the last few months – in fact, the last two years – making peace with the fact that we are not meant to be together. I've got a new business, I'm helping Mum and Dad move down here. Do you really think this is the right time to bring this up?"

I'm saying the words but I can feel a grin spreading across my face.

"You're damn right I do," he says gruffly, his hands finding their way inside my coat and holding my waist. I shiver, and laugh, and I find I am shaking.

In the bitterly cold tail end of the year; the Christmas stars shining brightly above, I kiss Sam. His mouth is welcoming, and so familiar. His body warm against mine. While his hands move up my back, his lips slide across to my ear. "Be with me, Alice."

"I will," I whisper back, and repeat the words once more. "I will."

As he pulls me tight so I feel the thudding of his heart, I know exactly what's been missing, in this year of weddings, fresh starts, fear, and misunderstandings. And I know that I never want to lose it again.

Thank you very much for taking the time to read
As Boundless as the Sea.

If you've enjoyed this book, a positive review on Amazon
or Goodreads would be much appreciated.

In case you missed them...

Books One and Two of the *Coming Back to Cornwall* Series

A Second Chance Summer

Alice knows that coming back to Cornwall means she will have to see Sam, the man she fell in love with aged 18.

How will he react to her return, and what changes have the intervening ten years meant for them both?

Still recovering from a toxic relationship, Alice realises she has allowed life to become too predictable, while Julie has just ended things with the man she was due to marry. The two friends decide to throw caution to the wind; coming back to Cornwall, where they spent a long, happy summer before life got serious. As they return to the same small flat in the centre of town, and seasonal jobs at the Sail Loft Hotel, Alice harbours both hopes and fears of finding Sam, while Julie is determined to enjoy the freedom she's been missing.

After the Sun

Sam and Alice, only recently reunited, face separation when Sam's only option in order to continue his studies is to leave Cornwall while Alice is committed to her new job managing the Sail Loft Hotel in landlady Bea's absence.

Sam's visits see him split in his loyalties between his daughter Sophie, and spending time with Alice. Sophie's mother, Kate, seems to be doing her best to make things difficult.

Meanwhile, Alice's friend Julie faces a similar challenge as her new partner, and Sam's best friend, Luke, is working in London. Struggling to keep herself in work now the summer season has ended, Julie has some big decisions to make.

Can these fledgling relationships pass the long-distance test, and can Julie and Alice make life in Cornwall work for them now that the summer sun has gone?

Acknowledgements

In May 2017 my family and I were staying near Fowey in Cornwall and I was fully intending to develop my younger readers' stories, when inspiration struck - for something entirely different. Just eighteen months later, this third and – I think – final instalment of the Coming Back to Cornwall series is ready to release and I have become very attached to Alice, Julie, Sam, Luke and the others. I was determined there would be a happy ending but some of my brilliant beta readers are suggesting this should not be the end. We will see…

Speaking of beta readers, I'd like to say a huge THANK YOU to Claudia Baker, Denise Armstrong, Katie Copnall, Janet Evans, Helen Smith and Wendy Pompe for their time, support and invaluable feedback.

Thanks also to my dad, Ted Rogers, who has read and proofread this book, and offered his excellent advice, in record time.

And finally, thanks as ever to my fantastic friend and talented cover designer, Catherine Clarke, for making this set of books (and all my others) look so blooming beautiful.

Writing the Town Read

You can currently get an ebook of *Writing the Town Read* for FREE on Katharine's website: www.katharineesmith.com.

On July 7th 2005, terrorists attack London's transport network, striking Underground trains and a bus during the morning rush hour. In Cornwall, journalist Jamie Calder loses contact with her boyfriend Dave, in London that day for business.

The initial impact is followed by a slow but sure falling apart of the life Jamie believed was settled and secure. She finds she has to face a betrayal by her best friend, and the prospect of losing her job.

Writing the Town Read is full of intrigue, angst, excitement and humour. The evocative descriptions and convincing narrative voice instantly draw readers into Jamie's life as they experience her disappointments, emotions and triumphs alongside her.

Looking Past

Sarah Marchley is eleven years old when her mother dies. Completely unprepared and suffering an acute sense of loss, she and her father continue quietly, trying to live by the well-intentioned advice of friends, hoping that time really is a great healer and that they will, eventually, move on.

Life changes very little until Sarah leaves for university and begins her first serious relationship. Along with her new boyfriend comes his mother, the indomitable Hazel Poole. Despite some misgivings, Sarah finds herself drawn into the matriarchal Poole family and discovers that gaining a mother figure in her life brings mixed blessings.

Looking Past is a tale of family, friendship, love, life and death – not necessarily in that order.

Amongst Friends

Set in Bristol, *Amongst Friends* covers a period of over twenty years, from 2003 all the way back to 1981. The tone is set from the start, with a breathtaking act of revenge, and the story winds its way back through the key events which have led the characters to the end of an enduring friendship.

Both of Katharine's first two novels are written from a strong female first-person perspective. Amongst Friends takes her writing in a different direction, as the full range of characters' viewpoints are represented throughout the story.

How to Run a Free Kindle Promotion on a Budget

Written primarily for other indie authors, this is a great guide to making the most of your 'free days' in the Kindle Direct Publishing KDP Select programme.

With BookBub deals hard to come by, not to mention pricey, *How to Run a Free Kindle Promotion on a Budget* takes you step-by-step through the process, from planning to record-keeping. It also includes real examples to illustrate the success or otherwise of the techniques described.

20685196R00192

Printed in Great Britain
by Amazon